I0674108

Aphrodite Mine

Regency's British Empire, Volume 1

IreAnne Chambers

Published by IreAnne Chambers, 2024.

APHRODITE MINE

First edition. September 10, 2024.

Copyright © 2024 IreAnne Chambers.

ISBN: 978-0996414685

Written by IreAnne Chambers.

Table of Contents

To the family I love both in the U.S. and in Greece
and my best friends of forever.

Secrets, intrigue, betrayal...
and belly dancing!

ALL REBEL INFORMANT Nikolas Stamatelopoulos needs to do is deliver Lady Mara Wingrove to safety in British occupied Corfu. He can handle dangerous travel through rebel territory aboard a pirate ship. He might even be able to keep Mara from falling prey to the Greeks and Ottomans who each want to leverage her for their cause. But keeping himself from falling for the lovely little belly dancer who has more charm—and family secrets—than even she realizes?

That might prove to be the only task Nikolas *can't* accomplish...

AUTHOR'S NOTE

THE INSPIRATION FOR Aphrodite Mine is patterned after pivotal dates in history during the Greek War of Independence. However, some artistic license is used to fictionalize settings, people, and events. Any discrepancies between fact and fiction is intentional and used strictly for this work of fiction and for the enjoyment of readers.

In addition, please note this story is set during a time of war and unrest in 1821. Heinous acts of violence were committed by all parties involved on each side. This story reflects fictional events based on word-of-mouth accounts and/or published events of conflict. Any perceived partiality on the author's part toward one side or the other is wholly unintentional.

The characters and events portrayed in this book are fictitious or are used fictitiously. Any similarity to real persons, living or dead, is purely coincidental and not intended by the author. Pivotal dates in history, places, and relevant historical figures may be mentioned or make cameo appearances, but the details associated with these dates, places, and people as they pertain to the story are a work of fiction for the enjoyment of readers and not intended to portray actual events in history.

Care has been taken to avoid dialogue/narrative that may be considered offensive to some readers in modern times. However, please know the words and thoughts in this book are portrayed by characters in the time of 1821 in the Mediterranean area. Any use or perceived use of any such offensive dialogue/narrative does not reflect specific viewpoints of the author, but may be used very minimally to create historically accurate content. It is not the intention of the author to promote or condone anything that may be considered offensive in modern times.

GLOSSARY

Agape mou - my love.

Ai sto diaolo - to the devil.

Anathema tous - Damn them.

Angaria – forced labor.

Chiftetelei – Greek for belly dance.

Chupas - shepherdess, meaning girls.

Flokati - handmade wool rug.

Hilopites - square-shaped egg noodles.

Kaftan – robe or tunic.

Kagianas - scrambled eggs, tomato, and feta.

Katse – sit.

Kefi - slang for mood.

Kilij – a single-edged, curved sabre.

Koritsi - young girl.

Ksenes - foreigners.

Maraki mou - my little Mara. An endearment.

Na parei euxei - an exclamation of frustration.

Nai - yes.

Oxi – no.

Pasha – Turkish Officer of high rank.

Plateia - Town Square.

Rouncey – an all-purpose horse that could be trained for war.

Stifatho - lamb stew.

Then milaei Ellinika? -Doesn't she speak Greek?

Trahanas - soup made with wheat or bulger with sheep or goat's milk.

Tsai tou vounou- mountain herbal tea.

Vlakas – stupid.

Yelek – bodice or waistcoat of a female or male.

Yatagan – Ottoman knife or short sabre.

Yiasas - good-bye.

Yiayia - gramma or elderly woman.

CHAPTER ONE

Island of Cerigo—April 1821

WAVES CRASH HARD AGAINST the rocks of the cliffs below. I curl my toes into the dirt and gravel. The dry grass tickles the side of my feet. I flex my calve muscles. Deep sea air infiltrates far into my lungs when I breathe in. I raise my hands above my head and exhale. Wind rips through my hair. I don't move. My eyes are closed. Warmth winds its way around my body in a spiral going up. Up to the sky. I peek down into the blue, deep water slamming against the rocks. I move my arms so they're parallel with my shoulders. I fall forward, pushing off with my legs. Free.

VICTORY AT KALAMATA! Nikolas Stamatelopoulos increases his pace along the path leading to the British Resident's Castle. Nikolas' meeting with the Maniotes this morning at the harbor brought the news. There's no doubt Captain Heathcote will wish to speak on the subject at the earliest opportunity. Best to be close to the British Resident's Castle.

The rugged terrain edging the cliffs never fails to increase energy. Training in the mountains of Morea prepared him well for his assignment. The assignment his father and uncle planned to be his from the start. His assignment on Cerigo? The Klepht connection to the British Resident. Regardless of Nikolas' preference to remain on the mainland. There is no choice. Klepht Chiefs will not allow their instructions to be ignored. And these Klepht Chiefs would not be swayed when a decision was made. Images of his uncle, Theodore Kolokotronis, leaving him on this island swirls in the backdrop of his memories. It was his father's orders. Nikitaras Stamatelopoulos.

"Nikolas," he said.

"For protection," he said.

"You are one of the elite," he said.

"A Klepht Captain trained by Nikitaras and Kolokotronis." Nikolas was proud of the rank given him then.

It's been months since he's heard from either of them, but their orders still rage havoc in his head. Orders on how to deal with the British Resident. Orders on what to do with the locals. Keep them from rebellion against the British. For now. This practice of angaria is slavery. But, it's a necessary means for now. Nikolas knows as soon as the news spreads of Kalamata's victory, he'll need to prevent an uprising until preparations can be made. It's close, but it's not time.

Nikolas steps up his rhythm to a run. He must keep his stamina engaged for easy and quick access to the mountains. Morea is mountains. Morea is home. Navigation through the foothills is the only way to prove he still belongs. It's a rite of passage in his clan. A way of life. A way of freedom. Free in an age when Morea is not free. Nikolas fills his lungs full with the air of the sea. Every morning running. Running along the rocky cliffs edging the Island of Kythera. Let the English call it Cerigo. This is Kythera. It will always be Kythera.

Nikolas' mind clears as he runs, but the sight of her brings him confusion. A woman. At the edge of the cliff. Looking down.

Confusion turns urgent. "Stop! Don't do it!"

She's naked with her arms raised. What is she doing? His subconscious already knows.

Her arms fall level with her shoulders, and she falls forward. "No!"

Nikolas runs harder to reach her in time. He doesn't. His arm swipes the air in a line when he reaches out to grab her waist. Nikolas loses his balance, slips, but just misses falling over. Her body is straight and rigid, like one unafraid. She plunges like an arrow, pointed and sharp, barely a splash. Will she come up to the top or be carried away by the current? What could have made her want to end her life in this way?

Nikolas becomes aware of his shallow, hard breaths. Her picture, intense and powerful, stains the places behind his eyes. Long, brown hair, and dark skin, vivid against the backdrop of deep blue sky. Then, nothing. Gone. Into the depths.

Nikolas wastes no time. He needs to find out if she survived. He surveys the edges of the cliffs for a quick route down. There isn't even a beach. Where will she go if she does survive? Still no sight of her. There must be a way down. Nothing. The area around him is deserted. Was anyone with her? There is no one. Nikolas looks down again. Down into the deep, white crescents below. Nothing.

"TAMARA WINGROVE!" WONDERFUL. Another attempt to keep Nana occupied for the morning fails. Again. "What are we to *doo* with you?" Mara can't help smiling whenever Nana emphasizes "do." Nana Lovina has never been able to completely let go of her Indian accent. Nana tries, and has been more insistent on her efforts since father moved us here to Cerigo. Nana's accent can stay the way it is as far as Mara is concerned. She loves the sing-song fluctuation of her Nana's Indian accent, though not so much when she scolds.

"Nana, you know I always leave extra clothing in here, and I always send servants to pick up what's left at the top."

Nana shakes her head while she pleats a length of light pink cloth laced in silver. "And you also know your father wants you dressed as an English woman, not wearing only the sari."

Mara takes the cloth and wraps it around herself to complete the skirt garment and fasten it in place. "Nana, you know how much more comfortable it is."

Mara begins the process of finger-combing through her tresses of tangled hair.

"I know nothing of it." Nana pulls Mara's arm, forcing her to sit in front of her on the rocks at the entrance of the cave. The sun is warm. Nana takes over the untangling, strand by strand, while the sun dries it. Each strand is straightened, allowing the wind to flow through it. Wisps tickle Mara's cheeks in the process. "I see you are using the elixir I gave you to lighten your hair."

"Of course. The lighter brown suits my complexion."

"You're right. It also highlights your blue eyes to match your father's."

"Nana, father's eyes are green."

"Oh? I thought blue. No matter. Still my beautiful girl."

Nana twists my hair into a low messy bun and fastens it in place with a long piece of whalebone pulled from a pocket inside her own pelisse.

"Nana?"

"Yes, Maraki." Maraki. This is the Nana I love, using the Greek endearment of my name.

"Do you miss Ceylon?"

"Why do you ask?"

"Because you always dress in the English way, and you try to speak without your accent." Nana sits silent. "And I love your accent." The heavy silence forces Mara to glance back over her shoulder. Nana's eyes are glossy. She hugs her tight. "I didn't mean to make you sad."

"I'm not sad. Not really. The truth is, I've not thought much about it. It's not Ceylon I miss as much as people I miss."

"It must be hard for you here."

"Believe me, Maraki. I would not wish to be separate from you. I have known you, and been with you, since you were a babe. You are as my own child."

I hug her even tighter. "You know I love you too, for I have never known my own mother." Mara stands up, pulling them both up together. "Let's dance. That has always brought us joy, yes?"

"Where? Here?"

"Of course, here. I have another sari up there hidden on that rock shelf."

"No, no. I cannot. Not here. And what do you mean you have another sari? You keep more than one?"

"I mean I store extra clothing there." Mara climbs up to a spot carved into a group of rocks where the water doesn't reach during high tide. She grabs a leather satchel shoved tight in the back, unbuckles the front, and pulls out her favorites. A dark purple sari with gold lace and matching choli. Nana will look beautiful in it with her dark skin. "I need to make sure I always have something to wear, don't I?"

Mara shakes out the purple clothing and holds it up for Nana to see.

"Tamara Wingrove!" Back to formalities again.

Mara decides to tease her and do the same. "Nana Lovina Aponsuwa, it's perfectly all right. No one is ever around." Mara jumps down from the rock ledge. "I've been doing it for years."

"For years. I know. And it must stop." Nana shakes her head and forefinger. "Come." Nana motions me to follow her out. "We must get back to the manor before the tide comes in." Nana grabs on to my hand and tugs.

No. Mara plants her feet where she stands. "We have plenty of time."

Nana shoots her the you'll-be-sorry glare. It never works. Mara places her hands on her hips and stares back with her usual I'm-just-as-stubborn-as-you-are reply.

"Mara, we don't have plenty of time. We must return."

"And, when will we have a chance to dance again?"

Nana's eyes glimmer. Mara knows she wants to give in. "We will dance, child. But, not here."

Nana tries to pull again. Mara doesn't budge. "Please, Nanoula?" Greek endearments. Will it work? Nana pinches her lips tight and shakes her head. She snatches the sari from Mara's hands and begins the process of undressing herself from her morning dress.

Win. Nana is beautiful. Still very attractive for a woman in her late thirties. Nana replaces her petticoat with the matching choli and wraps the cloth to form the skirt. "You're lovely." Mara holds their hands out together forming a circle between them. "I wish we could wear these clothes all the time. English clothes are too tight."

"Yes, well. Let's dance." Nana's excitement is evident now. "Do you remember how I taught you to hear the music?"

"Absolutely. In here." Mara places her hand on her heart. "It's the rush of the waves crashing against the rocks, the wind as it whistles between the cliffs, and the cry of seagulls surfing the air..." Mara spins around still holding one of Nana's hands and ducks under her arm completing an underarm turn. "I hear the beat of the drum in my heart like this..."

"THE CAPTAIN WILL SEE you now." Captain Heathcote's secretary holds an arm out in front to signal Nikolas permission to enter the dining room.

"Nikolas, sit. What can I do for you this morning?"

"Forgive me, sir, for intruding on your breakfast. There is an urgent matter in need of your attention."

Heathcote stands and walks around the table, wiping his mouth with his napkin before depositing it on the table. "Come with me to my office so we may discuss this in private."

Heathcote closes the double doors and motions for Nikolas to sit, then takes a seat behind his desk. "I believe I'm already aware of the information you wish to provide. I've had a letter this morning from contacts in Morea that Kalamata has been overtaken by the rebels, am I right?"

"Yes, that is correct. I also want to speak with you about another matter I thought to be more pressing at the moment."

"Oh?"

"I was out early this morning by the cliffs and observed a young girl fall over. I tried to stop her but was unable to. There is no way down the cliffs from where I was. And I'm sorry, but I did not see her surface. I'm concerned she may be washed ashore at some point and so wanted to report what I saw."

"Bad business, indeed. I'll dispatch a man to go with you where you last saw her. Maybe we can come up with where she may surface. And you've no notion as to who the girl might be?"

"None, sir."

"Right. We'll need to check the local villages and see if anyone is missing. Can you manage this task and report back here?"

"Yes, of course."

"Good." Heathcote calls for his secretary and instructs him to assign a man for the day.

"Thank you, sir."

"Now. Tell me. What do you think about this fall of the Turks in Kalamata?"

"I don't know if I can say anything. You know there have long been rebel forces against the Turks."

"Yes, but have you heard any news from your father or your uncle, specifically?"

"No, I have not." That is the truth. Nikolas hasn't heard from either of them. Heathcote leans back in his chair. He's waiting for more information. What else can he want to be informed on? Nikolas weighs his options. He'll not betray his country, but he must keep his position balanced with the British, at least for now. Greeks and Ottomans have been in conflict with each other for years. It's only a matter of time. Heathcote's contacts in Morea will tell him the same. Nikolas remains steady. Waiting. Heathcote breaks silence first.

"Well, then. Keep me informed and let me know about that gel. Can't have this become another masada."

"A what?"

"Never mind. Find out who she was and why she did it."

"Yes, of course." Heathcote's secretary escorts Nikolas out of the castle. A man is standing near the doors. Nikolas recognizes him instantly.

"Georgi! What brings you today?"

"Angaria."

"Hmm, right. So, it's you they've called up then. At least it's only today. Better than angaria every day, right?"

"Forced work is never better."

"Did they tell you what we're going to do?"

"No."

"Ah. Let me explain what I saw. On the way to my meeting with Heathcote, a young girl threw herself over the cliffs."

Georgi stops. "Wait. Do you mean Cape Grosso or Cape Trachillas?"

"Over on Cape Grosso. Do you know it?"

"Are you sure she was real?"

"Of course, I'm sure she's real. I saw her! I ran to her. I tried to save her but I missed as she went over. I'm not mad."

"It's because I've heard this before."

"You mean others have jumped? And no one reported it?"

"I don't know. If they're girls maybe they believe it doesn't matter."

"Still, they'd be missed by someone, don't you think?"

"It would seem so, but I also heard talk of the Gods."

"The Gods? What do they have to do with anything?"

"Some villagers still believe this island is a favorite of Aphrodite. They go to temples. Believe it's her, because she's, you know. Naked."

"All the incidents you've heard of, the girl was naked?"

"Ah, yes. Beautiful Goddess, they say!"

"Yes, she was beautiful, but I'm telling you she is not a Goddess. She was flesh and blood. Same as you or I."

"And you know this for sure?"

"Georgi! I thought you were a Christian. How can you believe in the Gods of Olympus and be a Christian?"

"I know. I know. I'm only telling you what they say."

"There has to be an explanation. I know what I saw."

"Let's hurry to get down there to see what we can find."

Nikolas' mind cycles through images of what he saw, trying to generate reasons why she might have jumped. "It's not far now. It's just past that rock mass."

A horse drawn carriage is aiming straight in their direction forcing them to the side of the road. An English coachman nods as he passes. Two ladies look out the window, their faces are veiled. Turkish veils? In a British carriage? Strange.

"DO YOU SEE, MARA? ARE you not glad I had the carriage waiting to take us back?" Nana straightens her back, not requiring a response.

Mara has no intention of leaving the conversation where it stands. "It makes no difference. I doubt those two would have done anything to us."

"You cannot know that. And dressed the way you are. If I had not come, you would be walking alone, dressed in your sari. It's hard to tell what might have happened to you."

"You're dressed in a sari too."

"That is neither here nor there and you know it."

"Nana, really. I admit it would have been a strange meeting on the path just now, but I have never met anyone before on the road back. We are so tucked away from everyone on the island anyway. We don't visit. Only with the British."

Nana's face remains firmly fixated out the window. She will not back away from this like she did with the dance. Mara places her hand on top of Nana's. "I will take care to watch myself in the future. Will that make you happy?"

Nana looks down at Mara's hand resting on top of hers. "Only if you don't do it anymore."

Nana still won't make eye contact. The carriage rattles side to side in a steady rhythm, keeping pace like the beat of a musical instrument.

"But, Nana."

"No more, Mara. I mean it. You see now what could happen. Your father does not need the added anxiety of your welfare. It is already hard enough living in this country holding the position he has. I never should have taught you." Nana closes her eyes and shakes her head back and forth in between the jostling rhythms.

"Don't say that." Why won't she open her eyes? She must know the serious nature of what she's asking. Mara tightens her grip. "I'm happiest when I dance. We've shared the best of times dancing together."

It works. Nana holds Mara's hands between them and turns to look. "Your safety must come first. You must take care not to let the men see you. And your father." Nana shakes her head some more. "The difficulties he would face."

Mara doesn't like to admit that Nana is right. She must be careful, for her father's sake. Living on so many islands in the Ionian states, an Orientalist's duties require him to be available for use in many instances. If there is trouble— Mara doesn't want to think about it. She lets go of their grasp, closes her eyes, and faces the opposite direction.

Nana reaches over to turn Mara's face back in her direction. "Promise me, Tamara."

Mara knows what Nana says is true. Knows she must agree. She doesn't want to give in. She waits a few extra minutes, on purpose, before responding. "I promise."

Nana exhales like she was holding her breath. Mara inhales deep. "Can we please, at least, find somewhere to go privately? To dance? Like we did today?"

Nana smiles, calm and happy. She takes back Mara's hand and holds it on the seat between them. "Of course, Maraki. Of course. I will schedule it. The footman can play the music for us. We'll dance in our private parlor." Nana sits back and closes her eyes. Mara sits back and does the same, holding her Nana's hand for comfort.

The pitted road to Livadi continues to sway the carriage. Mara relaxes and allows her body to rock with the flow of the movements. The carriage slows almost to a halt. Deep, anxious voices swarm outside. Greek sounding words ricochet against the sides of the carriage. The accent is somehow different. Hard to understand what they're saying. *Boom!*

CHAPTER TWO

THE CLIMB TO THE BOTTOM of the cliffs proves to be the challenge Nikolas knew it would be. He combs the edge and locates a foot trail worth attempting a descent on. Georgi leads. The path is narrow, slippery, and rocky, close to the edge. One misstep is all it will take to be lost to the white caps below. Not unlike the mountainous terrain climbed his entire life.

"Georgi, how often have you made this plunge?"

"Not often."

"Your footing suggests otherwise."

"It used to be more frequent when I was younger; not now, though. Used to dive for mussels, there by those rocks."

Nikolas follows the line Georgi is pointing. "I can't see anyone from here."

"I told you, Nikola. Aphrodite. Or, the girl's long gone with the current."

Nikolas reaches the bottom of a ledge that juts out over the water. Waves wallop the edge and splash over the top. Nikolas' boots absorb the moisture. He can feel it through the leather. Cold. He looks up to the top of the steep ledge. The vision of her fall replays in his mind. The drop is enormous. How can a person survive a fall of that distance? Nikolas removes his boots. Then his tunic.

Georgi grabs his arm. "You cannot be thinking to dive in?"

"That's exactly what I'm doing."

"It's too cold."

"I won't be in long. We've had enough warm days already. It's starting to warm up for summer. I've already seen some villagers beginning their summer swimming." At least this is what he tells himself as he prepares to dive.

"I think you're trying to be the hero again."

"Don't be stupid. I need to find out what happened to her."

"I'm telling you, Nikola, there is no girl. If there was, she's gone to open water by now."

"I need to be sure." Nikolas dives headfirst into the sea. His hands break the water first. It's not cold. It's frigid. He fights the urge to suck in air. Blurs of blue and green reflections appear in front of his eyes. Nikolas arches his back to reach for the top. Bright light glares white through the water's rim. Closer. Brighter. The strength of his upper body hauls him steady to the top until he breaks free. Nikolas sucks in all the air his lungs will hold. Another wave rolls over his head. He plunges deeper and swims a length. Searching. Searching for a clue. Some clue of her body. Nothing. Nikolas comes up for air and lunges immediately into the depths again. Each time he comes up for breath, he sees Georgi hunkering on the ledge, one knee resting on the rock and one knee supporting his elbow. Georgi is right. She's lost.

MARA LEANS FORWARD to peer out the window. Men dressed in black surround the carriage. Their cries intensify as the carriage slows. Loud blasts explode up in the air, one after the other. She covers her ears from the sound. Nana's eyes open wide. What is going on? Mara leans forward to open the door. Nana stops her halfway.

"*Nooo*! Stay here."

"What are we supposed to do here? Wait for them to drag us out?"

"Maybe they will leave us alone."

"I doubt it. I must see what the fuss is about."

"Mara, no. You heard the guns."

Mara unlatches the door and opens it. The first thing she notices are rifles. Then men. Men stampeding. Men shaking their rifles in the air. "I also see them pointed to the sky and not us."

Roaring, chanting, men encircle the carriage. "Victory to Greece! Victory for Morea!" Mara stares at the scene in front of her for a minute and then up at the coachman. Coachman shrugs. A short man with a black bandana wrapped around his head jumps up close to her face yelling, "Victory, Madam, Victory!" Each one shouts in her direction as they continue to blaze their trail down the road, shouting and blasting their rifles into the sky.

Mars looks at Nana. "What does this mean?"

"I don't know. We need to get home and see if your father has returned from Kerkyra and his dealings with Lord Maitland and Ali Pasha."

"I'm worried."

"Shh, child. Your father will be fine. He's assigned to the United States of Ionia, not with Greece."

"But he is much used by Ali Pasha and the Grand Vizier of Egypt here, where we are."

"Don't worry." Nana pats Mara's lap twice. "That is his job. He knows what he's doing. Let's get home where we will be safe."

THE MANOR HOUSE BUSTLES. Ali Pasha's party swarms the gates. Lord Conrad Wingrove knows this is only the beginning. Ibrahim Pasha arrives from Egypt in the next days ahead. Kyria Vasiliki enters the house. She immediately exacts her position in the household.

"Come now, Conrad Wingrove. How do you expect us to remain here in these small spaces?" She must believe her use of his full name somehow elevates her status. It doesn't, but Wingrove isn't going to be the one to tell her.

He follows her example and responds in like manner. "Kyria Vasiliki, forgive the meager amenities."

The lady raises one eyebrow and surveys the room around her. "His Highness the Pasha must have larger space than this." She raises her hands in an upward motion and spins around. "Where will you put the Egyptians when they arrive on the morrow?"

Wingrove wishes he could have left them to fend for themselves in Morea. Maybe a taste of life at the hands of the rebels would ease her comforts. He folds his hands behind his back, tapping the heels of his feet together, bowing slightly before her. "I'm sure we will arrange for suitable accommodations."

"Indeed, and you call these suitable accommodations for Pasha?" The lady crosses her arms across her chest and steps one foot back.

What the devil does this woman expect? Doesn't she know he's not royalty? Allowing them safe haven in his home is a *favor* to Maitland. He doesn't owe them anything. God only knows what will happen when Mara returns. Wingrove peeks at the bronze clock above the fireplace. It must be wrong. Mara should have been home by now. He pulls out his time piece to compare the time. The clock is not wrong. Kyria Vasiliki's rambling continues. He must put her straight. "My lady, His Highness, the Pasha, was not expected in this, my humble home. However, if you wish to make arrangements elsewhere on the island or to return to Morea— "

"No, no. This will do, I suppose. Pasha will meet with the Egyptians and make arrangements with the Sultan on what will be done with this, this Kalamata business." She raises her chin like the English heiresses from home. "We must endure the hardship." She looks around the room and clutches her clothing tight to her chest. Hardship indeed. Every comfort known to English high society is available to them. Miss "high in the instep" will need to adapt. Wingrove wipes his forehead and rings the bell for his servant. He will need to be advised the moment Mara returns. She is late.

NIKOLAS STANDS WITH GEORGI in front of Captain Heathcote's large mahogany desk, waiting.

Heathcote strums his fingers on the wood and stares at the missive he's holding in his hands. "We're going to have a rebellion." Heathcote flicks the letter down and pivots his glare from one to the other while he speaks. "Twenty workers did not show up for their angaria today. We need to get a handle on this."

Nikolas knows it will not stop there. The Turkish fall at Kalamata is only the beginning. No doubt his father and uncle are behind it.

Heathcote snaps up the letter and throws it across his desk. It glides along the edge and stops before falling to the floor. "Lord Wingrove advises me Ali Pasha has arrived today for an extended stay on the island while he meets with the Grand Vizier from Egypt. They are to consult to determine what should be done and collaborate on their reports to the Sultan."

"Ali Pasha's here on the Island?" Georgi's face is pale and his voice cracks when he speaks. The reason for his question is clear. Many Greeks fear the Ali Pasha's rule. They will not like the idea of him on the Island. No doubt they also will not like having the Grand Vizier visit either. Regardless of his fear, Georgi presses the matter further. "What business does he have here? Cerigo belongs to the United States of Ionia."

Heathcote stands up and walks around his desk to sit on the corner. "Yes, Georgi. And, it will stay that way. Lord Wingrove is one of the Dragomans used by High Commissioner Maitland. This Kalamata situation must be addressed in a neutral setting."

"Here on Cerigo? Is dangerous." Georgi shakes his head. His broken English and Greek accent is more emotional and pronounced. "Too close to Morea and too far away from the rest of Ionia." Heathcote looks at Georgi without responding.

Nikolas needs to help Georgi settle his nerves. At this rate, there lies risks of being compromised. "I'm sure the Captain and the High Commissioner are aware, Georgi. Maybe best to go and see to those in your village. Make them see the importance of neutrality." Nikolas nods at Heathcote for a silent acknowledgement.

Heathcote picks up on Nikolas' attempt to refocus his friend. "Yes. Quite right. I advise the same." Heathcote wraps his arm around Georgi's shoulders, moving him in the direction of the door as he continues to address the subject. "Impress upon them the importance of keeping the angaria. There are already too many men who now need to do two days for missing today. Let's not make it worse, or I will need to send for reinforcements. We don't want that, do we?" Heathcote stops and waits for Georgi to reply.

"I understand, sir. All I can do is let them know your position. I cannot guarantee compliance." Heathcote's eyes narrow as soon as Georgi finishes the last word of his sentence. Not good.

Heathcote drops his hands to his sides, straightens his back, and clicks his heels. His words are now stern and command obedience. "They will regret any disobedience, I can assure you. I'm counting on you to make them understand. We have plenty of troops. I need only send word."

Georgi's jaw tightens. He needs to hold his tongue. Heathcote is not in a mood for any guff at this moment. Nikolas short-nods his head to give the subtle warning to Georgi. Don't speak.

"Very well." Georgi heeds the warning. Nikolas can hear the sound of his own breath pass through his teeth. He must have been holding it.

Heathcote resumes his escort of Georgi to the door and closes it after him. He heads back to his desk and takes a seat behind.

"Nikolas, I need you to do something for me."

Another breath hisses through Nikolas' teeth.

CHAPTER THREE

ENGLISH FORMAL WEAR. Not as accommodating as what's worn by the Klephts. How does one wear such fashions daily? The shoes. Heels and buckles, most annoying. Nikolas scuffs the tips of the shoes with each step until he reaches the manor. Heathcote expects a full recap of this evening's events. Nikolas cannot fathom what can be so important, requiring his attendance at a formal dinner. In the dining hall, Nikolas hands his walking stick to Wingrove's butler, and is led into the study. No one stands except Wingrove. Not surprising.

"Welcome, Nikolas. Thank you for joining us." Wingrove motions for him to follow. "Come, sit here next to the fire." Wingrove moves to the side to allow Nikolas to pass. Judging from attire, one of the men sitting must be Ali Pasha. Things are beginning to make sense.

Wingrove extends his hand in the direction of his guests. "May I introduce to you, His Excellency Ali Pasha of Ioannina." The elderly man does not stand up, his long white hair is pulled back and fastened. His pointed beard covers his neck and reaches his waist. Ali Pasha barely bows his head in acknowledgment. So, this is the famed Lion. Ali Pasha's eyes squint. He glares at the top of my head and ends at the buckles on my shoes. The woman sitting next to him is dark-skinned and much younger. Thirties, maybe? She lifts her chin high in the air in a failed attempt to look down at me. This is his

"Greek Queen?" It could be said she was not given a choice with the Turks. They take. They always take, but she appears content in her position by her Pasha's side.

Wingrove then introduces a much younger man. "And, also, the Grand Vizier of Egypt's representative, His Highness, Ibrahim Pasha." This young man immediately stands and offers Nikolas his hand. A notable difference of behavior. Ali Pasha is less than pleased from the look of it. He turns his white, maned head to the side and mumbles in tones resembling insults. Wingrove stands silent while the younger stares down at His Excellency, smiles, bows, and sits.

Nikolas seeks to break the awkward silence. He has no desire to encourage the display of two rivals vying for dominance. He bows to each of them, smiles at one, and then the other. "I am pleased to meet you both."

Wingrove steps forward between them. "Gentlemen, welcome to my home here on Cerigo. It is my hope we may enjoy the evening tonight in preparation for his Lord High Commissioner's arrival within the week."

What? Nikolas snaps his head toward Wingrove. Did he hear correctly? "His Lord High Commissioner is coming here, to Cerigo? Maitland is coming here?"

"Yes, yes. He'll be staying at the Castle, of course, but he will join us as soon as possible after his arrival."

"I see." Nikolas doesn't actually see at all. What is Heathcote up to? Is he expected to spy on the Turks? Possibly. The only instructions were to appear for dinner, tonight, at Wingrove's invitation.

APHRODITE MINE

The door to the sitting room opens. A young lady enters. Her hair, a familiar color. Blue eyes, the color of the sea at midday. Nikolas' stomach churns like the waves of the ocean that engulfed her. Only it didn't. She's here. The lady who fell over the cliffs. Maybe she's a twin? Possible, but doubtful. Nikolas wants to run to her. Touch her. Make sure she is real and alive. But he holds himself back.

Wingrove's voice brings him back to present company. "Gentlemen, I would like to introduce you to my daughter, Lady Tamara Wingrove, Hostess of tonight's evening." She curtsies and smiles. The Turks are staring.

How can Wingrove stand it? They're looking at her as if she were for sale. He must recognize it on their faces. Something must be done.

Nikolas steps forward to impede their view. "My lady, I'm delighted to make your acquaintance." He offers his hand and she takes it. Her eyes meet his on level ground. Tall and elegant. The height of a Klepht. "May I offer my seat over here by the fire?" He must get her to the farthest seat from the Turks in the room. Ali Pasha takes two seats at least. He will stand by her side if he must.

"Thank you." She does not look away from him when she speaks. Nikolas doesn't either. He continues his hold of her hand, glued in its place between them. He senses the rivets of glaring eyes surrounding him. He doesn't care.

Wingrove clears his throat and gently separates them. "Mara, my dear, may I introduce Nikolas Stamatelopoulos. He is assigned here to the Island by the Lord High Commissioner Maitland and reports to Captain Heathcote. He is representative for the Greeks."

"Ah, that explains it." Explains what? What does she mean?

The young one called Ibrahim sits up straighter in his chair. His obnoxious whine of a voice leaves no doubt as to his thoughts about Greece. "A representative of the Greeks? The Greeks have no need for representation."

Wingrove turns to meet Ibrahim's announcement. His head is bowed slightly when he answers. "Of course, I did not mean to offend. As you know, there are the Greek *armatoli*, or militia, who help and support the Pasha with their requirements."

Ibrahim turns to Ali Pasha. "Is this true? If this is so, why not use them to stop the rebels?"

Ali Pasha's rivets are removed from one scene and squarely pointed at Ibrahim. "It is. We will discuss this more with the Lord High Commissioner when he arrives."

"As you wish." Ibrahim's leers are not silenced. His eyes are redirected to Nikolas and roll from the top of his head until they reach the buckles of his shoes. "If you belong to these, how do you call them, *armatoli*, how is it you dress as an Englishman?" Ibrahim puts his hand to the side of his face and tilts his head. He thinks he masks his insults by feigning innocence. Turks. Nikolas wants to knock the jeweled, green turban clean from his head. As if this Turk's attire is any less astonishing.

Nikolas summons the experience of his training. He swallows hard, focused on remaining in control when he speaks. "Your Highness, if one wishes to associate in polite society, one must adapt." Nikolas maneuvers his hands in sync, on either side of himself, in such a way as to highlight his own attire from top to bottom as if showcasing a prime piece of horseflesh. "I assure you, when worn correctly, English attire is more than accommodating. Should you wish to try out a pair of breeches, tailcoat and shoes, I'm sure Wingrove might find something that meets with your approval." The experience of his training is lost.

Wingrove's eyes roll to the ceiling.

Ali Pasha slams his mace to the floor.

A second woman enters the sitting room at the same time as Ali Pasha roars "Enough!"

This woman falls to the ground. Her black tresses weave through her fingers as she covers her head.

"NANA!" MARA KNEELS to where Nana has fallen to the floor. What is wrong with her? Dreadful Pasha. Mara seeks out her father for help. Dragoman or not, he needs to keep his Ottoman guests in check. Mara lifts her governess's face so that she can see her. "Nana, are you okay? Talk to me." Wingrove helps Nana to her feet. She's sobbing now.

"Forgive me. I, I did not mean to react so." Nana's face is pale and her eyes glossy. Her voice is shaky. "It was so very sudden. I had not expected..."

Mara moves the hair away from Nana's face, gentle and kind. "Of course you didn't. No one did." Mara stares blades at the Pasha. He's sparring back with dark blades of his own, eyes that glow black onyx. His long white beard hides his mouth. The mouth of a goat. And, he's evil too.

Nana's soft voice brings Mara's attention back to the task at hand. "Don't worry, Maraki, I will be okay. I was just startled." Nana lets go of Wingrove's steadying hand and swipes her hands down the front of her gown.

Mara wants to get her out of this room. Away from those who frightened her so. "Come. Let us leave until dinner. I'm sure the men can find some topic of conversation to amuse them."

"No, Mara." Lovina takes Mara's hand and pats the top twice. "Let us sit as we should." Nana bows down to the Ali Pasha and Kyria Vasiliki. "Forgive me Your Excellency for my clumsiness." What is Nana doing? Clumsiness? She should not be asking his forgiveness! He should be asking for hers.

Kyria Vasiliki moves closer to her Pasha and taps the seat opposite her. "Come, sit. Tell us your name. We get acquainted."

Wingrove stumbles forward to intervene. "Allow me. May I present Lovina Aponsuwa. She is companion to my daughter."

"Companion? Hmm, come now. You must sit. Let us discuss this island we find ourselves in, shall we? I'm sure we must have much in common, yes?"

Mara is not happy. How can her father allow it? Nana is much more than companion. Nana raised her. Has always been a mother to her. Lovina must not be devalued.

"My lady, may I engage a further moment of your time?" Nikolas pulls at Mara's elbow. What can he possibly want? Mara isn't sure she wants to know. She means to turn away when he tugs again. "I assure you it is of a pressing nature."

Ibrahim Pasha attends to her on the other side. "You must be chilled. Come sit here by the fire. It will soothe you after such an episode." Episode? Mara isn't the one needing soothed. Ibrahim extends his arm for her to follow. Of course, the seat he offers is next to his. What does he seek to gain? Slimy newt!

Mara tangles with the idea of leaving them all and taking Nana with her. With her to the safety of their sitting room. Never in their travels has she been in such demand. Why doesn't her father intervene on their behalf? In that moment, her father's words, and her Nana's, echo in Mara's head. The Ottomans treat their women different than the English. She must be careful not to offend. The Klepht's company is preferable. And Lovina's voice is calmer. Mara can hear her in conversation with Kyria Vasiliki. She'll need to gauge the situation for herself.

Intense pain slams the back of her legs. So intense that her balance is lost and she falls back. Mara's feet leave the ground so fast, the only thing she's aware of is one firm chest pressed hard against her mouth. The decision is made.

THIS IS NOT GOOD. NIKOLAS knows immediately that he should have acted sooner. Ibrahim Pasha's intent was clear from the moment Mara walked in the room. And it's also clear she doesn't know what to do. If she offends him, Ibrahim will exact the punishment. Nikolas must do something. Doesn't she know to 'swoon?' English ladies always swoon to avoid circumstances they don't wish to address. Nikolas will have to teach her. Furniture and dress fabric will hide his part in the action. Hopefully. "Lady Mara, are you ill?" Nikolas clips the back of her legs with his foot and scoops her up in his arms, in one movement flat.

"Mara?" Wingrove rushes over. His brows are furrowed. He takes her hand in his to lead the way to Nikolas' seat, vacated earlier. He lowers her so she can sit and helps her to lean back. Wingrove calls for servants to bring water. Her eyes are closed. She's breathing heavy. Did he hurt her? Lovina scrambles to a place on her other side. "Maraki, what is it, dear?" She smooths the hair from the edges of Mara's forehead with a mother's touch.

Ibrahim Pasha clops his heels together once, walks over to stand above the two women, and then clops again. Nikolas moves to the side so Wingrove and Lovina have more access, replacing Ibrahim's view with his body. Is it a face-off that he wants? Nikolas is all too familiar with his kind of menace. The Klephts have trained him well. Nikolas towers over Ibrahim's short stature. As expected, Ibrahim breaks frame first.

Mara whimpers from her chair. "What happened?"

Nikolas watches a servant pour a glass of water and hand it to Wingrove. "I believe you may have fainted, my dear." Wingrove places the glass gently against her lips. "Here, take a sip of this to help you feel better." Wingrove nods at Lovina and she takes over the task.

Wingrove stands and announces, "Maybe it's best we all move into the dining room. Dinner will no doubt provide us all with the strength we need for the evening."

Nikolas stays by Mara's side. He's not moving first. Not until he's sure Mara is alright. Ali Pasha and Kyria Vasiliki leave first. Nikolas waits until Ibrahim Pasha follows. He doesn't.

Wingrove shuffles prominent members into the dining hall first. "Come, Your Highness, if you please." He extends his arm for Ibrahim to follow. Ibrahim huffs in the direction of the party leaving the room to follow Ali Pasha.

Nikolas offers his hand to Lovina. Wingrove helps Mara to her feet, escorting her into the dining hall. Her hand presses Nikolas' forearm when he passes. The words "Thank you." drift from her lips.

Lovina curls her arm into Nikolas' elbow to take their turn last. "Thank you for your kindness."

"I only hope I did enough." One thought sticks in Nikolas' brain. Ibrahim Pasha will not stop until he gets what he wants.

IT IS DIFFICULT TO focus on the food on her plate. Mara can't shake the feeling. Nikolas' embrace. His protection. Thankfully she was able to ascertain his intentions soon enough. But what about her intentions? His rugged, Klepht appearance conflicts with his English comportment. He'll not fit in London Society. He is too dark. Too tall. Not unlike herself. For she is also considered too dark, too tall. These things are often overlooked on her account, having the benefit of English parentage. But where did he go to school? So many questions infiltrate her thoughts but she dare not ask. One must not show too much interest.

Mara squirms in her seat and stares at her plate as it's placed before her. If only the vile man sitting across from her would stop gawking. Ibrahim Pasha licks his lips every time his eyes meet hers. He isn't even acknowledging her father and his attempts to keep the conversation neutral and at a steady pace. Will this evening ever end?

"Do you not like the mutton?" Soft and kind is the voice that yanks her back to the present. The dimples on each side of Nikolas' smile draw Mara's thoughts into a more positive stretch. She watches him place a bite into his mouth and chew. So focused, she forgets to respond. "Am I to take that as a yes?"

Mara shakes her head to clear the confusion clouding her brain. "Um, yes. I like it." Now it's his smile that's pulled her in. A perfect, straight-tooth smile. "I must still be overwhelmed by earlier events."

"Understandable. I'm surprised you were not confined to your rooms for the evening to recover."

The reality of his words return her to the seriousness of what almost happened. Mara speaks in an undertone. "That may have been an insult to our guests, I imagine."

"Surely they could not object to you being ill?" Nikolas does not follow her example, unless he doesn't understand the need for discretion. He forks another piece of meat.

Mara glances across the table. It will not do to become the center of attention again. Everyone is eating. She exhales a deep breath. Relief. Mara continues speaking barely above a whisper. "I don't know. We need to be correct in our protocol while entertaining members of the Sultan's Empire. I'm sure *that* is first and foremost on Papa's mind."

"And, have you always entertained the Turkish dignitaries?" Does this man have no concept of discretion? It's almost as though he's speaking so on purpose.

Mara remains firm in her efforts to coax him into softer tones. "Actually, no. This is the first I can recall."

"It must be the rebellion." Nikolas places the meat in his mouth.

"Rebellion?"

"You haven't heard?" Nikolas raises one brow. "Of Kalamata?"

Of course she's heard, although she's not inclined to explain how she's heard. Best to maintain a sense of innocence. "I had heard something mumbled by servants, but wasn't sure exactly what it meant. I haven't spoken with Papa as yet about it. What happened?"

"Maybe I should not have brought it up." Nikolas sits back in his chair and wipes his mouth with his napkin.

"No." Mara places her hand on his forearm to urge him to continue. "Now you must tell for I won't stop until you do."

A closed mouth smile spreads across Nikolas' face, almost as nice as before, but not quite. "Kalamata has fallen to the Greeks."

"Oh, my! That is news. No wonder Papa is on edge and the Pashas are here. Do they think it will continue? Will they come here?" Forget undertones and hushed whispers. Mara gulps her water down complete in one instant. The heat in the room is stifling.

"Calm yourself. I don't think they will come here. Cerigo is British, not Ottoman. It's somewhat of a neutral base. It's why they're here."

Mara waves a cloth napkin in front of her face. Her fan is nowhere to be found. "Yes, there is that. I forget at times since we're surrounded by Greeks mostly. Except, of course, when

I'm home. Even then, socializing is often among the Society of Avlemona." Mara replaces the napkin across her lap. Why is she babbling on?

"Ah, I see." Nikolas raises his glass for the footman to refill with wine.

She must attempt to change the subject. "And, may I ask how you came to be, well...you clearly are not British. How is it you are so well educated in English customs and manners?"

"That is an easy question." Nikolas wipes his mouth with his napkin and takes a drink of wine. "My father and uncle wanted to protect me from the Turks. They are of the Greek rebels. Klepht Captains." So he does understand an undertone when it suits him.

"Oh. You support the rebellion."

"I did not say that." Nikolas turns slightly in his seat to face her. "My uncle made arrangements with the Lord High Commissioner for me to have an education in Kerkyra. I am to hold an Ambassador position in the future."

"So, you do not support the rebellion."

Their conversation is stalled when a servant brushes past to hand a note to her father. He reads it, folds it, places it in his pocket, and stands to address the party. "If you will excuse me for just a moment." He leaves the room. This cannot be good. Mara watches Nikolas. If the set of his jaw is any indication, he too is concerned. Her father never leaves the room during dinner. Especially, with guests of this caliber present. Mara wipes her palms down the length of her skirt. Instinct tells her something is amiss.

"Are you alright?" Why is he asking this? Is he going to carry her away again? More swells swirl in her stomach, for a different reason entirely.

Mara answers before allowing him a chance to consider anything of the sort. "Yes. Fine, thank you." His gaze lingers and the warmth of it freezes any reaction. Mara wants to lean closer. Very improper. What would Nana say? He's not even titled. Titled. Titled gentlemen are nowhere to be found anywhere near the place her father serves. Mara drifts close.

"I must insist!" Kyria Vasiliki is standing. The talk between them is broken. Nikolas snaps his attention to Vasiliki. Drat the woman. What is she complaining about now? "The host has left us. There is no hostess I can see of age so I must take the initiative. It is time for His Excellency to recline." Kyria Vasiliki calls out instructions to the servants to bring in massive floor pillows along with the nargile. "Come. We must leave the men to their pipes and relaxation." Kyria Vasiliki stomps a foot to the floor to demand compliance.

Nikolas leans in. His breath tickles Mara's ear when he whispers. "Best do what she asks."

Nana stands. Mara has no choice but to follow. Kyria Vasiliki leads the way. Once the doors are closed behind them, she turns and stops. "Well? Now where do we go?"

Mara watches Nana for a reaction. This Kyria of the Turks commands the room and then asks for direction? Mara isn't sure if a response is the correct course or not given the woman's status, but decides to respond anyway. "We could retire for the evening? Or...what does Her Excellency wish to do?"

"Her Excellency? Please. If Ali heard you, he would have your head." Mara's stomach burns. Ali Pasha is cruel. Especially against people who displease him. Kyria Vasiliki stands before them and laughs. Not the reaction Mara expected. Is the lady joking?

"You must call me Vaso. Come. We go to my room. I have my own nargile." Vaso pulls Mara's one hand and links it with hers. "Have you ever smoked from nargile? No? Probably not. I show you." Mara looks over her shoulder. She doesn't want to lose Nana. She's following behind with her eyes to the floor. Vaso moves them both forward. Her bangling bracelets keep pace with her walk. "We will dance. Servants will play music. But, not the English dance." Vaso stops to shake her forefinger in front of Mara's face. "I show you that too." Vaso laughs some more. "We will enjoy. My tobacco will relax you. It is the best. You will see."

NIKOLAS DOES HIS BEST to avoid the pipe. He's seen its effect too often on its users. His clan especially. He knows he'll have to accept it at least once. What happened that forced Wingrove to abandon his party? It must have been important. Wingrove must know Ibrahim Pasha will not relinquish the prize he believes he has acquired in Mara. His displeasure with Nikolas is apparent. And Ali Pasha is allowing it. That is not a good sign. Nikolas does not like the direction of the conversation. Where is Wingrove?

"Ibrahim, you wish to convey the Dragoman and his household to Egypt. This is your recommendation?" Ali Pasha's words are more a statement than a question. Ibrahim has fixed his interest in Mara, this much is clear. How can he persuade the topic to something more neutral?

"Yes. And you, also, your Excellency may return as well while we continue to execute the rebels." Ibrahim's sly, accommodating manner makes Nikolas' blood boil. Execute the rebels.

Ali Pasha draws in deep on the nargile, holds it, and exhales the smoke in the direction of Ibrahim. Nikolas wants to execute him. Here. Now. But that's not his mission. He does the only thing he can. Use his words.

"If I may ask, His Excellency, how will this benefit the Ottoman dynasty if you and your household are not nearer to the conflict to address any concerns and direct matters in the way it should be done?" His words meet silence.

Ali Pasha's glassy eyes stare through him without blinking. He rolls the wooden mouthpiece between his fingers. His eyes narrow. "This reyah speaks truth. How is this beneficial to me if we are not here to kill them where they stand and build towers of their skulls?"

A vision of slitting the old goat's throat will have to suffice. And Ibrahim's. For now, he must follow instructions. Observe and report. No harm must come to the ladies in the house. They are not bred in the ways of the Klepht women. These women are genteel and unaccustomed to the atrocity of war. No. He must stand down and keep control. No matter what.

Ibrahim's whiny laugh doesn't help. "Of course, you are right Your Excellency. We shall move this Lord High Commissioner to take us to Kerkyra."

"No!" The mace slams to the floor. "Are you not listening? I will not leave Morea. I come here only to meet with you and the Ionian States. Leave Morea? I will not. It will not be given over to these reyahs."

Wingrove enters the dining hall. Finally. He looks at the table where no one is seated and walks to the end where the floor pillows are spread out for reclining. "Ah, here you are. I'm glad you have made yourself at home. I apologize for having been called away for so long. We have a minor incident we must attend to." Wingrove lowers his hand to Nikolas. "I will need you to join me in my study immediately."

The Pashas are not happy. "What is this minor incident?"

Wingrove addresses Ali Pasha's question. "It is a matter we need to deal with regarding the angaria. Please continue to relax. The servants will attend to you and provide anything you require. Nikolas, come."

Wingrove walks to the door. The Pashas' words echo through as it closes. Once more Nikolas must fight the urge to shoot them where they stand or, as the case may be, where they sit.

The study is dark and damp. A man sitting in front of the desk with his back to the door turns. "Georgi! What happened?"

"It's bad. I did what I could. The villagers will not stand down. They're ready to revolt like they did in Kalamata. They say reinforcements are on the way. Captain Heathcote sent me here with instructions."

"What instructions?"

Wingrove motions for the men to sit. "I've already gone over them with Georgi. I need you both to escort Lady Mara and Lovina to the Lord High Commissioner's palace in Kerkyra."

"And you? Are you not coming?"

"Not at this time. I will need to continue here as Dragoman for the Turks. It's important to avoid any miscommunications. I must ensure the ladies' safety."

"Is the Lord High Commissioner arriving before we are to depart?"

"No, you will need to leave as soon as passage may be secured. I've just been informed Sir Maitland will not be back in Kerkyra for a few more weeks."

"So, he is not on his way here?"

Nikolas looks at one and then the other. Georgi shakes his head and Wingrove answers. "No. Plans have changed. He's on his way back from a mandatory meeting with the Regent."

This is not what his father and uncle had in mind for him. Wingrove is desperate. Worried. "Please. Nikolas, Georgi, I need to ensure my daughter and her companion are safe. Can I entrust them to your care?"

Nikolas isn't sure this is a task his father and uncle would approve, but he cannot refuse. "We'll need to leave at once to begin the preparations." Nikolas stands up to go and Georgi follows.

Wingrove escorts them out. "I cannot tell you how much I'm obliged to you."

"We may need to use unconventional means to get off the island depending on how far the rebels' reach is." It's more absolute than probable but Nikolas doesn't tell Wingrove. From the look of his face, he most assuredly already knows.

"Just keep them safe." Wingrove shakes Nikolas' hand and then steps out into the hallway. The door is closed. The light from two torches near the entrance dims.

"Georgi, do you think you can get in touch with the Maniotes? Are there any that would help us?"

"Probably. For a price."

"You heard her father. Whatever it takes."

"I'll look into it." Georgi heads for the stables to get his horse.

The clong, clong, clong of drumbeats echo around the side of the house. Nikolas follows the sound. Laughter and giggles chime above his head. The veranda is round and wide atop a glass enclosure below. It's Mara and Lovina. Another woman sits lower to the floor. They're smoking a nargile. With Kyria Vasiliki! Nikolas is glued to the grass where he stands. Mara. Her dark hair flows long below her waist. Her bare waist. Her hips move with the beat of the drum. The shimmy of bangles jingle when she moves in one direction, then the other. She lifts her hair with her hands and leans back letting it flow through her fingers in the process. The drumbeat intensifies. She shimmies her shoulders and then her breasts to the rhythm. He should leave. But he can't. He sits down and leans against a tree. Mara's movements flow with force and grace into each beat of the drum. His heart races with it. Mara turns and lifts her leg to rest on the edge of the veranda. Her bare leg. She bends back so far all he can see is the ripple of her stomach moving in time with each tap of the music. When she straightens and returns to an upright position, her arms are curved, but level with her shoulders. She slings one arm and then the other like a quiet whip and then she stops, dead stops. Looking straight ahead. Can she see him watching? Watching her in the dark?

CHAPTER FOUR

Ionian Sea

"PAPA, I WANT YOU TO come with us." Mara inches close to her father and cuffs her arm around his. The cold, crisp air whistles around them. Her stomach is a twisted mess.

Her father pats her hand resting on his elbow. "I know, my dear. But, I must stay here. You know this. As Dragoman, I must be available to ensure there are no miscommunications between the parties."

"But it's dangerous."

"Listen. I will be fine. Captain Heathcote and his men are here. And, as you know, the Pashas are here as well. For now, I believe I am well protected."

"But..." Mara's father kisses her cheek and helps her up into the carriage. Worry prickles her insides. She looks over at Nana already seated and ready to go. How can she be so calm?

Nikolas is mounted on his stallion beside the carriage. His black stallion. He's also wearing black. Black like the rebel pirates in the stories her father shares about some of his adventures. Mara swallows hard and clenches her eyes tight for a minute, but it doesn't help. Tears seep out of the corners of her eyes and down her cheeks. Why won't her father come with them?

Nana moves closer to Mara's side. She immediately falls into her Nana's arms. Nana's words are whispers in Mara's ear. "Maraki, you must not be so upset. You know the dangers of staying another day here. Kyria Vasiliki was very vocal on her observations yesterday."

"Kyria Vasiliki. You mean Vaso. I don't know if we should believe a word from her mouth. I think the tobacco we smoked had something in it."

"Maybe. We don't have to have her with us anymore. But she is right about her warnings of Ibrahim Pasha's intentions. He has set his eye for you. It is good we will be out of his reach soon."

"What? Do you really think he would kidnap a British diplomat's daughter? And take her for his bride?"

"I don't know, but I don't want to stay and find out." The carriage jostles from one side to the other. Mara leans her head on Nana's shoulder and lets the comfort envelop her. Creeks and forests pass by the window on the way to the harbor. She may as well accept it. Mara is determined to find out more about where they're taking her so she leans out the carriage window to speak to Nikolas.

"Do you know who will be providing the passage to Kerkyra?"

Nikolas answers without turning in Mara's direction. "Georgi will be meeting up with us shortly with the specifics."

"Georgi?"

"He's sent by Captain Heathcote."

"Is he also a Greek?"

"Yes."

"Hmm. Can you trust him?"

Finally, the man turns in her direction. "I've known Georgi for as long as I have been here on Cerigo. He has always been honest and loyal. I trust him."

Nana pulls Mara's sleeve from behind. "Mara, sit back now. You'll hurt your neck the way you're leaning out."

Mara twists back into the carriage. More black. The carriage is fitted in black velvet throughout. Bland and boring. There is never a thing to do when riding. Mara slides open the window and leans out again. She has an idea that will boost her spirits.

"Can we not switch for a while? You ride in here and I will ride your stallion?"

"Mara, no!" Nana grabs her sleeve and pulls hard this time. Nikolas laughs. That got his attention. He bends down to look inside.

"I don't think it wise. My job is to keep you safe, remember?" He's wearing the same warm smile he had a few nights ago at dinner. Mara's stomach zings. Nana bends across Mara to talk to him.

"Thank you. We are most grateful."

Galloping horses interrupt the conversation. The carriage stops and Nikolas meets the riders ahead. Mara tries to hear what they're saying. It sounds like Greek but she can't be sure. What she does see is the hard line of Nikolas' jaw. He's staring out in the distance. What is he trying to see?

Nikolas dismounts, opens the carriage door, and pulls Mara out so fast she doesn't have time to blink. "You're getting your ride on my stallion after all."

"What?" Nana's voice is sharp. "No. She will not."

Nikolas pulls Nana out next. "I'm sorry, there's no alternative. You'll have to ride too."

"Absolutely not. We are not dressed for it. How do you expect us to ride?"

"It doesn't matter, and we don't have time." Nikolas moves quick and slick. She's out of the carriage before her next breath.

Nana tries to hold firm by grabbing the stallion's reins. "No. I won't allow it. We must stay in the carriage where it's safe."

Nikolas' voice is more severe. "Miss Aponsuwa, Greek rebels are on this road as we speak. They will not be kind, I can assure you. They are intent to follow the example set in Kalamata. Captain Heathcote has already detached a unit to address the situation. We cannot be on this road and the carriage cannot go into the terrain."

Mara watches paleness creep into Nana's face, at the same time her own fear grips her insides. "Nana, we must do what Nikolas says."

Nikolas takes charge of his stallion's reins.

Nana shakes her head. "I don't like it, Maraki. I don't like it at all."

Mara watches Georgi coax Nana into the saddle of his horse. He looks at Nikolas. His lips are tight. "It's not going to work like this."

Nana adjusts her seat in the saddle. "What do you mean?"

At first Mara isn't sure what the problem is, then she sees it. "Nana, you can't sit sideways. You have to ride astride."

"What? No. I have not ridden astride..."

"I know Nana, but you must."

"We need to move." Nikolas grabs Mara around her waist. The sudden sensation of his hands on her hips traps her breath in her throat for a short second. He hauls Mara up and holds her there. Mara grabs the horse's mane and tosses her leg over. The movement is fast. She doesn't think, it's automatic.

Nikolas puts his foot in the stirrup and pulls himself behind her. He takes the reins in one hand and wraps his other arm tight around Mara's waist. Her back is so close to his chest, she can feel it when he breathes. His solid, muscular form touching every part of her. From the neck to the back of her heels.

Mara looks to the side and sees her Nana Lovina riding astride with Georgi. Now her fear intensifies. Nana reaches out to try and touch Mara's hand but misses because Georgi takes off into the trees. Nikolas yells to the coachman to return to the manor to warn them, and then follows Georgi into the woods.

APHRODITE IS IN NIKOLAS' arms. Rather the girl the villagers believe to be Aphrodite. If only it wasn't to save her life. He enjoys the closeness of her body against his. She's strong and firm, not frail and limp. It's hard to focus. He needs to keep his mind on task. From Georgi's account, the band of men headed in their direction cannot be reasoned with. They have one goal. Independence. They will not stop for anything or anyone.

Echoes of shots sound from the direction they came. Captain Heathcote hasn't been able to catch up to them yet. Low, angry cries bounce toward them as they ride. Nikolas steals a quick look back and sees the group of men weaving through the woods in their direction. Some are on foot and some on horseback.

Nikolas kicks to move faster and line up with Georgi. Lovina's face is pale and mask-like. Georgi is trying to maneuver and keep her in the saddle at the same time. The hill they're climbing is rocky and the horses struggle for a steady footing.

If they can just reach the Harbor. Men there will help them board while keeping these rebels at a distance. Mara's grip on his horse's mane tightens. She trembles against his chest. Her breaths are heavy, but so are his. Momentum is what they need. At least the rebels are having the same difficulty. Another shot explodes through the air. Mara screams. He must get out of range. Another shot, then another. He doesn't have to kick too hard to keep moving up. The horses want out of the way as much as they do. More shots. Another scream. Close. No, it wasn't. It was a direct hit.

Georgi is bleeding from his right shoulder. Nikolas pushes his stallion forward still. Georgi's horse falls. Mara turns to look back.

"Don't."

"What do you mean? Nana!" Mara tries to see behind and struggles in her seat. Hard fists slam down on Nikolas' thighs. He holds Mara as tight as he can. She must not see them.

"Stop it. Mara! We need to get over that ridge. It's our only chance."

"We can't leave them." She tries to slap and misses. Shots start firing again. Mara stops and curls herself against his chest.

"Mara, trust me. We can't stop."

BRUTE...SAVAGE...MURDERER. He's not warm or kind. He left them. Forced her to leave Nana. Her nose is dripping. She doesn't care. Let it drip all over him. Let the rebels shoot them. She doesn't care.

Mara's body falls forward and away from the man holding her back. She looks up and sees the descent toward the sea in front of them.

"There! In the bay. That's where we need to get to." Mara doesn't want to hear his voice. She doesn't care what he has to say. "The maniots are already in port. If we get close enough to them, they'll give us cover while we board."

"They'll probably shoot us too."

"They've been paid. Paid well. They have a reputation for being pirates."

"Pirates? We're sailing to Kerkyra with pirates? Does my father know?"

"Your father tasked me to escort you safely to Kerkyra. I'm using whatever means available. If there was a British frigate in the area, I'm sure Captain Heathcote and your father would not have needed my assistance." Nikolas looks behind. "No one's coming over the hill yet. We need to move fast."

Mara has never in her life been this afraid. What was her father thinking? She'd much rather be with him. With Nana. "Can we please go back and check before we leave? Maybe they realized Georgi and Lovina aren't worth anything to them. Maybe they left."

"No." Mara tightens her hands so hard her fingernails dig into her palms like pins in a pincushion. "Georgi will take care of Lovina."

Mara wants down. Down off of his horse. And down off of this hill. "What if he's hurt?"

"Listen." Nikolas' voice is heavy and hard against her ear. "They will not hurt either of them. It's you they want."

"Me? Why?"

"Because they want the British to support their independence. Now, loosen your grip and relax or you'll have us both thrown."

"I don't understand. How can taking me help them? I've never been anything but supportive."

"This is the beginning of war." Nikolas looks back again.

"Is anyone coming?" Anxious breaths separate her words.

"No." Nikolas' one word stills the churning in her stomach.

A group of men are walking towards them as they reach the bottom, ragged and rough. These are the men who will protect us? Nikolas waves and they wave back.

The closer to the ship they get, the more details are clearer. It's not small. It's quite massive. Tall masts spear the center. Raised cabins are built on the deck. Windows line the sides below deck. Will that be where they stay?

As soon as Nikolas and Mara hit the bottom, men surround them. The mountain they just scaled has dots of movement, picking their way to the same spot they just came from. Mara shoves Nikolas to look where she points. Words are hung in her throat.

"I know. They won't get to us in time." Nikolas bends close to Mara when he stands up in the stirrup to swing one leg over and down. The strength of both his hands on her waist is in the same place as before when he helps her off the horse. It's not as before.

Nikolas greets each man with a bear hug and rough kiss to each cheek. "Good to see you, Manny."

"You too, Nikolas. I've heard many things of your father and your uncle." Manny's smile is wide and his lips are thick. His skin is dark like all the Greeks, but his eyes are green.

Shots splice the air. Manny and his men take an immediate stance behind rocks, pistols in position. "Don't worry. We're out of distance. They want to scare us. We show them."

"Nikolas! Hurry!" A female rebel yell bounds in their direction. "We need to set sail out of the harbor and into open water, far away from these mad men, yes?"

"Rachel?" Nikolas turns and looks at the woman standing on the deck of the ship. "What are you doing here?"

"Plenty of time to catch up. Move!" Rachel grabs the reins of Nikolas' stallion and rustles him on board. "Let's go! Both of you, don't stand there."

The men shooting at the rebels run past and start helping raise the sails. Others are pulling anchor. Rachel is shouting orders from a deck above. Nikolas is watching. Land begins to distance itself from the ship. How will she endure all this? Endure it without Nana.

Rachel jumps back down in front of where they're standing. "So Nikolas, are you going to introduce me to your wife?"

"WIFE?" MARA'S INCREDULOUS voice matches her wide eyes glaring the same question.

Nikolas stops her before she gives up his ruse. He grabs her hand to pull her close and wraps his arm around her shoulders. "Yes, my wife." He nods in her direction. She must understand his meaning.

"Wife?" Mara repeats, raises her eyebrows and bows her head. "Of course. Nikolas, dear, you must introduce us."

She's not dimwitted after all. "Yes, of course. Rachel, my wife..."

"Yes, we've already established she's your wife." Rachel is laughing at him. It's been years and she's still laughing at him. Rachel extends her hand to Mara. "Rachel Flessas."

"I am pleased to meet you. Tamara Wingrove." Mara curtsies and Rachel laughs. "You don't need to be doing any of that around here. Just watch you don't lose your balance and we need to fish you out of the sea." Rachel yells for one of the deck hands. "Give them the deck house. It's the nicest space for a couple." Rachel winks, turns around, and runs up the wooden ladder, giving sailors orders at each step. She stations herself in front of the wheel with her legs apart and hands behind her back.

"Are you coming, husband?" Nikolas follows the voice to Mara, who is now accompanying the deck hand taking them to their quarters. Nikolas inhales a deep breath. It's going to be a long voyage.

CHAPTER FIVE

THE DOOR CLOSES BEHIND her. Mara surveys the small cabin. A square desk is built into the side of the wall, above it is a curtained portal. Mara tries walking forward to look out; it's like she never learned to walk.

Strong hands grip the side of her hips. Again. "Whoa, easy." Nikolas holds her steady. The ship rocks. "It'll take time to get used to. Best to sit before moving around too much."

"I have been on a ship before you know." His hands do not move when she circles to face him. Warm, tingling sensations from his hands as they pass over her midsection and across the small of her back leave a circling trail around her waist. His face is so close to hers Mara can feel his breath when he breathes. Then she remembers. Remembers Nana. Nikolas left her. Left her to the rebels. The vision of Nana's face is still fresh in her mind. Mara slaps her hands on top of his and shoves them to his sides. She crushes them between her fingers in the process.

"Ow! I only meant to offer my help."

"Your help? What about Nana?" Tears well up in the corners of her eyes. Mara brushes them away. "And Georgi? Are they not good enough for your help?"

"Mara, please." Nikolas attempts to take her hand. She pulls away. "Georgi will take care of Lovina. I promise." Nikolas tries again to take her hand. This time she lets him. "He'll get her to Kerkyra." His reassuring words soothe the ache in her chest. "There was no choice, but to split."

Mara pulls her hand away again. "What do you mean? Split?"

"I mean he and I agreed your safety comes first. You're the one the rebels want. You're the one they hope will get the Lord High Commissioner's attention."

"Me? Why?"

"You must see your value is more than that of your companion?"

"No." Mara turns her back to him. "How can you say such a thing? My life is of no more consequence than someone else's."

"Mara, listen." Nikolas tries to turn her around, but Mara squeezes herself away refusing to allow him to touch her. "I agree. All life is priceless. But, this is war. And there is no limit to what some will do to get what they want. War brings out the worst."

Mara knows what he says is true but she doesn't want to agree. There's a knock on the cabin door. This gives her time to move closer to the desk and farther away from Nikolas. Mara holds on to the back of the chair to steady herself.

"Come in. It's open."

The same deck hand who showed them in earlier slips inside.

"Captain wants you to join her at her table for the evening meal."

"Right. Thank you."

"I'll come back when it's time to take you to the dining room." He slips out the same way he came in and the door closes. The rocking of the ship lulls the silence.

Mara waits to see if Nikolas will try to continue their conversation. He doesn't. The silence makes her uncomfortable. She searches for something to break it. "They have a dining room on the ship?"

"I guess this one does. Come, rest before dinner."

Nikolas takes a step closer to Mara and reaches for her hand again. His movements are slow. He pulls one finger into his palm, testing. Mara watches him pull each of her fingers into his grasp until they're tangled together. She doesn't know why she lets him. Something to do with the crazy sensations charging through her body each time he touches her? Something about the calm, reassuring way he comforts her? She's safe. Nikolas leads her to the bed. Her mind screams stop, but she knows she's safe. Mara sits down and lays back. He releases her hand and walks to the door. All of a sudden fear takes hold again. Mara sits up.

"Nikolas, wait."

"Don't worry. I'll be outside. It's alright."

The door closes. She waits for a minute before laying back down. How can she rest with all that's happened? She closes her eyes and then opens them repeatedly. The slow rocking of creaking wood and crish-crash of waves against the hull lull her eyes closed. Maybe sleep will come. Her breaths are even now and her body begins to relax. She rolls onto her side. She opens her eyes one last time. This room only has one bed.

SEA AIR CUTS ACROSS Nikolas' face. Cool temperatures calm the heat rising in his chest. Mara has reached places in him no woman ever has. He exhales deep breaths. He must control his actions, even his thoughts.

"Nikolas!" Rachel yells over the balustrade above. "Come up here. Join me. I have wine!"

Nikolas looks up at Rachel and waves. It'll be good to catch up with her. Nikolas climbs the pegs of the ladder two by two.

"Sit." Rachel motions for him to sit on a bench built near the edge. In the seat are wooden compartments holding different items of necessity. One holds a bottle of wine. Definitely a necessity. Rachel reaches in and grabs a wooden vessel, pours wine into it, and hands it to him. It's red. Good, red wine. Nikolas drinks down most of it in one swig. Rachel drinks from the bottle.

"Tell me." Nikolas leans back on the bench and puts his feet up along the seat. "How long have you been Captain of this ship?" The *kefi* that comes with the wine begins to flow through him.

"Not long. How long have you been married?" Rachel swings the bottle back and forth in one hand while keeping her other one steady on the wheel.

"Not long." Typical. Avoid the question and ask another. She did the same thing when they were children living in the mountains. He's learned a thing or two since then. He's not going to let her avoid this question. "And how is it you happened to become Captain of this ship?"

"How do you think?" Is she going to answer his every question like this? More wine. He needs more wine. Nikolas finishes what's left and hands it back for a refill.

"If I knew the answer I wouldn't be asking."

Rachel lifts the bottle to her lips and drinks it like water. "Do you think it improper for a woman to be ship's Captain?"

"I did not say that."

"Yes, but you're thinking it."

Always trying to argue. "Rachel, you know me well enough to know if I were thinking it, I would not hesitate to say it."

"Hmm. So you say." She drinks more wine before she answers. "Laskarina Bouboulis. Have you heard of her?"

"No." Now she's really toying with him. Nikolas has no plans of backing down. He crosses his arms over his chest. She'll need to explain.

"Don't look at me like that. I'm not lying. It's true. Karina is showing them all how it needs to be done, a true warrior."

"Tell me more." Rachel knows how to create drama. Always has. No doubt this will be another of her imaginations.

"What would you like to know?"

"How is it that a woman is able to appoint you as Captain of a ship?"

"That's easy. She owns this ship."

"Owns it?"

"Yes, and three others. She even Captains her own."

"And how did she obtain these ships?"

"She inherited a fortune. And a trading business from her husband when he died."

Nikolas watches his friend. He's not sure if he should believe her. "You're not making this up?"

Rachel throws her empty wine bottle over the side. It almost hits him in the head in the process. "What was that for?"

"I should do to you what I do to the crew who are insubordinate."

"Insubordinate?" Nikolas barely has time to laugh before another item goes flying by his head. What is wrong with her? That one would have knocked him out if he hadn't ducked. "Alright. I believe you. But, you have to admit it's very odd to think a woman is able to build ships, captain them, and appoint another woman as captain. Are all her captains women?"

Rachel puts two hands on the wheel now. "I don't know if all her captains are women. I know she is captain of her ship, the Agamemnon."

The wind is picking up. Rachel begins to wield the ship to her will. The strength in her arms tightens with the sails as she molds the ship to the direction she wants to go. This child he once knew is now a grown woman with the strength of a man. It's time to take her serious. "I'm still confused. How was this Karina able to build these ships under the nose of the Turks? And, they let her keep them?"

"That's easy. She bribed them."

"Bribed them? I can't believe that is all it takes. If that was all it takes, others would have done the same."

"It may also help to have the ear of the Sultan's mother."

"What is this nonsense?"

Rachel locks the wheel in place, turns, and places both hands on her hips. "It is not nonsense. It is actually brilliant. No one suspects a woman. And, Karina did go and meet with the Sultan's mother who convinced her son to leave her property alone. What they don't know, I'm sure, is how large the Agamemnon actually is. Wait until you see her."

Nikolas stares at Rachel, sure this must be some silly game, but it's not. Rachel's serious. Not even a slight lift of her lips ready to laugh. Dead serious. Nikolas cannot believe a woman is able to accomplish this. But then he recalls the strength of the women in his clan. No doubt any of them can take on a band of Turks if necessary. They've been trained to do it. "Does my father and my uncle know?"

"Kolokotronis? *Pfft*. I don't know. Probably, by now. As far as your father? I haven't heard from him in a while." Not surprising. "So, tell me Nikolas. What is this business with your wife? Why are those bandits after you?"

Rachel stares down at him. Waiting. Can he trust her? What if she decides to take Mara instead? Nikolas stands up. Now he's looking down at her. This is Rachel. They grew up together. Trained together. Fought together. The decision is clear. "They want to use her to leverage the Ionian States to join them."

"And she's someone of importance?"

"She's British. And the daughter of the Dragoman on the Island." Rachel remains silent. She squints her eyes, but doesn't remove her gaze. What is she contemplating?

"I knew it! You're not married."

"What? Of course we are. Why do you think we're not married?"

"You forget, Nik. I've known you, how long?"

The wind is slapping the sails above them. Why won't she turn her attention there instead? "And, that means what, exactly?"

"You do not handle her like a man who's taken his wife."

"And you know these things how?"

"Look around. I'm surrounded by men. I know men. I know how they act when they've taken a wife. You have not taken her."

"Fine." Anger boils inside him. Rachel pushes her forefinger into his chest until he sits back down.

"Now." Rachel props one leg on the bench beside him. "What are we going to do about her?"

Nikolas refuses to cower to her like one of her deck hands. He stands back up forcing her back on two feet. "What do you mean?"

"I mean, if you're going to get her safely to Kerkyra, you'll need to make some changes." Rachel walks back behind the wheel.

"What kind of changes?"

"First, she'll need to change her clothes. Her English finery stands out too much, not that it's all that fine anymore."

"Agreed." Nikolas walks closer to where Rachel is standing. "And where do you suggest we get these new clothes?"

"I have some clothes that will probably fit her. She can have those."

"Good. Anything else?" He takes another step closer.

"She'll need to begin self-defense training."

"Self-defense training? What are you talking about? Mara doesn't need self-defense training. She has me." Nikolas turns around to begin his climb back down the ladder.

"Yes, but what if something happens and you're not around to defend her? What if you're separated? Anything can happen between now and Kerkyra."

Nikolas stops right before he's no longer visible. "What can happen on a ship to separate us?"

"You won't be on the ship the entire time."

"Rachel, you make no sense. Where else are we going to be? Are we not on our way to Kerkyra now? Aboard this ship?"

"No, and yes." What the devil is she up to? Nikolas climbs back up to find out.

CHAPTER SIX

IT TAKES MARA A MINUTE to realize where she is. She can hear movement near the door. She doesn't open her eyes, they're still heavy from sleep. Her breathing cuts the silence. She can hear someone else breathing near the foot of the bed. Mara doesn't move. If he thinks she's asleep, maybe he will leave her alone. She can hear shuffling and floor scrapes in different directions. The bed sags next to her. Is he lying in the bed with her? Mara wants to scream out, but can't. Paralyzed and frozen in place, how can she sleep with him in the same bed? Next to her? That close. What if it's not Nikolas? Mara's afraid to open her eyes to check. It must be him. Anyone else would have woken her up. She decides to peek one eye open a slit. Nikolas is staring right at her. Awake. His wide-eyed, creepy face so close scares her witless. Mara can't contain the shriek that follows. She sits straight up and pulls the blanket up to her neck. It doesn't budge. He's leaning on one elbow and watching her.

"What's wrong? Did you have a nightmare?"

"A nightmare? One might call it that." She tugs again for more blanket. "What are you doing?"

"I'm trying to sleep." Nikolas yawns. "What are you doing?"

Moonlight shines through the window. He's not wearing a shirt! Mara's heart races more, if that's even possible. "You can't think to sleep in the same bed as me. It's not proper."

He sighs and exhales a deep breath. "I know. I'm sorry. It can't be helped."

"Of course it can be helped. Get up!" Mara shoves him, but all it does is sling him a few inches backwards and he pops back in place.

"I'm not sure you want me to do that."

"What? I said get up." This time Mara slaps him on the shoulder.

"If you insist." He stands up.

The blanket he was laying on top of is released and I pull it to my neck. He's not wearing pants! Mara covers her face and turns away. Her insides twist. "You got in bed with me naked!"

"Mara, I'm not naked. I'm wearing my..."

"I know what you're wearing. You're still naked."

"I did remain on top of the covers. That is until you told me to get up."

I throw him the blanket lying across the foot of bed. "At least cover yourself."

He wraps the blanket around his waist. His chest is still bare. Mara purposely stares in the opposite direction. She can't fathom looking at his broad chest. His muscular chest. "Not exactly what I meant. Will you at least sit down?"

"Is here alright?" Mara takes a chance and looks. Nikolas is pointing at the side of the bed, smiling. At least it looks like he's smiling. Maybe it's the moonlight casting shadows on his face. Maybe it's casting shadows on his chest. And his arms, the upper part. Strong and solid. The memory of him holding her on his stallion pops in Mara's head. She needs to turn away, again. It's hard to breathe. The bed sinks when he sits back down next to her. He's inches from her face. "Mara, please don't be afraid."

Nikolas is serious now, not smiling. "I'm not afraid." Mara doesn't recognize her voice when she speaks. It's high-pitched and weak. Nikolas covers her hand with his. Mara watches his fingers encase hers in the shadows of the night. His hand is warm and coarse. A warrior's hands. Mara tilts her head to look up into his face. So close. His lips, so close.

HER FULL LIPS ARE A finger's breadth away. Any man in his position would have kissed her by now. Any man on this ship would do more than kiss her. And that is the whole point. Nikolas must protect her. Keep her safe. "I promise you are in no danger with me. But, it's important the men aboard ship and elsewhere believe we are married. Do you understand?"

Mara nods. "Can't you sleep on the floor or fashion a hammock between the pillars?"

"I could. But, there's not a lot of materials aboard and bed linens are scarce. And what will happen if the cabin boy comes in to bring breakfast and finds us sleeping separate?"

"I doubt a cabin boy will discover us. Can't we lock the door?"

"I latched it shut, but they can still open it when necessary. Thievery is not uncommon." Nikolas still has her hand covered with his. He doesn't want to move it. She hasn't moved either. Her hand is soft and instinct moves him to caress the top. She still doesn't move.

"Can you at least put on some clothes?"

"I can. But, it's like I told you. They need to believe we are married. Which means you will also have to change."

"Change what?"

"Your clothes."

That prompted a quick retraction of her hand. "I will not. I don't have anything else to wear."

"Rachel gave me a selection for you. I put them over there on the desk." Mara looks at the pile on the desk, stands up, and walks over to inspect them.

She raises one piece in the air into the moonlight. Then another. And another. "These are men's clothing. I can't wear these."

"You can and you must. They're not men's."

"Of course they are." Mara raises a piece in the air and holds it out. "These are clearly men's breeches." She twists them around. "Or, something like them."

"It's a salwar. And, trust me. There is plenty of cloth to it. It will feel like a dress."

"Feel like a dress? How can you know what it will feel like?" Nikolas doesn't say anything. She waits for him to respond. He's not going to. "Have you worn it?"

Nikolas laughs loud and low, almost like a roar. "No. But, men wear something similar."

"I'm not wearing it. I simply cannot."

"Come now. I know you are not like the other English women. I have seen you."

"What do you mean?"

"On the veranda of your house. You were dancing. And you were not wearing anything like what you are wearing now." She doesn't respond immediately. He can't tell if the color on her face is the moonlight shadows or the innocent blush of a young woman.

"That was not for you to see." Her voice is softer than a whisper.

Nikolas doesn't believe her. There was no mistaking it. Innocent or not, that dance absolutely was for someone to see. It unraveled him from the inside. It still unravels him to remember. He moves to where she's standing and takes the salwar from her hands. "You need to wear these." Nikolas throws it on the desk and turns her to face him. "And you need to learn to protect yourself."

"Protect myself?"

"Yes."

"Isn't that what you're for?"

"Yes, but things happen. Things that are not planned. Like what happened on our way to the harbor." Wrong thing to say.

Mara's eyes fill with tears. "But, I thought we're safe here."

Nikolas cups her face in his hands and wipes her wet cheeks with his thumbs. "We are. For now. But I want to make sure you will at least have a chance if something happens to me."

Mara backs up into the moonlight. Each expression is highlighted. "What do you mean? You know the Captain. And we'll be in Kerkyra within a couple days."

"Not exactly."

"What do you mean?"

"Rachel advised me passage is paid to the mainland first."

"No! She must take us to Kerkyra. You have to tell her to take us there first."

"It doesn't work that way. We'll have to wait until they can take us the rest of the way or we can continue on land and find other means."

"Other means? How far up the mainland? How far do we need to go on our own?" Mara spits out the last question and sucks in a heavy breath.

Nikolas steps as close to her as he can without touching her. "Calm yourself. I have a plan. Trust me."

"You keep telling me to trust you. I don't know that I can."

"Mara, listen." Nikolas lifts her chin, forcing her to look at him while he speaks. She grabs onto his wrist when she does. "I promise it will be okay. I'm taking you where I grew up, where I lived before I went to Kerkyra. These are my people. We'll be safe."

"Your people? Isn't Rachel your people? What if they see me like the rebels did on Cerigo? As a way to get what they want. What then?"

"That's why we need to continue pretending. Pretending to be married. Trust me."

TRUST HIM. NIKOLAS keeps telling her to trust him. The only man she's ever trusted is her father. Mara's head is spinning.

"Mara?"

She refocuses her attention to the man standing in front of her and drops her hands to her sides. "You keep asking me to trust you. I don't know if I can." Mara's hands begin to shake. She clasps them together in front of her. Cold rushes through her to her very bones.

Nikolas reaches out to take hold of her hands. He holds them gentle and firm between his own. His warm, firm touch soothes her while he speaks. "Listen. Your father entrusted me to get you there safe, right?" Mara nods her head, unable to speak. "You trust your father and he trusts me."

The warmth resonating from just the touch of Nikolas' hands holding hers continues to calm her. Mara looks down, staring at their molded features. Nikolas releases one and lifts her head so she can see straight in his eyes. His face is clear in the moonlit room. His eyes are an amber-ish color, like dark honey. Mara is overwhelmed with an intense feeling of security. Security in the knowledge that she is, in fact, safe. "I trust you."

This time the inches separating them are closed. Closed in an instant. Mara's mouth is covered with his. Soft, gentle kisses are splayed across her lips. Nikolas' hand under her chin unfolds and envelopes her entire cheek.

Mara raises both of hers and places them on his chest. His naked chest. He wraps his free arm around Mara's waist pulling her tight. Tight against the length of his body. She is lost. His kiss deepens. Her stomach flutters and tickles in the strangest way. A pleasant way. Mara tries to kiss him back. He moans from deep in his throat and tightens his hold around her waist. Mara moves her hands from his chest to encircle his neck. She's never been kissed before. Not like this. Not by a man. Don't stop.

Nikolas lifts his head slight and slow. Mara leans back in for more but he pulls away. "We must stop. I'm sorry, I shouldn't have kissed you."

"I'm glad you did." Mara's voice is raspy, unsteady.

Nikolas smiles wide enough to see the dimples on each of his cheeks. "Even so, we have a long road ahead of us."

Something must be done. All Mara wants to do is smother him with more kisses. That certainly will not do. She unfolds herself from his arms and turns her back to him. "So how do you propose we do this then?"

"To start, you need to get rid of your clothes."

MARA LOOKS OVER HER shoulder. Her straight nose and full lips give her a perfect profile. "What, now?"

She pulls her hair to the front over one shoulder and begins to unfasten the back of her dress. Nikolas is mesmerized. It takes him a minute to realize what she's doing. "No, stop. Of course not now. But, you'll have to wear the clothes Rachel provided tomorrow."

"I understand." Mara continues her attempts to unfasten.

Nikolas places his hand on hers to stop her before she gets too far. She's going to drive him mad. "Don't. Wait until tomorrow."

"Now it's you who doesn't understand. Help me unfasten a few more. I need to show you something." What can she need to show him that he doesn't already know is there? "Please?"

Nikolas inhales a deep breath and exhales slowly. Mad. He's going mad. One by one he unfastens. One by one he grapples with his desire to simply rip it off. Mara pulls at the front and removes her bodice, exposing her shift. She shuffles with the front. Nikolas envisions her father standing in the room next to him to help keep his sanity intact. Mara reaches for one of the tunics Rachel gave her. She pulls it on. It hangs below her waist. She turns around and hands him a flat wrapped package.

"What's this?" He takes it. Mara steps out of her skirt and kicks it aside. More thoughts of Conrad Wingrove are conjured up. Thank God her shift reaches almost to her ankles. Very beautiful ankles.

"Are you going to open it?" Nikolas looks at the unopened package he is holding.

"Yes. Of course." He still can't take his eyes off of her. Wingrove be damned. The moonlight highlights the gold strands in her hair. Brilliant. Nikolas stares at the package again. "What is it?"

"Open it."

Nikolas tears open the edge and flips through bills of money inside. "There's a fortune here."

"Papa wanted to make sure we had money if we need it."

It's going to be needed. Maybe not all of it. But it's going to be needed. "When exactly were you planning to tell me about it?"

"I wasn't, unless pressed."

"And now you're pressed?"

"Well, not exactly. But, I do need to keep it safe. And since I can't be wearing my clothes anymore. What do you suggest I do with it?"

"We can't leave it here. That's for sure. It's too easy for someone to find."

"If I'm to wear these clothes, I no longer have the use of my hidden pocket. You'll have to keep it in yours."

He did ask her to trust him. This is a lot of trust. Nikolas doesn't like the idea of being responsible for this amount of money. He hands it back to her. "We'll come up with something."

Mara takes it. "Don't you have a pocket somewhere?"

So what if he does. He's not taking her money. He walks over to the desk where the pile of clothes is and starts picking through them. He scans the area on the floor where some of the clothes were strewn. There. That's what he's searching for. He picks it up and hands it to her. "Try this."

Mara holds the garment up, turning it in one direction then the other. "What is it?"

"Try it. You can probably wear it with the tunic you have on."

She flattens it against her chest and runs her hand along the front. "It's a vest. The embroidery is remarkable. Gold, I think."

"It's called a yelek." Mara puts it on and rubs her hands up and down on each side of her torso feeling the fabric. If she doesn't stop doing that, all thoughts of Wingrove won't stop him from doing a whole lot more than kiss her.

"Can we light a candle so I can see it better?"

"I'm not sure where they are or if they gave us any. I'd rather wait and not call anyone in here tonight."

Mara moves closer to the window. The moonlight is bright, but still she can't wait to see it in the light of day.

"Let me show you what's important." Nikolas tugs open the front and lifts up the fabric inside. Mara is watching closely. Nikolas stays focused on showing her where to put the money. It's not easy. "The envelope fits snug inside the lining along the seam."

"What a perfect idea." Mara smiles when he closes the vest in the front.

Nikolas pulls it taut around her waist. She's watching his every move. Her curves send zings all the way through his body. Everywhere. He doesn't want to stop touching her. Everywhere.

"I think it will work." She takes both his hands and holds them. "It's good. Really." She's still smiling. She's not looking at him when she speaks.

"Right." It takes him a minute to decide what to do next. Nikolas releases her hands and steps back. He turns around and stares at the bed. "Now, we need to figure out how we're going to sleep."

Mara rummages through the pile on the desk and grabs another tunic. "Here. Put this on and I think we'll be fine." She throws it at him across the room. It hits its mark. His face. Her laughter swirls around him like bees swarming in spring.

Nikolas does what he's told. Mara removes the yelek, walks over to the bed, straightens the blanket, and slips under. Nikolas' legs are rooted where he stands.

"Are you coming? You asked me to trust you. I trust you to keep your promise to my father." Mara rolls over so her back is facing him. It takes him a minute before he's able to lay down beside her. Nikolas is not at all sure if they'll be fine.

CHAPTER SEVEN

WARM. THE ENTIRE LENGTH of Mara's body is filled with warmth. She can't remember the last time she felt this content. The bed careens back and forth in slow even motions, rocking. There are no more crashes of the waves against the hull. Slow even breaths tickle the side of her cheek. She can lay like this forever. A cocoon of complete comfort. She opens her eyes a slit. Nikolas' hand is folded across his chest, just below her face. His other arm is locked tight around her shoulders, holding her in place. Mara lifts her head up to try and push herself up. It doesn't work. Nikolas moans and rolls them both to the side tucking her tighter against him, cradling her. Mara can't move. His body is now sealed to hers, shoulders to feet. One thing is sure. Mara must separate herself. And fast. How can he sleep? What if he's not? Mara rolls her head back to try and look at him. His eyes are closed. His breathing is even. He looks like he's sleeping.

What if she rolls over and faces him front to front? Then she could see him in the light. Nana. What would Nana say? What would Nana do if she knew she kissed him? Spent the night in the same bed? Slept this close with him? In the same bed. Better not push it. But, right here, right now, Mara has never felt more protected. More secure. Maybe she'll stay put just a little longer.

NOT YET. NIKOLAS ISN'T ready to let her leave. He rolls over and pulls Mara tight against him at the same time. He tucks his arm between her and the bed for leverage. It wasn't long before she snuggled up to him after they went to bed and he's not ready to let her go. Just a little longer. If he can get her to stop wiggling, he might get her to stay curled up together all morning. The door slams open. Mara squeals and Nikolas jumps out of bed fast. "What the...?

"Breakfast." Rachel enters with the cabin boy carrying a tray. He sets it down on a wooden bench under the window, shifts the clothes on the desk to the side, replaces the empty space with the tray, and leaves the room.

"What? You don't knock?"

Rachel stands at the foot of the bed with her hands on her hips. She gives Nikolas a top-to-bottom perusal. "It's not like you've anything to hide. Since when did you start wearing a tunic to bed?" Her laugh is no more than a disguised giggle. Next, she looks at Mara. "Well, then. Get up. We've got a lot to do. Might as well get started."

Mara glares at Nikolas. "What does she mean?"

Rachel answers. "Plenty of time for explanations. Come and eat. Oatmeal." She pulls a chair to the desk and waits for Mara to sit. "Also have some boiled eggs. Cook boiled them special for you at my request. Even peeled them."

Rachel motions to Nikolas as soon as Mara is stationed at the desk. "You too. I know you like eggs for breakfast." Nikolas keeps his eyes glued to hers when he walks past her to sit next to Mara on the bench under the window. Rachel's smile doesn't flicker. "There now. We'll have some ale to drink later. Before we start your training."

Mara winds around in her chair. "Training? Today?"

What is Rachel up to now? "I don't think we need to start it here on the ship. Best wait until we make land."

Rachel hits him with a hardboiled egg. It bounces off his shoulder. Nikolas tries to catch it, but misses. "What the devil is wrong with you?"

"Nothing. What the devil is wrong with you?" Rachel picks up another one and whips it across the room. This time he catches it and bites it in half. Mara is watching them with both her hands folded in her lap.

Rachel pops an egg in her mouth. "We're stuck."

"Stuck?" Nikolas is sure he's not going to like what comes next. He tosses the rest of the egg in his mouth.

Rachel throws an apple in the air and catches it. "No wind. It shouldn't last long. This is the Mediterranean. Doldrums don't last long here. Maybe a day, if that." She bites into the apple.

"You mean we're not moving?" Mara's voice squeaks when she speaks.

"Not at the moment." Rachel takes another bite of the apple and grabs an egg. "Eat up, get dressed, and let's get moving. It'll be fun." She walks toward the door.

"Fun?" Mara looks at Nikolas for help. He's not sure how he can help so he doesn't say anything.

"You'll see." Rachel opens the window, tosses the apple core out, then fastens it shut again. "And I promise you. Once you get used to these clothes, you won't want to wear those English contraptions again."

"Excuse me? English contraptions?"

"You'll see." Rachel opens the door, stops, looks at Nikolas and shakes her head. "I'd suggest dropping the tunic. *Au naturale* is much better." She leaves. The door clicks shut.

"*Au naturale*?"

"Never mind."

MUCH MORE THAN FRIENDSHIP. There must be. Maybe trusting him is not a good idea. What choice does she have?

"Come. Eat." Nikolas' voice is kind. He kneels in front of her placing his hands over hers. "I'm sorry you have to do this. But, you need to."

Mara knows he's right. "It's not the training. It's the thought of needing to use it." Running from rebels on Cerigo is not something she wants to repeat. She never wants to face that kind of clash again.

"I know. But isn't it better to be prepared rather than succumb to them? Morea is at the beginning of war. We don't know what we might be facing."

"Surely, the Turks won't harm me once they know I'm the daughter of Conrad Wingrove. They must know him as Dragoman."

"Like I said. We don't know." Nikolas stands up and begins to remove his tunic. Mara hurries and turns around. She starts eating her oatmeal. She can hear him behind her dressing. The oatmeal is cold. It needs butter. At least the eggs are fresh. Mara eats another and pushes the tray back. Where might Nana be right now? Is she safe? Is she with Georgi?

Mara turns around in time to see Nikolas sit on the side of the bed. "Is there any way we can find out about Nana?"

He stares flat at her before he answers. "Not right away." Not the answer she's hoping for. "Once we know how things stand, I can look into it. But I know Georgi. Our goal is to get you both to Kerkyra. We split up, but the goal is still the same."

Nothing about this trip is close to what Mara hoped for. Her stomach lurches. She wants to vomit. What if she never sees Nana again?

Nikolas hangs his head before he stands up. "We may not know until we get there. I'm sorry." He opens the door to leave. "I'll come back in a few minutes, so you have time to dress."

Mara listens for the door to latch. She sits immobile, searching out the window in front of her. The sea is calm. Smooth like glass. Mara can barely feel the movements of the ship. Doldrums. Either that or she's acclimated to the water. The yelek Nikolas showed her last night hangs on the edge of the desk. She picks through the different garments until she finds a long skirt. Mara slips it on over the salwar. She tucks the tunic in, wraps a sash around her waist, then pulls the yelek on last.

Mara inspects the embroidery. It's stunning. Who may have worn it before it ended up in a pirate ship's bounty?

Mara messes with her hair. It must be atrocious. She searches for a mirror. There isn't one. She can't do anything else but braid it and tie it back with a piece of cut cloth. She decides to take another piece and make a headscarf instead.

Nikolas knocks on the door before he opens it. He walks in and doesn't say anything.

"What do you think? Is this suitable for training?"

"Hmm. Probably. You might get hot with the headscarf." Mara takes it off. Nikolas hands her a pistol. She's never held one before. It's heavy. "We're going to start with this."

"I've never shot one before."

"It's alright. I'm going to teach you." Mara doesn't know how to tell him she doesn't want to learn. Doesn't want to shoot it. Doesn't want any of this kind of adventure. She stares at the metal instrument weighing down her hand.

"Here." Nikolas hands her a knife.

She doesn't want to stab anyone either. "A knife too?"

"It's a yatagan. And yes. You need to learn how to use them also. The Turks still use them and so do the Greeks."

Mara's heart races and she can't catch her breath. Wielding weapons is not something she thought she would ever be forced to do. Only a few days ago she was free, happy, dancing to her heart's content. It doesn't feel like only a few days ago. Mara touches her forehead to wipe the beads of sweat forming. She tosses the pistol and the knife, sword, yatagan, or whatever it's called, on the bed. "I can't do it."

"Yes, you can. And never throw a pistol. It could have fired if it was loaded."

"I don't want to do it. I can't take the life of another."

Nikolas turns her to face him. His grasp is firm on each of her arms. "Believe me. I don't want it to come to that. But you must be prepared in case." Mara tries to sit. Nikolas holds her in place. "No, Mara. We need to do this. You need to do this."

"No. I said I'm not. You need to do what you were hired to do. I will not be wielding knives or yatagans or whatever else. I won't." She squirms hard and fast to free herself from his grip.

"I'm sorry for this, Mara."

"For what?" She turns around. Nikolas angles forward. His shoulder meets her hips. His arms circle around, bending her in half, hanging her over his shoulder while he carries her out the door.

MARA'S FISTS FLAIL against Nikolas' backside. In other circumstances, he may have enjoyed this. The crew on deck are whistling and heckling. Probably a good thing. She belongs to him in the eyes of the crew. He'll keep that piece of information to himself. Nikolas puts her down. He's not prepared for the slap she whips across his cheek. He deserves it. He rubs the spot where it burns most. "We can do hand to hand combat if you prefer." Nikolas can't resist challenging her.

"I do not prefer." Mara crosses her arms across her chest and stares out into the open water.

Rachel jumps down from the upper deck and yells at her crew to stop slacking. Then she turns to Mara. "What is it you do prefer?" Rachel circles around Mara like a hungry lioness protecting her prey.

Mara isn't daunted. "I *prefer* to go to Kerkyra. You were paid to take us there. Not some port along the way."

"I see." Rachel folds her hands behind her back and continues to circle. "And you think you're of greatest importance during this time we are living in?"

Nikolas doesn't like the tone of Rachel's voice. He needs to find a way to intervene.

"Of course, I understand." Mara's smug tone isn't helping. "My father is heavily involved in what is going on *during this time*." Not good.

"Really? And does your father know what it is to be a woman among the Turks? What it is to be slaves to them?"

Nikolas can't let her continue. "Rachel, I'm sure..." Rachel raises her hand, forcing him to stop.

Rachel stops circling and stands in front of Mara. They're the same height. "Let me enlighten you. Maybe then you'll understand why you need to be able to protect yourself."

"Rachel, please I don't think it's necessary to—" Rachel's hand stops his words again.

"Come here." She grabs Mara's hand and pulls her to the side. She glares at Nikolas with each step. "It is necessary. Very necessary."

Rachel's eyes shoot fire and molded indignation. "She and I will have a chat."

Nikolas checks the area around them. Most of the crew are busy. Some still stand near the edge of the boat watching. Watching and smiling. Nikolas needs to get Mara from Rachel, but he can't risk the crew's ire. He must find a way without putting Rachel in a difficult position. Rachel's animations overwhelm Mara. She is not dauntless now. Her head sulks. Rachel rants around her in a circle. He can't take it any longer. Let the crew do what they will. He's ending this one-sided conversation.

"Enough." It comes out softer than it sounds in his head.

"Yes? Do you have something you want to say?" Rachel is taunting him now. He's not about to give in to it, but he lets her know he's serious. Nikolas takes Mara's hand and positions her behind him.

Mara interrupts his standoff with Rachel. She moves him to the side. "It's alright. I will learn what you ask me to." Mara is calm, almost sad. Rachel went too far. Nikolas shoots her a look meant to take down Zeus.

Rachel says nothing, only laughs. Nikolas lowers his voice so only she can hear me. "What did you say to her?"

Mara tugs his arm. "It doesn't matter. I understand now." Nikolas walks with her back to the center of the deck where there is open space. He turns so they're standing face to face. "I'm not comfortable with weapons yet. Can we start with hand fighting?"

"Alright." Nikolas moves her into a ready position in front of him. "Let's start with something simple. I know you have strength because I have felt it. Instead of a slap I want you to make a fist."

Mara fists her right hand following his example. "Like this?"

"Yes, now hit me." She swings, he moves, and she misses. "Good. Try again." Another miss. "Keep trying. Put some force into it." She misses again.

Mara stomps her foot. "If you would stop moving."

"That is the point. Your opponent will not stop moving, will be stronger, and most likely more experienced. Keep trying."

Nikolas begins to circle and she follows him. He raises both hands in front of his face. "Put both your hands in fists now and raise them. Like this."

She swings and claps him square on the jaw. It hurt. "Better. Keep going. Give it more. As hard as you can." She misses. She's getting angry. Good. There's more force behind her swing. Rachel motions something to Mara but he can't tell what. The next swing hits its mark.

INSTINCT? MAYBE. RACHEL'S howls from the upper deck don't help. What if she hurt him? Really hurt him. "Nikolas, I'm sorry." Mara tries to help him sit up. It's not working. "I didn't know that would happen. I remembered what Nana always told me."

Mara's concern for Nikolas is replaced with frenzy as soon as she feels the wind whip across the deck and slap the sails on the mast. Rachel's commands to her crew to lift the sails adds to the chaos. Rachel slides down the ladder to where she and Nikolas are in the middle. "Nikolas, you need to get over to the side and out of the way. Now." He stares up at her holding his midsection and groans.

"Here, take my hand." Rachel grabs hold of his elbow and helps Mara lift him up so he can stand. Mara wraps her arm around his waist. "I did tell you this training wasn't necessary."

Nikolas stops. "I assure you. They will not all be as easily beaten." They reach the side and sit by the rail.

Mara isn't sure what she can do to help. "Shall we return to the room? Maybe you would like to lie down?"

"No. I'll be fine." Mara sits beside him. They watch the crew scramble to release the sails. One by one they climb the mast like ants on an anthill. Moving with one goal in mind. Once the cloth is loose, the sail billows like a pillow on its side. The ship lurches ahead with more speed each time a sail is released. Rachel is stationed at the wheel. She spins it around until it reaches the direction and position she wants it.

Mara peers over the side at the open water. Nothing. No matter what direction she looks there's nothing except open water. The lookout in the crow's nest starts yelling. Mara can't understand what he's saying. She follows his line of sight and still sees nothing.

Rachel pulls out a telescope from an inside pocket of her yelek. She stretches it out and looks in the direction the lookout is pointing. She spouts off instructions to the man standing next to her and he takes the wheel.

Rachel hurries to where they're crouched against the side. "Here." She hands the telescope to Nikolas and points in the direction she wants him to look. He peers into it scanning the horizon and hands it back. "Who do you think it is?"

"The Turks."

Mara's stomach begins to swirl. Her mind is suddenly focused on the sway of the ship. She watches them both discuss what to do next.

"How do you know?"

"The flag." Rachel looks through the telescope again.

"Can we outrun them?"

Rachel stands alert in front of us. She looks again. "It's hard to tell at this distance." She places the scope back in her vest. "Do you want to take the chance?"

Nikolas is not slow to answer. "No. What else can we do?"

Dizziness sets in while Mara watches Rachel consider the options. She takes her time, paces a length in front of them. "I could give you a few of the men. Take the lifeboat and head for shore. We can keep them busy here to give you time to reach land."

Mara hears what Rachel says, but she doesn't comprehend it immediately. As soon as the comprehension of it all catches up, her stomach somersaults sideways, dizziness aside. "Wait. You expect us to row our way for land we can't even see yet?"

Rachel's stare only serves to straighten the somersaults playing havoc with her insides. "It's either that or take your chances with us against the Turks. If they capture us, you will be the one to suffer the most. They like blue eyes."

Mara refuses to give in to this fear anymore. "I've no intention of being captured. I'm sure once they know who my father is they will behave."

Nikolas whirls her around to face him. "Look. I agree with Rachel. We need to take our chances in the lifeboat. I doubt these Turks even know who your father is." His words serve up another tumble in her stomach.

"The land is there. I can see it through the spyglass." Rachel pulls it out and hands it to Mara. "Take a look."

Mara pulls it straight, she looks at one end and then the other before placing the small end to her eye. There is land. She removes the end from her eye to see if it's visible without the spyglass. It's not. Mara looks again, and it's there. "Fine." She's still not settled, but it doesn't matter. "As long as we have enough hands to get us there. I don't trust the wind to last and I don't want to be stranded on the sea in a small boat."

Rachel smiles. "I'll give you my strongest rowers." Mara pretends this makes her feel better.

Nikolas takes hold of her elbow. "Good. Let's get moving then." Mara doesn't fight him. She allows him to guide her to the boats.

Thunder bellows from a distance. Nikolas and Rachel turn to look. It isn't thunder.

CHAPTER EIGHT

MARA HAS NEVER BEEN afraid of the sea. This is different. Open water is different. Colder, darker, heavier. The boat wobbles. "Stop moving." Mara holds tight to the edge of the boat. They're sure to topple over if they don't stop moving. She tries to control the panic. This is not just somersaults.

"Mara, relax." Nikolas' voice is soft.

"I am. I can't." She doesn't look at him. Her eyes are focused in front of her. "We're not even close to shore." All she wants is to see the land as soon as it appears.

Nikolas pries one of her hands from the edge. Mara squeezes hard. She's losing balance. "Mara, we'll get there, I promise." His voice is calm. Mara is most definitely not.

The sickness catapulting inside is creeping up her throat. She swallows to make it go back down. It doesn't. "You can't promise that. The cannons are still firing."

"And look, the ship is still visible and afloat." Mara can't look. She's not moving until they reach land. "Mara, Rachel will win. Those cannon balls aren't reaching the ship. They're warnings designed to instill fear."

"It's working." Mara is more terrified than she's ever been in her life.

Nikolas holds out the telescope Rachel gave him. "Here. Take a look."

Mara stares at it and listens to the rowing of the four men Rachel assigned to them. They don't speak. They simply row. In unison. The wind isn't strong enough to take them as fast as they want to go. Mara is afraid to let go.

"Mara, take it. Trust me."

She finally lets go and grabs it fast. She puts the small end to her eye. "It's land!" Oh my God. Mara starts to take deep breaths as she hands back the spyglass to Nikolas. She replaces her hands on the edge of the boat.

"I told you. We're not far."

"I still can't see it without the spyglass."

"But, it's there."

"I know." Mata breathes in deep, the sailors row, the boat wobbles.

Nikolas stands up and points the telescope in the direction of the Helles. Something's wrong. His brows are furled. Nikolas sits down facing her. His movements rock the boat. Cold water splashes across her side.

"I'm sorry." The cold chills her already trembling bones. Uncontrollable shivers follow. "Here. Let me sit next to you."

"No." The thought of any more moving sends her into full blown panic. "It's alright. I'll be fine." She clenches the side harder. Her breaths are short.

"Trust me, Mara." Nikolas tries to coax her into letting go.

"No." Mara shakes her head while Nikolas unclenches her fingers one by one and fits her hand in his. It's not the same. Mara starts to rock forward and back, squeezing his hand.

"Shh..." Nikolas moves very slow to come over to her side and sit beside her. "Move over just a little."

"No." Mara can't move one more muscle. She's frozen. He nudges her gently so she has no choice but to slide over. The freeze is broken the minute she makes warm contact with his arm wrapped around her shoulders and her body pulled tight against his chest. The sailors row. Waves slosh against the back of the lifeboat.

"It won't be long. We're close enough to shore. The waves will help pull us in." Mara buries her head against Nikolas' shoulder and closes her eyes. His voice continues to reassure her. She wants to look behind, but doesn't. Instead, she listens to the rhythm of the waves and the rowing of the rowers.

MARA'S HEAD IS HEAVY against Nikolas' shoulder. Her eyes are closed and her breathing is even. She's no longer trembling from the cold. It won't be long before they reach shore. At least then he'll be able to get her to a safe place. A warm, safe place. How can a woman fall over a cliff into the water with no fear, but be terrified in the sea? Strange. Mara shifts. Smoke rises on the horizon from the direction they came. Rachel. He should not have left her. He needs to get Mara to Kerkyra. Rachel understands. It's probably the Turks' ship in blazes. He hopes it's the Turks'.

The lifeboat scrubs the bottom of the sea floor. The sailors stop rowing and jump out to pull the boat further in. Mara lifts her head and looks up at him.

"Hold on. We're here." She looks around. Nikolas leaves his arm in its current position around her waist. It's perfect where it is. She's perfect right where she is.

"Where's here?" Mara pushes herself back.

Nikolas has no choice but to let go. Feather strands of hair are loose from the cloth holding her hair back. The mountain range in the distance shows him exactly where they are. His clan may be spying on them at this moment. "Not far from my village."

"Do you still have family there? Is that where we're going?"

"It wasn't my plan, but I think it's best we do." Nikolas decides not to reveal his concerns about whether she'll be able to make the trek into the mountains. Better to just go.

"And how much longer until we get to Kerkyra?"

"It's farther than I anticipated." They're too far south to make it on foot. Best to keep that to himself. The next port of harbor is all they can hope for now. "We need supplies and transportation." Lines streak Mara's forehead. "I know this has been hard on you."

Mara straightens her back and fists her hands. "Hard on me? Really? It's a lot more than hard on me I assure you."

Nikolas doesn't doubt it. Hard is an understatement for anyone being chased by Turks at sea. Most of her acquaintance with them having been through her father who is on good terms with them. Nikolas takes his time to respond. He's tired. And needs rest. Mara needs rest. He can't risk the possibility of needing to throw her over his shoulder again. "Look, Mara. We have no control over this. All we can do is make the best of it."

"Make the best of it? How does anyone make the best of this situation?"

"You know what I mean."

"Actually, I'd like you to explain it to me."

Cursed child. Nikolas stands up in the boat. He doesn't care if the rocking scares her at this point. "You know I had no idea of Rachel's plans to take us ashore sooner than Kerkyra." It works.

Mara grabs the edges but she doesn't back down. "Do I?" Stubborn child. "You yourself said you grew up together."

It's true. But he hasn't seen her in years and had no idea she'd become Captain of her own ship. He's not sure how to respond so he does the only thing he knows to do. He jumps over the side of the boat into the knee-deep water.

"What are you doing?"

Nikolas doesn't respond. He lifts her out before she has time to react, carries her to shore, sets her down, and prepares for what comes next. He snatches her wrist before her hand reaches his face.

Anger flares in his direction but he holds her hand in place. She stares and waits. Nikolas catches her other hand on its way to the same destination.

Mara shakes herself free. She stomps in place. "The next time you try to carry me away, I promise you I won't miss."

Nikolas knows she means it. He decides to let her have her minute to gather her thoughts. She walks past him and scans the area. He follows her. There's nothing but barren rock around the shore. She walks farther inland and sits on a boulder molded smooth from the water. Nikolas sits next to her. He says nothing. They watch the sailors push the lifeboat back out into the water. "Where are they going? Aren't they coming with us?"

"I thought they were."

Nikolas jogs to where the men are jumping in. "Where are you off to?"

The larger one of the four answers. "Back to the Helles."

"You can't make it back in time. I know you saw the smoke."

"That's why we're heading back."

"I don't understand. She could be sunk by then."

"No, that'd be the Turks."

"How do you know?"

"Green smoke."

"What?"

"Captain gave us orders to come back if the smoke is green." He points to the horizon. Green tufts of smoke mixed with black blow up the sky. "It means all's well. They'll wait for us to row back." All four men are in and start rowing out to sea.

"Wait! We'll come with you." Nikolas runs back in until the water is up to his knees. Too cold to go further. He yells with his mouth cupped between his hands so they can hear him. "We'll come with you!"

Their synchronized rowing quickly pulls them out of earshot.

"*Vlamenoi!*" Maybe they'll hear him calling them idiots. Nikolas backs up out of the water. He throws them a few fist punches in the air. Maybe they'll see that. Mara touches his arm as soon as he reaches the sand of the beach.

"Why are they leaving? Wouldn't it be better if they came with us?"

Nikolas walks them back inland past the boulder. "You would think."

"So, what are they doing?"

"It seems they had orders to return to the ship." He's not about to tell her they stranded them here on purpose. It will only make the climb into the mountains harder.

NIKOLAS GRABS MARA'S hand. Rough callouses rub against the palm of her hand but his firm grip is reassuring. "Come. We need to find a place to stay for the night and make a fire. It's going to be cold."

"We have to stay the night in the woods?"

Nikolas swings his free arm around in a circle in front of them. "Look around. Do you see any houses?"

"You don't have to be so sharp. It's only a question. I have never spent a night in the woods in my entire life."

"I'm sorry. You're right. Listen." Nikolas motions for her to sit on the edge of a fallen tree. "It's not going to be an easy journey."

He kneels in front of her. He doesn't let go of her hand. Instead, he reaches for Mara's other one and cradles them between his own. He bows his head before he speaks. Goosebumps creep up Mara's arms. "Do you think it's been easy so far?"

Mara remembers everything that's happened so far and it makes her shudder. "No, it hasn't."

Nikolas rises to sit on the log beside her. "I'm sorry to tell you it's going get harder." Not what she wants to hear. At least he's honest. She likes that he's telling her the truth. Not hiding the worst. Nikolas' arm wraps around her waist. It reaches all the way around to her front. She can feel his fingers reach her navel. Trembles creep through to her spine. How would it feel if she were wearing her sari and choli? He would be touching bare skin. Her bare skin. As soon as the thought enters her mind, she can't sit still.

"Are you uncomfortable?" He's sitting so close. Too close. His breath brushes her cheek when he speaks. Mara doubts what she's feeling qualifies as uncomfortable.

"No. Not exactly."

"Not exactly? Is there anything I can do?"

"Yes. I mean no. I mean, I'm fine."

Nikolas' eyes sparkle and the dimples in his cheeks appear. "Good. Because I'm going to need to get a fire going. You can either stay here or come with me and help gather the wood."

"Stay here? Is it safe?" His deliberate stare answers her question. "I'll come with you."

"No. You're tired. Stay here and rest. I'll not go far." Mara exhales a deep breath. Relief. She doesn't want to go and doesn't want him to leave while he traipses around in the woods. Not after he almost toppled them over in the lifeboat.

Mara watches him walk into the trees. He's far. She can still see him in the distance picking up one branch and then another. His hands are full, but he is still searching. What else can he be looking for?

Mara decides it's not important and moves over to lean against a tree. She closes her eyes. The rustle of the wind in the trees crackles the leaves above. A lone bird squawks far away. What if there are animals? Dangerous animals. Mara hears Nikolas' steps coming back. She opens her eyes. Tall men wearing turbans surround her. She opens her mouth to scream. A cloth is shoved inside. She can't make a sound worth hearing. She's lifted off the ground. She kicks. Punches. Scratches. One man is holding each of her legs. Mara writhes her entire body upward, sideways, and down. Nothing works. Where is Nikolas? Will he find her? She needs to break free.

Mara fists her hands and swings hard and low. She hits her mark. The man holding her mouth stops and falls to his knees. Something hard hits the side of her head. Her vision blurs, darkens, and then turns black.

CHAPTER NINE

Navarino Bay

NIKOLAS DROPS THE WOOD at his feet and hunkers behind a tree. Mara is surrounded by a group of Ottoman soldiers. One, two, three...at least twenty he can see. Where did they come from? What are they doing here? There is no way he can take them all down himself. He'll have to follow them to their camp and try to slip in undetected. Now they're carrying her away. Good for her. She's fighting. Not good for the one kneeling on the ground.

Ai sto diaolo! He's going to kill them all! Mara's body goes limp. It's taking all he has to stay put. Nikolas knows if there is any chance at all, he will need to be patient, wait, and follow. Once he knows where their camp is, he'll elicit the help of the Klepht Captains from his clan.

MARA HEARS THE VOICES arguing in circles above her. She can't understand what they're saying, exactly. It's Turkish. She's been around her father and his translations enough to know she is definitely in the hands of Turkish military. But, exactly what are they saying? What are they arguing about? She doesn't want to open her eyes. What do they want with her anyway? Do they know who she is? She's no longer dressed as an English woman. It's doubtful they would believe her anyway, even if they do speak English.

A sharp kick in her side forces her to open her eyes. "*Ksipna*! Wake up!"

Mara sits up and scrunches in a ball, wrapping her arms around her bent legs. Three men in turbans stand above her. One yells at her in Turkish. She keeps her head down. Maybe a show of submission is best right now.

"This is the one." Mara turns to look at the one speaking English. "I told you. She understands English." He bends down and tucks a strand of her hair back behind her ear. Her headscarf is gone. He puts his face directly in front of hers. "Tell me who you are." She remains silent. "Come. You must tell me so we can help you get where you need to go." His slanted eyes squint and open in intervals.

"Mara."

"Mara. You know it is dangerous for a woman to be alone in the woods. Do you not? If my men had not rescued you, there's no doubt you would have frozen to death tonight." Rescued? The Turk is mad.

"I did not need rescued." Mara's voice cracks. She clears her throat.

"Oh? And, do you normally wander the woods alone at dusk?"

"No. I was not wondering the woods. I was..." What can she tell them she was doing? "Resting."

"Resting? And, where do you live?"

Mara looks down at her clothes and pinches the fabric between her fingers. Now what? She must think of something.

"In a village in the mountains."

"Of course you do." The man slaps her across the face. "You need to stop lying if you ever want to see your father again."

"What do you mean?"

"You're the daughter of the Dragoman Wingrove, yes?" How can he possibly know this? The man scales her face with his fingers, the cheek where he slapped her. She can't possibly admit to this. Thoughts fly through her head. What can she say that he will believe?

"Do I look like the daughter of a diplomat?"

"So, you deny this?"

"Of course I deny it. If I were this girl you speak of, the daughter of a diplomat, why would I be here?" Maybe she can trick him into giving her some information.

"Because you run to hide from the Greeks that want to use you to push the English to support their cause."

"I am not this woman you seek."

"I'm afraid you must do better than that." He rises and ties her hands in front of her. "You must come and appear before the Pasha."

He pulls her up and drags her out of the tent. She stumbles and he tugs hard at the rope. Hopefully, she will not know this Pasha from her father's dealings. They stop in front of a large tent. Two soldiers are positioned on either side of the entrance. Her captor hands the rope to one of the soldiers and enters the tent leaving her behind. Mara's head hurts. She wants to sit, but there is no slack on the ropes. The soldiers are eating her alive with their eyes, from the top of her head to the end of her toes. They growl and smile, eyes droopy with lust. Chills and fear build in Mara's stomach. She's not prepared. She needs to get out of this camp. Their intentions are clear from the leers on their faces. The curtain flaps open and she is dragged inside.

There he is. The Pasha. Mara doesn't know this one. This is good. Maybe. At least he will not know immediately of her deceit about who she is. He inhales from the lit nargile. Smoke hangs in the air. The Pasha stands and waves his hand for everyone to exit the tent. Not good. He walks around her smiling and smoking.

"You do not look like the English. Tell me the truth. Are you her?"

Mara bows her head. "Who do you suppose I am?"

"We are looking for the daughter of Dragoman Conrad. Do you know this person?" He smiles and stops in front of her. He lifts her head with his hand and pulls her to him with her chin. "I think you are she."

Best to remain silent and find out where this goes. If he knows already who she is, it is no use what she says.

"Tell me." His fingers tighten and pinch the skin of her chin together. She doesn't say a word. The Pasha shoves her face away and scoffs. "Insolent rayah! You will answer me or you will regret it."

The Pasha yells Turkish commands and two men enter the tent and stand on either side of her. One takes out a long whip and slaps it in the air. Tears well up in her eyes. What can she do? She must endure the pain. She can't tell them what they want to know. It's clear things will be much worse if she does. They will use her to get what they want. But maybe they will respect her and treat her better? No. She doesn't believe that either. Mara straightens her back in an attempt to appear strong and willing to endure the pain. But the tears will not stay back. One leaks down her cheek.

The Pasha smiles. His voice is soft. "Come now. All you need to do is tell me the truth, hmm?" He smokes his nargile.

"I don't know what you want me to say." Her voice is weak and feeble.

"I want you to tell me the truth." He blows smoke in her face.

"I'm telling you the truth." The whip slaps in the air next to her and she jumps. "How can I prove it to you?"

"Hmm... Prove it. This is good. Prove to me you are not the English daughter we seek."

The crude sound of his voice claws in her ears. She wants to slap his face. He continues to inspect her.

"What would you like me to do? How can I prove it?"

"So, you cannot?"

The evil man snaps his head in the direction of the door. "Take her and put her with the others for now."

"NIKOLAS, IT'S BEEN three days. I hope you know what you're doing." Spero crouches next to Nikolas while they spy from the edges of the camp. "There is no sign of any females."

"No doubt, they'll have them housed near the Pasha. We just need to find out which tent is his and focus our efforts there." With only the two of them, they will have to be extremely cautious. Spero being the only one the clan would provide him.

"Come, let's go to the edge across the field. Too many are gathering there. Something is going on. We need to find out." Spero follows close behind. They meander around the trees and bushes, careful not to give away their position. One crack of a tree limb and they'll be discovered. It's almost nightfall and it's beginning to be hard to see. Nikolas is focused on the fire being stoked to high flames. He and Spero crouch at the edge of the camp. What are they doing?

"What do you think it's for?"

"I don't know. We'll wait here and see. It may be the diversion we need."

The Turks gather around the fire. Large lounging pillows are skewed about. A tall one dressed in a long kaftan with gold designs moves to the center and reclines against a purple pillow in the center and the rest take seats around. Some are still standing behind. Nikolas searches the edges of the camp for a way in. Maybe their guard is down now that so many are gathering for what seems to be some kind of celebration.

Another group of men move around to a second row at the end. They're not dressed in the usual regalia. They take their seats. They are each handed instruments.

Spero's eyes squint. "Is that a duval?"

"No, it's too small. It's a nagara." The men begin to strike the drum in rhythm. Another one begins playing the baglama.

"That looks like a bouzouki." Spero crosses his arms in front of his chest, more sure this time.

"No. It's close, though."

Spero shrugs his arms to his sides. "What are they celebrating?"

"Good question. I think we need to step up our attempts to locate Mara."

"Agreed, but how?"

Three girls are dragged into the circle. They're dressed in different colors. Their faces are veiled, and it almost looks like they're dressed for dancing. Unbelievable. One is of particular interest. The way she moves, the color of her hair. Mara. There is no mistaking her. The other two girls have black hair. It is as he fears. They have taken a liking to her.

"Let's get closer." Nikolas tugs at Spero's elbow to get him to follow. They still have to be careful how they step. Guards are still posted at the edges. But, not as many. The girls begin their dance. The wicked smiles of the men cause anger to boil inside. He needs to get her away and to safety now. He yanks his pistol from his belt. Spero holds him back.

"Nikolas, now is not the time."

"What? Of course, now's the time. It's clear what they intend for those girls."

"We need to wait." Spero presses harder against his shoulder.

"No!" Nikolas pushes Spero and he stumbles backward. "This needs to be stopped."

Spero grabs his arm and jerks him around. "I can't let you. I'm telling you there's too many of them."

Nikolas takes a swing at Spero and misses. "*Kerato sou!*"

Spero swings back and connects his fist with Nikolas' jaw. His head is spinning now and he's dizzy from the impact. Spero's words are muffled. "Make sure you don't miss next time."

Yes. There will definitely be a next time. What the *diaolo* got into him? Now he has no choice, but to wait until the fog is free from his brain. He can't even see clear enough to aim the pistol. Nikolas tries to get closer. "Stay there." He shakes the pistol to point where Spero should sit. "I'm only going to get a better look."

"Make sure you keep your distance, at least for now. I won't hesitate to come after you and take you down myself."

Nikolas shrugs and puts the pistol in his belt. What the devil are they doing with those girls?

MARA'S WRISTS ARE RAW from the rope. It's no use trying to fight them. What was she thinking telling them she could dance the *chifteteli*. It was all she could think of as proof she wasn't the girl they were searching for. It's true she has been doing the belly dance with Lovina from a young age. But, never in front of men. The drums begin and then the baglama joins in. Mara hasn't heard this kind of music to dance to in ages. She may even enjoy this. What is she thinking?

Her hands are released. She follows in line with the other two girls stepping to the beat until she reaches the center. She allows herself to feel the music. Each step is pressed to the ground and followed with a pop of her hip. She listens to the sound of the bangles that were placed around her wrists and ankles. She raises her hands and tangles her fingers in her hair. Each of the girls begin dancing, paying special attention to the Pasha. Mara refuses to cater to this man. Rather, she will dance for herself, dance for her freedom. The clothing she was given doesn't have the cloth she is accustomed to. She is uncomfortable, exposed. The veil placed across her face gives her some security. Mara closes her eyes to take in the music. She rolls the muscles in her stomach, a move she has mastered very well over time. She must use her skills of this dance to her advantage if she will convince these brutes she is not who they are looking for. The only way to succeed is to allow herself to become one with the music completely, moving her body to its rhythm.

THE MUSIC WAFFLES THROUGH the air. Nikolas finally is close enough to see and hear what is going on. He'll need to keep very still at this distance. Mara is definitely one of the women veiled and dressed for presentation before the Pasha. This one is Benderli Ali Pasha. Benderli is newly appointed. It's yet unclear how his dealings go with the Greeks under his rule. One thing is clear. Mara must be removed from him. And soon. He watches Mara and the other two women swirling their veils in circles above and below their heads to the beat of the drum. Mara's skill is clearly marked and Benderli's eyes do not stray from her long before they return. Even Nikolas is stunned to silence when she rolls the muscles of her abdomen from low all the way up to the top of her ribcage. Her movements are flawless. He looks around at the guardsmen. They are all focused on the dancing. If he wasn't looking to grab the focus of their attention, now would be the best time to strike.

Getting into the camp is not difficult. The sentries have allowed their guard down in order to watch the spectacle. If only he had more help. Spero is not enough. He makes his way to the tent where the ladies were held. Good. It's no longer guarded. He opens the tent and enters. *"Vlamenoi!"* They didn't even allow the women somewhere to sleep. The restraints where they are held are still in place. No bed linens. No pillows. Only a bucket in the corner. He spews more curse words while trying to figure out how he will get Mara out. There's no choice. He'll have to retreat back the way he came and wait until later, when everyone has gone to bed.

MARA SHIMMIES HER HIPS, circling Eleni and Lela, the other two girls in Benderli's grasp. It's clear they are also not pleased with being forced to dance for the entertainment of the Turkish dragoon. Mara slides herself back to lower her body to the ground in slow methodical rhythms. Her eyes are fixed at a point above their heads although she is aware of their intense stares. Benderli stands and retreats to his tent motioning to one of the soldiers. Mara lifts up in time for one large hand to grab her arm and drag her to Benderli's tent. She looks back at Eleni and Lela who continue to dance. Their eyes lock with hers. Fear.

Mara's thrown to the ground at Benderli's feet. He circles and helps her to stand.

"Come. Let me help you." His words are brine. He looks down at her. Not in her eyes, but her chest. Mara pulls back. She cannot stand the thought of his hands touching her.

"Leave me alone." Her tone is firm. She remembers what she did to Nikolas on the ship. She will do the same to him if he comes any closer.

"Leave you alone? Tsk. Tsk. No, this cannot be done." He removes his kaftan. He removes his tunic. The sight of his round midriff causes her temper to flare. He reaches out to bare her shoulder and she smacks his hand. He retaliates and backhands her across the face. It singes burning hot across her cheek. She loses her balance and he wraps his arm around her waist to pull her tight against him. Benderli rips her sleeve clear to her waist leaving her naked. Mara covers herself with her arms and kicks where she knows she must, but he blocks her and laughs. Mara spits at his face. That stops him. "You will regret that."

Mara struggles to free herself, but his grasp is tight. She can't separate herself from him enough to be able to fight back. Benderli turns her around so that her back is to him. His growl penetrates her ear. She's going to be sick. He shoves her to the ground and she scrambles on all fours to get away. He puts his foot on her back using his weight to hold her in place, face down on the ground. "Why do you struggle so? This could be a pleasurable experience."

"Pleasure? It will be my pleasure to dagger you in the heart." Benderli presses her again to the ground.

"You will be still or I will make sure that no one touches you again after I'm done with you." Mara's heart is beating fast. Each tiny breath, in and out of her throat, scratches like sand in the eye. Mara wants to kill him, but she can't move. Any self-defense Nikolas and Rachel tried to teach her is useless. Why didn't she listen when she had the chance? Benderli begins unwrapping the sash used for a belt. He's going to take her and there's nothing she can do. Panic swells inside. Anger and fear build. The pressure of his weight on her back squelches her breath. Mara can't move. Her voice is failing her. Screams in her head will not come out. How can this be happening? Tears drip down her cheeks. Benderli replaces his foot with his hand in her hair yanking her up to her knees. She covers her bare chest with her arms and he yanks her higher. Pain gushes from her scalp to the tips of her hair. This cannot be happening. But, it is. He licks the back of her neck along her hairline. Mara cringes.

"Stop, please stop." She's begging now.

"No. I will not stop." He yanks her back against him. She can feel the swell of her own tongue in the back of her throat and gags. He's not wearing any pants. "You will find this pleasurable." His voice claws the air.

Mara closes her eyes. Please make it stop. Drumbeats match her own breath. Her entire body rages with trembling fear. She focuses on the beat sounding in her head. His hands grope along the thin fabric of what's left of her clothes.

Drumbeats stop. An explosion booms outside. Voices yell. Mara can't move. Benderli curses and puts on his kaftan.

"You will stay here. If you leave, I will find you and kill you. And then I will kill everyone you care about. Do you understand?" Mara stands still. Another explosion. More curses. Benderli shoves her to the ground again and ties her hands and feet with cloth from her veil. "You will stay here."

He leaves the tent yelling commands. Voices blend. Clanking swords, gunshots, and sounds of muffled fabric surround the tent. Some are close, some far away. The crimson cloth of the tent waves back and forth with the wind. Or, maybe it's from fighting on the outside. Everything around her rages like a story someone is telling. Who they're fighting doesn't matter. It must be the Greeks. Who else could it be? Nikolas?

Another shot fires close, loud and piercing. The door to the tent ripples and a large man thumps to the ground. It's not Benderli. Now anger stirs inside. She's not going to let him win. She drags herself on her hands and knees to the body. His yatagan is unsheathed at his side. Perfect. In seconds she is free from the cloth confining her wrist and ankles. Mara grabs her veil and wraps the cloth around her chest to cover herself.

Mara peeks under the tent door careful not to open it too much. She doesn't want anyone to see her. There's fighting. In all directions there's fighting. She sees Eleni and Lela crouching together behind a row of seating where the musicians were playing earlier. Mara snatches the yatagan as she leaves the tent, careful to stay low to the ground. She reaches the spot where the girls are.

"Come. We need to find a safe place to hide." Mara pulls Eleni and Lela. The two sisters are frozen where they sit. Mara tugs at them. "We need to run. What is wrong with you?"

Eleni and Lela shake their heads in opposition.

"What do you mean you're not coming? Do you want to stay here with that Turkish bastard?"

Eleni answers for both using her broken English. "You don't understand. If Benderli catches us, he will slaughter us and our families."

Lela, the younger of the sisters, pleads with Eleni. "I'm going, Eleni. I would rather die than allow that pig to touch me again."

The chaos around them escalates. One thing is sure. If they're going to move, they need to do it now before there's any kind of clarity. Swords clank around them. Mara doesn't wait. She grabs one hand of each of the sisters. "I'm not waiting. We're going and we're going now."

Dark smoke surges low across the area. Intense whiffs of gunpowder permeate the air. Eleni and Lela are running as fast as Mara now. She doesn't know which direction to go, but a dense forest must be their best hope if they want to find a place to hide.

A familiar voice screams, "Mara!"

CHAPTER TEN

Katafigio

"RACHEL!" MARA LETS go of Eleni and Lela to run back to where Rachel is standing. "What are you doing here? I thought you would have been on your way as far from here as possible."

"Really? Where else would I go?"

"I don't know, but when your men deserted us to head back to the ship, I was certain it was so that you could be on your way somewhere else."

"That was the initial plan. But, come. We can't be standing here. You need to get higher up."

"Of course. Let's go." Mara turns back in the direction of the mountain they were heading to. Eleni and Lela are farther ahead now, but their pace is slowing. Mara's breath is heavy from climbing. It doesn't look so hard from a distance, but now when she is actually on the hillside it's harder. She reaches the spot where Eleni and Lela stop to rest and sits down on a rock near them.

"I need a minute."

Rachel looks around. "This is not a good spot. It's too open. We need to find a more hidden spot."

"Why? I doubt they will come up here now. I can see the camp and they're still fighting."

"Yes, they are. And I need to put you to safety and get back down there to help."

"What? You're going back?"

"I have to. Nikolas and Spero are there. I can't leave them. I need to make sure my men are covered."

"Nikolas is down there?" Mara's heart stops in her chest. She watches the fighting and sickness erupts up again but for different reasons.

"Who do you think started it all?" Rachel pulls Mara up the hillside "Come on ladies, we need to move!" The sisters follow. "There, perfect."

Mara turns to see where Rachel is pointing before she jumps down the side of what appears to be a cliff. Mara bends over the edge and Rachel's head pops up. Rachel reaches her hand out to Mara. "Here. This is where you need to stay until we come back for you."

Mara slides down. Lela follows. Mara looks up at Eleni. "What are you waiting for?"

Eleni wraps her arms across her chest. "I don't want to go down there."

"Eleni, you must." Lela starts to climb back up to her sister.
"I can't."

"Yes, you can." Lela reaches the top. "I'll help you. Give me your hand."

"No, Lela, I can't." Lela reaches the top. She starts talking to her sister in words Mara can't hear now.

"What's wrong with her?"

"I don't know. I've only been with them a few days. We didn't talk much. Their English is not very good."

"Stay here. I want you to get as close to that fallen tree as you can. The roots will shield you from anyone passing by. And, if they get too close, you need to cover yourself with the branches and leaves. Understand?" Rachel begins to climb up.

"Where are you going?"

"I'm going to get them down here."

Rachel reaches the top. Mara can hear them arguing, but she can't make out what they're saying. Lela starts her descent again. Halfway down, she reaches up to help Eleni who's hanging on to Rachel's arm as they both descend again. The three of them form a train until they reach the bottom.

"Good. Stay here with Mara. Do what she says. Do what she does. It's important." The girls nod in agreement and Rachel is out of sight, up the hill.

Mara pulls a log under the tree roots so they can all sit and wait. All she can think about is Nikolas. She needs him to survive.

WHAT THE DEVIL IS RACHEL thinking? Nikolas watches her running back down the hill. Alone. What she should be doing is getting Mara to safety. Up the mountain as fast as possible. He points his last shot, pulls the trigger and misses. That was the last of the gunpowder. The pistol is useless now. Nothing left but fisticuffs. One smack into the jaw of the same soldier hits its mark. "Stay down!"

Another one comes from behind. Bodyweight slams hard on the ground when it flips over Nikolas' shoulder. It isn't enough to keep this one down. He starts to raise up and Nikolas kicks him hard in the face. Flat and motionless. Will he stay that way? More Turks are headed in his direction.

"Need some help?" Rachel. Nikolas looks around her to see the trail of fallen bodies she left behind. They stand ready, side-by-side, fists in the air.

"I thought I told you to get Mara to safety."

"She's safe."

Nikolas can't focus on Mara right now. It'll have to wait. He sizes up the men still standing. Most are Rachel's men. One soldier comes up from the side. Nikolas wastes no time. One jab to the right and he's down. No sign of Benderli. Nikolas walks methodically to each man lying on the ground. Benderli is gone. He walks back to where Rachel is standing. "What do you want to do now?"

Rachel follows the invisible line Nikolas created on his way to her. "We could put a bullet in them all. Make sure they're dead."

"No. I don't like it. Killing. We're better than that."

"Nikolas, you do understand it's a revolution? There's going to be a lot of killing."

"I understand what it means. I'm not taking a life in these circumstances. Let the dead be dead. If anyone survives, let them live another day." Rachel shakes her head. She doesn't agree. Nikolas doesn't care.

"They wouldn't be this easy on us." Rachel puts two fingers in her mouth and whistles. All the men left standing head in their direction. "How many have we lost?"

The one with a scar over his left eye answers. "We have two down."

Rachel kicks the dust. "Let's get them back to the ship. We'll bury them at sea."

"You're going back now?"

"Of course. We're done here, yes?"

"I thought you would come with us to the village."

"I can't. Ship still needs repairs and I can't be gone for that long."

"But Mara?"

"You'll find her. I put her in a ditch behind a fallen tree. Just follow the direction you saw me come from."

"Rachel, wait. What are you going to do now?"

"I told you. I'm going to oversee repairs and bury the dead."

"I know. But, then what?"

"I'll continue the mission given to us. What else?"

"Will I see you again?"

"Who knows?" Rachel smiles and laughs. She walks backwards causing the space between them to widen. "Go on then." Rachel turns to walk forward and waves her hand in the air. "You need to get to those ladies."

"Lad*ies*?"

WAITING IN THE ROOTS of a fallen tree is proving difficult. Every crackle, every pop, every sound slices the silence. Mara holds her breath waiting. Eleni and Lela are hugging each other close. Mara crouches near them. She tries not to let herself think of what she fears most.

"How long do we have to stay here?" Eleni hasn't stopped shaking the entire time. Lela is the stronger of the two. Eleni repeats her question. "What did Rachel tell you? How long do we have to stay here, does she expect us to stay here all night? I'm not going to do it. We're leaving. The farther into the mountains we can get the better it will be. The safer we'll be."

She's not wrong. "I think we should wait just a little longer."

Lela wraps her arms around her sister. "Eleni's right. It is getting chilly." Mara scoots closer and puts her head down to try and block the wind. Rushes of dirt and leaves scale the side of the ridge next to them. Mara's heart races. Don't breathe. Mara stares at Eleni and Lela and holds her forefinger in front of her mouth. There can be no sound or they'll find us. Mara puts herself in front of the girls, pinning them between the tree and her back. Mara jumps as soon as she sees one leg. She wraps her arms around his neck and pulls down hard. He's too strong. He loosens her arms in one sweep and turns to face her.

"Mara?" Her eyes are squeezed shut waiting for the blow, but she recognizes his voice.

"Nikolas?" Mara opens her eyes and excitement floods through her veins like a torrent of hot lava. She hugs him tight. "I'm so happy to see you."

His arms are snug around her waist. Her feet leave the ground. Warmth radiates against her ear. Nikolas lowers her slow and steady. Her body is sealed against his. Don't move. She doesn't want him to move. Did she speak those words out loud? Because he's not. Not moving. Lela speaks something to Eleni in Greek.

"I think you need to introduce me to your friends before they have us married."

"What?" Mara steps back and instantly feels the chill air slice the space between them. She makes the introductions.

"*Hairete.*" They giggle like two cackling crows. Nikolas shakes their hand one at a time. Now is not the time for games. They need to move. The farther the better. The best option right now is to ignore them. "Where do we go now?"

"There." He points to a peak of rock mass between a range of mountains.

He must be mad. "How are we going to get to the top of that? It's not possible."

"No choice. You will. Don't worry. Tonight, we're only going to the foothills. We'll overnight in the caverns."

"Caverns? You mean caves?" He can't mean caves. What is the man thinking?

"That's exactly what I mean. Spero will meet us there to assist in the ascent."

"Spero? Ascent?"

THE AIR IS LIGHTER with each step higher. Eleni and Lela are farther ahead. The grinding ascent burns in Nikolas' calves. They must not stop. They'll risk leg cramps, if they stop too soon. No break yet. Nikolas regulates his pace to help keep pushing them all forward, steady on. Mara stops to look around.

"No. We can't rest yet."

"What? I must." She starts to sit, but Nikolas stops her. "If you want me to continue, I need to stop for a minute."

He holds her arm above the elbow. "Not a good idea. It will be hard to get moving again after."

She looks at his hand holding her arm and then back at him. Nikolas lets go, and she massages her arm in the same place. "I'm sorry. I didn't mean to hold you so tight."

"How much longer?"

"Not far. It's best to keep moving ahead. Slow and steady."

Mara starts to walk beside him again. They don't get very far. Her breaths are winded.

"I can't breathe."

"It's the air. It's lighter the higher we go."

Mara looks behind again at the distance they've covered. Nikolas doesn't need to look. He knows exactly where they are.

"We've barely made...any...progress." He can hear the struggle in her speech. They still can't stop.

"I assure you. We are making progress." Mara looks back again. Nikolas looks back, too, this time. The edge of the forest is a dented line of dark green. "The hard climb will be tomorrow. We're crossing the foothills now, but they're elevated as we climb."

"How is it Eleni and Lela aren't finding it as difficult as I am?" Mara presses the back of her hand to her forehead and forces the air between her lips.

"They're probably accustomed to the elevation. They'll struggle more tomorrow. Come. You can do it. I know you can. Your dancing must have given you more strength than you are aware."

"My dancing?" Now what? No choice. He'll have to confess.

"I saw you dancing...in the camp." Her eyes droop and she stops. "I'm sorry." Nikolas decides not to push her to keep going. "I'm sure it's not a pleasant memory. I wish I could have prevented it."

Mara doesn't say anything right away. Her voice is soft now. "I hate that he forced me to perform for him. It's always been my joy. Now, I'm afraid my joy of the dance is ruined."

Mara's eyes glaze over. One tear breaks free. Nikolas doesn't think before he reacts. He holds her cheek in his hand and wipes it away with his thumb. "No. Don't say that. You will find it again. Something so beautiful cannot be hidden away."

Mara's tears pour down her cheeks. There is nothing to be done. He wraps his arm around her, and sits down with her on a large stone boulder. She leans into his embrace. "You don't understand." She sniffs.

"Then help me."

Mara studies his face. "The dance has always given me joy, helped me when I struggled through difficulties. An escape. Now..." Her voice cracks and more tears fall. Nikolas takes her hand in his. She doesn't pull away, but instead presses her face to his shoulder. Nikolas kisses the top of her head. "I'm afraid it's ruined. How can I find the same joy, the same escape when all I can think of are his disgusting eyes and—."

Mara doesn't continue. She doesn't need to. Nikolas knows exactly. He wants to remove the memory completely. He wants her happy and safe. He tightens his hold and says the only thing he can. "I'll help you." Her body tenses. Maybe that wasn't the best idea.

Her voice is muffled when she speaks. "You can't. You see, it's something I've done most all my life. Nana and I, and sometimes with other ladies."

"I know."

Now she pulls away. "How can you know?"

Nikolas takes a deep breath to help him release his own fear. He's never held a woman's confidence in a situation like this before. He wants to choose careful words. Kind words. Safe words. "Have you forgotten? I saw you on the veranda at your father's house the night before we left."

"Right." Mara stands up. Her fists are tight against her side. Nikolas stands up too.

"Wait! I promise I wasn't spying on you. Or anything of that nature."

"Then what? What would you call it then?"

"Please don't be angry." Nikolas reaches out to take her hands to try and hold them. Mara doesn't pull them back, but her fingers are still clenched shut. "I was drawn by the music, and when I looked up, there you were. Beautiful— the dance was beautiful." That's what he'd call it.

Mara's fists relax in his hands. He slips his fingers in between her palms and holds them both. "I still don't think you can help me. There's nothing you can do."

"I know I can't change what happened, but maybe I can help you find the joy again."

Mara stares at the ground and scuffles her feet. Nikolas isn't sure if he will be able to, but one thing is certain. He's going to try, but right now they need to catch up with the others. "Do you think you'll be able to continue now?" Eleni and Lela aren't too far ahead. They've also stopped to rest. "Come." He fastens his arm firmly under Mara's elbow, clasping her hand at the same time so they can begin their ascent up the hill again. "Watch your step here. It's slick from the erosion."

Mara squeezes his hand. "I don't seem to have appropriate shoes for climbing."

"We don't have much farther. We're almost to the caves where we'll stay the night."

Eleni and Lela stand up as soon as they reach them. Eleni speaks first. "How much longer?"

Nikolas points to the right. "There. Keep going till we reach that break between those rocks. There's where we're going."

Eleni scrunches her brows together. "*Ekei Mesa?*"

"Yes. In there."

Mara whispers in Nikolas' ear. "I gather she's not thrilled with overnighting in a cave either?"

"It's not as awful as you may think."

Mara looks up at him and smiles. "You may be surprised to learn I'm not at all put out by caves, but rather the thought of staying the night in one."

Nikolas pats her hand to reassure her. He tries to keep them moving. "We keep provisions in it for such occasions where someone will need to stay. It's a long journey from bottom to top. It's not uncommon to take two days."

Eleni and Lela reach the entrance first. Something's wrong. Their screams split the evening air. Mara tightens her grip on his arm.

"Stay here. I'll find out what's happening and come back." Nikolas runs as fast as he can, and as quiet as he can, to where they are.

Mara's voice is right behind him. "No, I'm coming with you." They reach the entrance.

"*Ti sto diaolo! Pali!* What the devil is going on?" Eleni and Lela are beating and punching at one man crouching on the ground. Two more are trying to pull them off.

Mara yells from behind me. "What is he doing here?" Eleni and Lela stop for a minute and both men turn around.

"Spero? Souli? What is going on?" Then he sees the problem. Benderli. He's still bent over, hands bound with rope, and a length of it trailing down. Spero bends down to pick up the end, pulls Benderli to his feet, dragging the man out of the cave, and shoving him down to sit. Mara goes over to Eleni and Lela. Both girls are holding each other, fire and daggers shoot in the direction of the men. Nikolas walks over to Spero.

"Why is *he* here?" Mara squawks.

"Spero? My question exactly. What are you doing with that man, here?"

"I didn't know what else to do with him. We caught him trying to get away, so we tied him up. We planned to keep him here while we speak with the Klepht captains about what to do with him."

They should have slit his throat where he stood, but truth be told, he probably should be brought to the Captains. Mara is not going to like it and Nikolas doesn't blame her. "If you need to keep him here, so be it. He can't be inside with the ladies."

Spero tugs the rope to get Benderli to move. "Fine. We'll set up over there under those trees for the night then move him into the cave after you leave."

Mara walks closer to where they're standing. She is not pleased. The lines between her brows tell him all he needs to know. "What are you going to do with him? I refuse to be anywhere near where he is."

"Come now, princess, is that how to speak to an old friend? Hmm?" Benderli's slimy words earn him a slap across the face by Spero. Nikolas positions himself between her and Benderli. He refuses to allow the man to even look at her. Mara pushes him aside. She stares silent at Benderli's globular presence. She says nothing, spits in his face, and walks away.

PIG! MARA CAN'T STAND the thought of him so close. How can Nikolas allow it? The man deserves much more than a spit in the face.

Mara's face burns hot. Anger erupts inside every pore of her being. She wants to hit everything in sight. No wonder Eleni and Lela hurled on him. Mara stomps her feet with each step to shake loose the crawling sensations in her skin. The cave is dark and cold. No way will she spend the night in there knowing that oily snake is only a few feet away.

"Mara, wait!" Nikolas yells at her from behind, but she's not stopping. She can't stop. She needs as far away as possible. Her quick walk turns into a run. Nikolas' footfalls are fast behind her. Nikolas continues to yell out to her. Mara increases her speed with all out paces. She climbs a low rock mass to put a barrier between them. It doesn't work. Nikolas overtakes her and is on top of her before she can clear the other side. His strong arm wraps around her waist, pulling her back hard against him.

Just in time.

Mara screams.

Rocks crumble at her feet and slide off the edge of a cliff. The rock mass is immediately followed by the low ledge they're standing on. Jagged edges line the sides of the ravine. Mara turns around and buries her face in Nikolas' chest. Uncontrollable tears pour out. She fists her hands and hits him on the chest. Nikolas tightens his hold with both arms.

"I can't believe they brought that repulsive man here. I can't stay there. In the caves where he is. I can't. Please don't make me."

"It's alright. We can work something out." Nikolas rubs his hands up and down Mara's back. "First, let's focus on getting to the other side of that rock, shall we?" Nikolas' breathing is heavy from running.

"Of course, I'm sorry. Thank you, again."

Nikolas bends his head down. Mara is lost for a minute looking into his eyes. "For what?"

Mara doesn't move. She motions in the direction of the edge. "For saving my life...again."

Nikolas smiles. "Oh that. Well, we would have both gone over if I didn't get a strong hold around you. It's good you have a small waist."

"Small? It is not small, not as small as most English ladies."

"Small enough then." Nikolas positions her to face the rock mass. "Come. Let me help you up. There's a foothold there. That should get you where you need to be to lift yourself to the other side." Mara follows each direction, putting her foot where Nikolas suggests. It's hard. She struggles to raise herself up. She begins to step back down when two hands firmly grip her bottom on each side. One shove and she's over the top enough to pull herself to safety. In any other circumstance it may have been inappropriate. But, not now. Not here. Not between them, not anymore.

Mara sits and leans against the rock mass and catches her breath. Nikolas pulls himself up and over with no difficulty. He crawls to sit next to Mara. Calm acceptance of what just happened sets in. Nikolas raises one knee and rests his arm across it. He stares at the empty landscape in front of them. The cave is not visible. There is nothing but wild green grass and grey rocks in mismatched patches. How far did she run? And in what direction? "Do you know where the cave is?"

Nikolas keeps looking forward and nods. "I do."

"I guess that's a good thing." Mara doesn't know what to say. What might have happened if Nikolas hadn't grabbed her is still playing out in her mind.

He smiles the smile she enjoys most. The one that shows his dimples. "I believe it is." Then it changes. Becomes serious. "Are you alright?"

"Yes, thanks to you." The cold begins to prevail now that she's caught her breath. Mara crosses her arms for protection from the cold.

In seconds Nikolas envelopes her with his arms. "I know you are physically unharmed, but do you feel all right?"

Mara doesn't know exactly what she feels. One thing is for certain. She will not be going back to the cave tonight. "I don't want to be near him. I can't."

"Fine. You don't have to."

"Can we stay here?"

"I don't think it's a good idea to stay here. The wind can be harsh at night. You can already feel the chill."

"I don't care. I would rather feel the chill of the night."

"Listen," his tone is even and calm. "We don't have to go back, but I know of another place we can go. It will offer some shelter against the wind. I'll build a fire for warmth and we'll stay there. Yes?"

Mara is still. She doesn't want to move from this spot. This warm spot. Here. In his arms. Nikolas leans her to the side. His eyes are watering from the wind. It's clear they must move to a better shelter. "Yes."

Nikolas stands up first and offers his hand to help her up. The strength of the wind shoves her against him. Mara doesn't mind. She enjoys walking with him. Her body against his. Nikolas holds her close to him while they continue along the edge of the ravine. It's visible now. Mara's head is more clear now, but what might have happened still muddles her thoughts. She inhales a deep breath and moves closer to Nikolas. Step by step she nudges them farther away from the ravine. His voice breaks into her thoughts.

"Here. We'll stay here. It's not enclosed like a cave, but it looks to be a clear night and the rock masses surrounding us will block the wind."

Mara inspects the area surrounded by the towering pillars. "I'm amazed how well you know this place."

"I should. I grew up here in these mountains."

"How far are the caves from here?"

"Not too far. But no one will see us, and we will not see them. Is that acceptable?"

"I suppose." Mara shakes her head. Visions jar her thoughts every time she thinks of the man. "I can't go back there."

"I know. I'll need to go and find out if Eleni and Lela want to stay here too. Do you agree?"

"Yes, definitely. Go. I'll stay here. I promise." Mara walks the area for a place to sit and settles on the ground leaning against a tall stone mass.

"I'll make a fire before I leave to cut the chill. I don't want you getting sick."

Nikolas circles the area to gather dried brush, twigs, and flint to start the fire. Once it starts, he adds larger wood pieces. "I'll leave a few larger pieces for you to add while I'm gone. I'll bring more from the caves. The village keeps it well stocked for overnight stays."

"Fine. Go. I'll be fine." Mara waves him off. The sooner he leaves, the sooner he will be back. She doesn't want to be alone in the dark with only a fire to light the night. She fights the recent memories of the last time he left her alone. Best she keep that information to herself, else he might make her go back to the cave with him.

NIKOLAS RUNS BACK TO the cave as fast as he can. He engages the years of training in these mountains, adjusting momentum as necessary so he doesn't tire too soon. Mara can't be alone when it's dark. He must hurry. He reaches the vicinity of the cave and Benderli is tied to a tree outside and out of sight. Good place for him. Spero and Souli are inside with Eleni and Lela. A fire is started and the cave is as it should be, warm and protected.

"You know you can't leave the man out there like that all night."

"Why not?" Eleni glares at him, her eyes as brassy as her hair.

"He'll freeze to death."

"Let him." She turns her back to the fire and Spero stands up and motions him nearer to the entrance of the cave. Souli and Lela are closer to the rear of the cave. Nikolas can't hear what they're talking about, but whatever it is must please Lela. She's very beautiful when she smiles.

"The girls won't stand for him to be in the cave with them." Spero's words bring back the problem of the Turkish invader.

"I know. It's what I've come to talk with you about. Mara and I are going to stay out by Hydra's peak. I've come to get some supplies from the inventory."

"Do you think it wise?"

"It doesn't matter what I think. She refuses and I won't force her. Not after what that bastard put her through."

"Understood."

"You, however, need to make sure your prisoner survives the night."

"I've no intention of letting him freeze, but he does deserve more than a little discomfort."

"Agreed. Now tell me what the blazes is going on with Souli and Lela?"

"What do you mean?"

"They haven't separated since I got here." Nikolas nods his head in their direction for Spero to understand.

"Oh, that."

"That?"

Spero shrugs. "They enjoy each other's company."

Nikolas stares at his friend kicking the dust and gravel at their feet. "Just be sure your own company is not a distraction for you." Nikolas claps him on the shoulder and walks over to the cellar built in the ground, where the village keeps provisions. He pulls out a number of *flokatis* and jars of dried fruit and olives. It isn't much but it will have to do. The wool *flokatis* are perfect to wrap up in and they'll make a soft bed to lay on. He tosses a couple jars to Spero. "Here. You're all probably hungry too."

"Thanks." Spero holds it up to look at the contents. "It'll do." Eleni grabs the jar from his hand.

"I'll take that." Spero reaches out to grab it back. She laughs when he wraps his arms around her from the back. Souli and Lela join them.

"Eleni! Watch you don't let it break."

"Don't worry, Lela, I'm not that stupid. Here." She hands it over to Spero and smirks at her sister. "Of course, now you pay attention when there's food."

"I was paying attention. You're just upset my attention wasn't on you."

"What? I can't believe you said that."

Spero interrupts their playful banter. "Souli, can you check on the 'guest' outside? Make sure he has a fire. A small fire. We don't want him too comfortable."

"Fine. I agree with the girls. He deserves nothing." Souli grabs some wood from the pile in the corner. Nikolas takes the opportunity to gather his wood next and ties it with a piece of rope left over from Benderli's binding. He wraps the food in the flokatis to make it easier to carry. He leaves the rest out for the others. They'll need them, too, even though the shelter of the cave will keep them warmer. He must get moving. The dark night is almost pitch black. It will be by the time he gets back to Mara.

"Spero, see you in the morning. You know where to find me if you need to."

Nikolas can hear Lela call out to him as he leaves, giggling in between her words. "Stay warm."

"Lela, hush," Eleni warns her sister.

"It's not like they won't. You know they will."

"It doesn't matter." Their voices fade in the distance. It's true. Nikolas does want to help Mara stay warm. And the way the evening feels at the moment, they will have no choice.

"What are you so happy about?" Mara's question startles him on his approach to their camp. He doesn't see her standing there. His eyes are focused on the fire leaving everything surrounding it black shadows.

"Happy?" He's not about to tell her what he's really thinking.

"Something has you smiling as wide as Grosso Bay. I can't imagine what. I'm certainly not thrilled with the idea of spending a night in this freezing weather."

"I told you to stay by the fire. It's warmer there." Nikolas lays out the flokati and throws another log on the fire. Orange sparkles float up in the darkness. "Come." He motions for Mara to sit on the flokati. "This will help keep you warm. It's made of wool."

"I am familiar with the flokati. My father uses them in his study on occasion."

"They will keep us warm tonight." Nikolas wraps a second one around her shoulders. A shadow of her smile enlivens her features. He kneels in front of her and pulls a corner around each of her shoulders, making it taut in front. "Is that good?"

"Yes, thank you." He doesn't want to move from where he is, this close to her. Mara looks directly into his eyes. Then she looks down at his lips. He can feel her warm breath on his face, they are that close. She doesn't say anything. Nikolas doesn't know what to say. Her lips are inviting him. She wants him to kiss her, he's sure of it. So, he does. The draw he feels when he is with her is magnetic. He keeps his hands on the flokati keeping it closed tight. She doesn't move, she is kissing him back. She pulls away first.

"I'm sorry." Why did he say that? Nikolas is not sorry at all.

"No, it's all right. I was kissing you too." Her words are delicate and kind. They resonate in his chest. Nikolas can't think clear because of it. He reaches behind her to grab a jar of dried fruit. Something to break the spell.

"Here, you must be hungry." Mara takes the jar and holds it. He sits down next to her and wraps another flokati around himself. She isn't eating. "Aren't you hungry?"

Mara hands the jar to him. "Can you open it?"

"Ah, of course." He opens it and gives it back to her. She holds it out for him to take one first. Then opens her mouth. Waiting. What is she up to? Nikolas places the dried fig on her tongue. She's going to drive him mad if she keeps it up.

Mara pulls another one from the jar and offers it to him. He opens his mouth this time. She giggles and places the fig on his tongue. He closes his mouth quick to catch one of her fingers. She smiles. Her eyes are bright with the glow from the fire. She doesn't pull back.

Nikolas grabs ahold of her hand and holds it to his mouth, kissing the palm of her hand and her wrist, then begins to chew on the fig. "Mm. Very good."

Mara's laugh encourages him. He kisses her full on the mouth. She melts against him. The fire crackles in front of them, Nikolas doesn't look. Doesn't care. He's only interested in the woman in his arms. Her lips, mouth, tongue. Her arms around his waist. Her hands with their light touch, soft and gentle. A low whimper vibrates from her throat, or was it his own? He must stop before it goes too far. Mara breaks first.

"I'm sorry." He can't help but smile a little at her apology. Nikolas doesn't believe she's sorry at all. He stretches his arms above him before fastening his hands behind his head and leaning back against the rock mass, crossing his legs at his ankles.

"What are you smiling about?" Mara tightens the flokati closer to her neck.

"Nothing, really." Nikolas crosses his ankles in the opposite direction.

"What do you mean nothing *really*?"

"Only now we're even." He takes a deep breath and continues his satisfied smile.

"Even?"

"Yes. First I was sorry, now you're sorry. We're two sorry milksops." It's true.

Mara scoots close and leans back with him, crossing her legs at her ankles. "I suppose we are." She bends her head, positioning it against his chest. Nikolas looks down at her.

"I'm cold."

That's all he needs to hear. Nikolas unfolds his arms and clasps them firm around her, grabs another flokati and spreads it over them. "It's going to be cold. Are you sure you want to stay here? We can still go back to the cave."

"No. Here is good. I don't want to be anywhere near that beast." Her voice shakes. Nikolas caresses her shoulder and takes her hand in his. She is cold. He rubs her fingers with his to get the circulation flowing. She begins to cry.

"Come now, it's going to be all right. He can't get to you."

"I miss Nana. I want to know how she is, if she's alive."

"Georgi will have taken her someplace secure."

"But, what if he didn't?"

"We must be positive. We must focus on getting you safe and secure."

"After what that beast did to me? I don't think I'll feel that way ever again." She sobs uncontrollable.

"Shh. I know it must be hard. I can't imagine." Nikolas can feel his hate for the man boil inside. He wants to go to him and slash his throat.

"If you hadn't come when you did..." Mara chokes. Her tears sparkle in the light of the fire. "I'm sorry."

"Listen. No more sorry." Nikolas wipes her tears with the back of his forefinger. "What that man did to you is unforgivable. You had no control over it."

"I tried to stop him, but..." Mara buries her face in his chest. He tightens his grip. Nikolas will never understand what makes some men do the things they do. Mara cries hard. All he can do is hold her until it subsides. She lifts her head up. Her voice is melancholic. "I can only imagine what he's done to Eleni and Lela. They were with him longer than I was."

"It's going to be all right. I promise." Nikolas kisses the side of her head. He refuses to allow anyone else to touch her.

"How do you know?"

How *does* he know?

Mara rubs her hands together, wipes them again on the flokati, as if trying to rub out a stain. "He's awful. His hands on me..."

"*Maraki mou*, don't. Don't give him power over you. He didn't do what he set out to do. He didn't win."

Mara sniffs and shakes her head. "How am I going to be the same again? Do you know what he was going to do? I think he was going to molest me."

"I know. And, the truth is, you may not be the same again."

Mara begins to lose control and pull away.

Nikolas doesn't let her. "No. Come here. Listen. I'm not finished."

"I think I've heard enough."

"No, you need to hear the rest. It's a fact you will not be the same again. But, you can be stronger from the experience."

"I don't know how. I feel like a broken piece of china."

"It's not going to always feel that way. With time, it will turn into something from your past. A small piece of history that dims with the passage of time."

"How can you know this?" This is a question he's not sure he wants to answer. But her glossy eyes compel him.

"Because I also have experienced tragedy at the hands of the Turks."

"What do you mean? They attacked you too?"

"No. Not me. My mother."

"Your mother? Nikolas, I'm sorry. It must have been awful for your family."

"What did we say? No more sorry."

Mara relaxes against him once more. "But, like you said to me. It was not in your control."

"No, it wasn't. But, I was the result."

Mara straightens to face Nikolas. "You mean?"

"Yes, my mother was left pregnant with me by a Turk."

Mara lays her head back again.

Nikolas is surprised at the ease of words flowing from his mouth. The circumstances surrounding his birth have always been difficult to articulate. "My father. He raised me as his own, but I can't help wonder at times how he can feel for me the same way he would for a child of his blood."

Mara takes a deep breath. "It's like you said. It was not your fault. You had no control over it."

"Right. But, I still endured the ridicule from those who knew. And, most knew."

"How could they blame a child?"

"It doesn't matter now. We lived through it and now it's a point of time in the past."

"Your mother?"

"She died when I was very young." The fire needs more wood. Nikolas must put a stop to this conversation before it riles up more emotion than he's comfortable with. He stands up, adds more wood, and returns to his place by Mara's side. Her face is streaked with the pattern of her fallen tears.

"Don't be sad on my account. I'm proof that you can become stronger regardless of some of life's less than pleasant experiences. And I know. I know with time you will become stronger."

Mara rests her head back on his shoulder. "You're right. No more sorries."

CHAPTER ELEVEN

THE FIRE IS OUT. THE cold ground threatens to chill him. The air is clean and clear. It's still dark, but Nikolas can tell it's almost dawn. The velvet darkness starts to slide open to allow a new day to peek through. The wool flokati is exceptional, but Mara glued to his side from top to bottom is much more preferable. He watches her while she sleeps. They'll have to get up soon, before anyone decides to meet them here. Doubtful, but possible. Nikolas can't remember ever feeling this close to a woman, not only physically, but connected on a different level. He doesn't want her to move, well maybe a little. He rolls to his side and props his head with his hand. She still sleeps.

He nudges himself against her, front to front. It's the warmth of her body that draws him. That's what he tells himself. Each breath she takes presses against him. He intertwines his legs with hers and runs his hand along the length of her arm resting on the indent of her waist above her hip. She still sleeps.

Nikolas is keen to every arch and curvature of her entire length. He leans down to lightly touch his lips to the pulse in the center of her neck, then moving up to her ear, her jawline. Mara opens her eyes when he reaches her lips. She's not sleeping.

Mara's kiss enlivens him. She wraps her arms around his neck allowing him the freedom to explore.

"Nikolas..." Her whisper is heavy and breathy. She throws her leg across his hip.

He helps it by pulling it higher than his waist, then moves his hand slowly up her back. Mara presses hard against him. Nikolas rolls her over on her back, intensifying their kiss with his tongue while cradling her head between his hands. He stops for a moment and Mara opens her eyes. Clear blue like the sea in the summer sun. The depth of emotion beckons him the same as the clear ocean floor. Nikolas twirls a strand of her hair around his finger, caressing her cheek in the process. "We need to stop or it will go too far."

"I'm not sure it hasn't already." Mara's dreamy eyes beckon him to kiss her again.

But he doesn't. "Believe me. It could go much further."

Mara runs her hands down his back, around his waist and up the front of his chest. "All right."

Nikolas doesn't move straight away. He kisses her lightly one final time before standing up. "All right." He turns his back to her while putting wood on the fire and stoking it to help the embers catch it on fire. There are no sounds from Mara. A brisk walk to clear his head is what he needs. "I'm going to see what the others are doing. I won't be gone long."

"Fine. I'll wait here."

Nikolas wants as much distance between him and Mara as he can safely get right now. If she only knew what her closeness does to him. Maybe she does. He'll need to keep better control in the coming days. He must get her to Kerkyra safe and intact.

Nikolas' thoughts begin to clear as soon as his steps take on the same brisk intensity of his training. The new day is rapidly opening. The sun is now low against the mountains to the east. He can see the smoke from where Benderli is tied up. Souli, or is it Spero? One of them is sitting opposite him.

Nikolas quickens his pace. He needs to get his head clear before he meets them. Souli. It's Souli outside. He waves, but he must not see him. Nikolas turns to enter the cave. Their fire is also dimmed to the embers. Spero is spread out on one side. Lela and Eleni are spooned together on the other. Early hours must have been cold in the cave also. Nikolas adds wood from the pile to the fire and stokes it to get it going. Spero grumbles when he rolls over.

"It's a good thing I'm not the enemy."

"I knew it was you." His eyes are still closed.

"You knew it was me? How?"

"You have a walk."

"A walk?"

"Yes, I can tell by the way you walk."

"Hm. I doubt that."

"I'll prove it to you one day. What time is it anyway?"

"Sun is up. We should get moving."

Spero sits up and yawns. "Yeah, all right."

"Souli been there all night?"

"Yes." Spero points to the sleeping sisters. "The older one insisted on it."

"Oh?"

"I can't say that I blame her. After you left, the younger one and Souli. They were getting a little too familiar if you know what I mean."

"And what about you?"

"What? I don't know what you're talking about." Spero stands up to go outside. Nikolas follows. They meet where Souli is sleep-watching Benderli. Spero kicks him in the side.

"Hey! Wake up. We need to get moving so we can make it to the village."

"I'm up. I'm up." Souli stands and kicks dust over the embers to make sure it is completely out.

Benderli grovels. "Isn't there anything to eat?"

"Not here. We'll eat when we get to the village. Although, I'm not sure when or where you're going to eat."

Spero and Souli look at each other and then at Nikolas.

Spero asks first. "What do you mean?"

"I mean I don't think it's a good idea to bring Benderli to the village. I think you two should stay here with him and I'll get the ladies to the village. Mara won't go near him and I don't blame her."

"I agree the last stretch of the way will be difficult to keep them at a distance."

"What are we going do with him then?" Souli scratches his head and then ruffles the scruffy chin hair around his mouth.

"I want to talk to my uncle and my father, if he's there. They can decide and then we'll send word. We need to restock the inventory in the cave anyway."

Spero and Souli are silent for a minute before Spero takes the initiative to speak first. "Fine. If you think it's best. Don't take too long. I need to make sure *yiayia* is well."

"I know Spero. I'm looking forward to some hot *trahanas* too."

NIKOLAS IS RIGHT. SINGLE file is the only way to navigate their ascension. The path is hidden between the mountain and the rocks jutting up at the edge. Amazing. A person would never find where to enter unless it's revealed to them. Mara goes first, Eleni second followed by Lela. Probably best because Lela can keep her sister from panicking and running back. Nikolas is leading. Each step brings them higher. Nikolas climbs the bluff with ease. His stride is easy and measured. Mara can feel her heavy breaths intensify with each step she takes. Eleni and Lela are not out of breath, but Eleni is not happy, her face is splotched, white and pink. At this rate, Eleni will cause them all to lose their footing.

Mara signals Nikolas with a touch to his shoulder. "We need to stop and rest. Please."

"This is not the best place to do that. Come. It's not much farther up this path. There will be a place we can rest."

"If you think best." Mara glances back at Eleni. Still the same. She reaches out to hold Eleni's hand. They continue the climb, linked together, but still one by one up. Nikolas was correct. They do reach a clearing. Not much of one, but it's something.

"Another cave? How many caves do we have to stay in before we finally get to the village?"

Nikolas laughs while Mara catches her breath.

"Actually, we didn't stay in a cave last evening, if we're counting, that is."

"True. But, another cave?"

"The mountainous regions here are full of them. It's to our advantage, truth be told."

Nikolas helps Eleni and Lela sit on a large boulder near the entrance. Then he comes to sit closer to Mara on the other side of the opening.

"How do you mean to our advantage?"

"I mean we know them. Know how to use them. And, they all have unique features that have become known to the Klephts over the years."

"Hm. So, what is so unique about this one?"

"For one, it's well hidden."

"Yes. I can see that. It's almost like we're surrounded by a barricade."

"You noticed?" Nikolas smiles and looks down at the ground.

"Of course."

"As it happens, the Klepht captains built this rock mass to hide the cave entrance from below. We needed a place to rest or layover about midway from the top to the bottom. This also serves as protection from wind and sometimes rain depending on how it's blowing."

"Very clever."

"Yes, I agree." Mara follows Nikolas' line of sight. Eleni and Lela have moved to the ground and laid down. Probably not the best idea. How will they want to get moving again?

Nikolas must have been thinking the same thing. "Come ladies. Let me show you something unique and refreshing."

"Refreshing?" Lela sits up and nudges her sister. "Eleni, come."

"No. I'm staying here. I'm not going anywhere."

"Yes, you are. We must. You know this."

"What I know is I'm tired, I'm hungry, I'm thirsty, and my legs burn."

Nikolas lowers his hand to Eleni, offering to help her stand. She stares at his hand, rolls her eyes and accepts his help. "I might be able to help with one, maybe two of those complaints."

"Really? Does this cave have a buried compartment too?"

"Maybe. But you'll be pleased with what I know it has. Come."

Nikolas enters and they all follow. It's cold and dark. Nikolas picks up a torch leaning against the wall of the cave. He searches the perimeter for something. He lays the torch on the ground and picks up two rocks at the edge of the cavern and strikes one rock against the other. Sparks fly and in no time the torch cloth is burning bright.

"There. Come now. We won't have too much time before it burns out."

"Where are you taking us?" Eleni's high pitch voice bounces off the walls.

"You'll see." Nikolas moves forward with the torch leading the way. He clasps his hand around Mara's and the sisters follow. His hand holding hers here, in the dark, in front of everyone. She doesn't care. She enjoys his possession of it.

"*More* climbing?" Lela calls out from behind.

"Lela, it's not that steep." Their constant complaining is getting tiresome. Don't they appreciate everything Nikolas is doing for them?

"Whoa. Look at that." Mara stops their trek to admire the engravings. Must be medieval or even earlier. She has only heard of such carvings. "Nikolas, do you know what they mean?"

145

"I suppose it is an early form of writing or maybe recording of history. No one I know has any idea."

"Astonishing." Mara rubs her hand along the rough edges. Maybe if she touches them somehow the ancients will give her meaning and understanding of their purpose. Some are vague and others are obvious recollections of a past event. Nikolas drags her away to keep them moving forward, but Mara keeps her eyes glued to the ancient art until the blackness of the cavern overtakes them.

Nikolas stops. "We're here."

Mara sees nothing surrounding them. "What exactly is here?" Nikolas raises the torch higher and places it on a perch. Now the entire cavern is lit in golden ambient light. The girls squeal.

"Oh my!" Mara has seen many caverns and caves in Cerigo, but nothing compares to the colors and beauty of the scene before her. A pool of clear water circles a rock island in the center. On the far edge there is a constant flow of clear liquid coming from a crack. White splashes of water rush out of it, landing in a puddle below before it makes its way to the pool.

"Now you know the secret of why this is the perfect place to rest. And, we're a little over halfway home."

"Can we drink it?"

"Of course. It's why I brought you in here. It's best to drink straight from the source. Like this." Nikolas walks over to the fountain, leans over, cups his hands under the flow of water and drinks. One by one they drink to quench their thirst. No more complaining. At least for the moment. Mara bends down at the edge of the pool to glide her fingers in the water's rim.

"It's warm!" She swishes her entire hand in the pool. Eleni and Lela join her to test the water for themselves. The girls begin to remove their shoes.

"What are you doing?"

"What do you think?" They raise the fabric on their salwar to knee length and hang their legs over the edge.

Nikolas walks nearer to Mara and kneels. His breath tickles her neck when he speaks. "We don't have a lot of time, but if you want to try it we can spare a few minutes."

Mara removes her shoes and rolls the fabric to her knees before he finishes his last sentence. Nikolas laughs. She kicks her legs and splashes the water. "Do you know why it's warm?"

"It's always been so as long as I can remember. They say it's from the volcano."

"Volcano?"

"These mountains hide volcanic activity."

"Have there been any eruptions?"

"Not that I recall. I've never seen one although I know where they are located."

"We're not in any danger here are we?"

"No. We're quite safe." His smile lights up his face through the dimness of the cavern. "Didn't I tell you they all have something unique about them?"

"Yes, you did."

"And, many have legends attached to them."

"Truly? Tell me one."

"One group of caverns are located near a place call Pyros. I've only been once, when I was a boy. Dirou. The caves of Dirou is what they call them. The colors you will see in those. Blues, greens, yellows. You can take a boat deep inside."

"You must take me there one day." The words are out of her mouth before she can stop them. Nikolas is silent. He must know once she's delivered to Kerkyra the chances of them seeing each other again are slim. Nikolas reaches forward and places a strand of her hair behind her ear. The light touch of the tips of his fingers linger as he traces the line of her jaw.

"Except in the caves of Dirou the water is cold and it's said there are giant eels that live in it." His boyish smile endears him more to her than he is already.

Eleni and Lela screech and swing their legs out of the water. "Eels!"

Nikolas stands up laughing. "Don't worry. Not here. The water is too warm for them. Here, the legend is that this is the bath of the Gods of Olympus."

Now it's Mara's turn to laugh. "Gods of Olympus. Do they still believe in these Gods?"

"Some do. Those that have lived their entire lives in the mountains and have had little contact with others outside their own village."

"Are there still such places?"

"Yes."

"How is such a thing possible? I mean with the Turks' rule."

"You'll see." Nikolas snaps his attention to the way they came in. Mara heard it too. A cry. Or something. Maybe an animal whimpering?

Eleni and Lela already have their shoes on. Nikolas helps Mara put hers on and then grabs the torch from its perch. "Come with me, but stay to the side and behind me."

"What do you think it is?"

"I'm not sure." Nikolas crouches to avoid hitting his head on a low hanging rock. Mara and the girls do the same. He shoves them against the wall behind a long rock jutting out on the side. The entrance is now visible. He hands the torch to Mara. "Stay here. Don't move." No arguments on that account. Not going anywhere. Nikolas continues forward. All Mara can see from this distance is another figure taller than Nikolas. He's wearing a small turban. His back is turned to them and she can see he has long hair. Is he a Turk? Nikolas presses forward, arms curved and out. Silent, calculating. Nikolas jumps the Turk from behind. Instead of bringing him down, Nikolas is slammed on his back with the Turk standing over him, knife to Nikolas' throat. Mara covers her mouth and leans back into the shadows. Did he hear her squeal? She turns to face the girls pushing them back into the cave to hide. Two men laughing cause her to turn back around. The Turk lowers his hand to help Nikolas up. What is this?

"Mara! Eleni, Lela! Come out. There's someone I want you to meet."

Mara wants to slap them both across the face. "You know each other?"

"Quite well, actually. This is my uncle. Theodoros Kolokotronis, this is Mara, Eleni and Lela. Mara is the Dragoman's daughter." Kolokotronis slaps his heels together and bows to each of them, kissing the back of their hands. Eleni and Lela giggle between themselves. Mara is not as enthralled with the man.

"I thought you were one of the Turkish soldiers coming for the men who captured Benderli."

Kolokotronis smiles and laughs, his mouth barely visible under the thick mustache sitting wild on his upper lip. More fitting would be the mustache smiles than the man, with its curled ends turning up. "Eh? What's this about Benderli?" Even when he speaks, it's the mustache doing the talking.

"We have him, sir."

"What do you mean you have him?"

"Spero and Souli have him at the cave near Hydra's peak."

"And, how has this come about?" Kolokotronis glares at Nikolas, then Mara, Eleni and Lela ending the inquiry on Nikolas. He doesn't seem pleased with the news.

"Your nephew rescued us from that evil man." Lela spits on the ground.

"Did he now?" Kolokotronis raises an eyebrow at Nikolas.

"I certainly didn't do it myself, uncle. I had help."

Mara interrupts now. "And, now we need to get rid of him."

Kolokotronis focuses his attention on Mara. He doesn't speak. His black eyes pierce the silence. Nikolas elbows her. "Why don't you take Eleni and Lela and sit outside for a moment while we decide what's to be done with him?"

Eleni and Lela leave and begin petting Kolokotronis' black courser stallion. Mara stays put. "I want to hear what you're going to do. I'm not going anywhere." She crosses her arms in front and pierces him back with her eyes.

Kolokotronis turns his attention back to Nikolas. "The details do not matter. What you must do now is arrange to have him taken to Ali Pasha."

"Ali Pasha? Isn't he on his way to Egypt?"

"No."

Mara interrupts. "But, that was the Sultan's instructions before we left Cerigo."

"Young lady, I do not know what his instructions were, but know this. Ali Pasha of Ioannina will never leave Morea. His favorite wife is Greek and he wants this land for his own."

"Yes, we met in Cerigo."

"Did you? It is of no great importance." He dismisses her entirely and speaks directly with his nephew. "Nikola, you will advise the captains of my wishes."

"Yes, sir."

"Good. I will continue down to Hydra's peaks and have a go at Benderli myself."

Mara wants to strangle the man. "How can you just release him back to the Turks? After all he's done to us? To all the Greeks."

"Mara, you need to let us handle it." Nikolas' warning is not like any she's heard up to this point. He's almost afraid. Well, she certainly is not.

She switches her look from one to the other in silent protest, ready to plead her case. Waiting for an answer. Kolokotronis responds first. "I am well aware of what this man has done and what he is capable of. I also know what the Turks have planned for him. And it will not be pleasant."

"What? How can you know such things? Are you with the Turks now?"

"Mara! Enough." Nikolas' voice is raised now. Commanding, not warning.

Kolokotronis raises his hand. "It's all right, nephew. Let me say, some Klephts have a unique relationship with them, allowing us to acquire useful information which will help us in the battles ahead."

"Uncle, you don't need to explain further. I will handle matters once we reach the village."

"Good." Kolokotronis turns to Mara and lifts her chin, slight and delicate. "He will get his due, I promise." He waves his hand goodbye and grabs the reins from Eleni. "*Chupas, yiasas.*" Kolokotronis continues to pick his way down the slope leading the way for the black stallion to follow.

Mara eyes Nikolas. "What did he mean he will get his due?"

"I don't know. But, he is always on the mark."

"Fine. And what did he mean the Klephts have a unique relationship with the Turks? Do you have such a relationship?"

"Me? No."

"Then what?"

"The Turks have been known to use the Klephts to help them keep the people under control."

"And you condone this?"

"Mara. It's like my uncle said. It allows us access to useful information. That is all."

"Such as?"

"Information I won't discuss with you. Come. We need to get moving or we won't make it before nightfall."

"Lovely."

MARA IS READY TO GOUGE Nikolas' eyes out. She sits down on the ground and crosses her hands in front. "I'm not going any further. I'm tired. I need to rest."

"If that's what you need." Nikolas continues on the trail. Eleni and Lela continue with him. Is he actually going to leave her here? She watches until she loses sight of their heads sinking behind the slope.

"Stupid man!" He doesn't care she's in the middle of the trail to nowhere. No matter. She can't take it anymore. She will sit here until it pleases her to leave. She moves over to lean against a grass mound. It is cooler now. The evening progresses. Her stomach begins to hurt. She's hungry. She takes a deep breath and drags herself to her feet.

"Would you like some help?" Two hands appear on each of Mara's hips. She recognizes the voice and whirls around to face the man who belongs to the hands.

"How did you get here?"

Nikolas smiles down at her. "Here? I came through the field."

"The field?"

He points behind him. "Yes, just across there. It abuts the village."

Mara peers over his shoulder but the swell of ground on the edge of the trail is too high for her to see over. "We're here? We reached the village and you left me?"

"My dear, it was clear to me you were not going to continue. We were this close so I allowed you the time you needed to relax."

"You could have told me how close we were."

"Would you have believed me?" His quirky smile outlines the edge of his teeth. Mara can feel the sudden release of tension from the long climb to the top. She places her hands on her hips on top of each of his.

"Probably not." She turns back around and he releases his hold, but she keeps one hand in his.

"Come. Let's go meet some new friends, yes?"

They walk hand-in-hand along the trail. The land is flat in sections, hidden by the mountains. Incredible. Incredible how well hidden it is and how well utilized the space is. The sun is making its way to set. The red and orange colors are vivid splashes behind the green and gray of the hills in front of low-lying plains. She looks back at the direction they came. At some points it looks like stairs for the Gods.

"Breathtaking, isn't it?" Nikolas' voice brings her back to him walking beside her.

"Yes, it truly is. I never would have believed this could be here."

"Wait till you see the village. Anyone who does is astonished at how it is situated."

"I can see why. And the Turks? Have they been here?"

"They know it's here, I'm sure. But, no. It is not a place they frequent. It's not easy to find or navigate as you have seen. And, of course, there is no purpose for them. They leave us alone for the most part."

Not far in the distance, a tall, slim figure dressed in black teeters against a walking stick firmly planted in front of her with both hands folded one on top of the other. The closer they get, the longer the smile on her face.

The old woman raises her cane and points to Mara. "Who are you?"

"Yiayia, this is Mara. Do you remember who I am?"

Her toothless grin widens. "*Nai*. Do you think I would forget my own grandson? Why did you bring a foreigner to the village?"

"This is Mara. She's a friend. Mara, this is my Yiayia Kanella. Everyone calls her yiayia."

"Another friend? How many are you bringing us today?" Nikolas wraps his arm around her hunched shoulders. She is almost as tall as he his.

"How many have you counted so far?" Mara watches one, then the other. Nikolas' teasing enlivens the old woman more. Her voice raises with each response until finally she hits the side of his shoulder with the back of her hand. "What was that for?"

"You know. I raised you better than to tease an old woman." Yiayia stops and fixes the knot holding her scarf around her head, balancing her cane against one leg. "You need to come to the house. I will make you coffee."

"I was looking forward to your coffee." Nikolas turns his head to Mara. "How about you? Coffee?"

Mara hesitates. Coffee isn't her first choice. "I suppose. But, do you think she will have any tea?"

"Probably not black tea. But, *tsai tou vounou*? Most definitely. In fact, I will probably have some too."

"What is it?"

"You haven't had mountain tea? You can drink it plain or add some honey. I highly recommend it."

"Maybe I have had it. Surely they have it in Cerigo."

"Most assuredly."

Yiayia knocks Nikolas' arm again. "*Then milaei Ellinika*?"

"No, she doesn't speak Greek." Yiayia shakes her head.

"Ksenes." Tsk. Tsk. "Ksenes."

Mara watches yiayia. Yiayia isn't happy about something. "What's wrong?"

Nikolas moves her hand to the crook of his arm and pats. "Nothing important."

"But, what did she say?"

"She's complaining about foreigners."

"Really? Foreigners?"

"Yes, I'm afraid so."

Mara bends forward to see yiayia on Nikolas' other side. The woman is still shaking her head. "She must know Morea has many 'foreigners' as she puts it."

"She knows. But she doesn't see it up here every day."

"She will need to move past this, of course."

"Ha! If only that were the case." Nikolas wraps one arm around Mara's waist and the other around yiayia. "Can one easily move a donkey when it refuses to move forward?"

"I see your point. No matter. It's not like I'm not used to being thought of as a foreigner. But, she makes it feel so vulgar."

"The truth is, many here feel the same. They are very embroiled in the politics and patriotism."

Mara knows it's true. She's experienced it in Cerigo, albeit somewhat controlled thanks to the protection of her father. "I find it very tiresome at times."

"You must see they have little other recourse, yes? With everything they are being forced to do?"

Yiayia bolts ahead of them. Mara stops mesmerized. The speed with which this yiayia moves is a wonder to watch. The outskirts of the village is clearer. Mara begins to see what Nikolas meant earlier. Houses built of stone topped with clay shingles line the edges of cobblestone streets winding in different directions and raised at different levels all along the side of the mountain. She can hear a lone church bell echo in the distance. Nikolas nudges her to begin moving again. "There it is."

"What?"

"The church bell. It's a signal."

"What do you mean?"

"The priest will have the bell rung whenever there are new arrivals to the village, when a new baby is born, or when someone dies."

"So, that is a signal for what?"

"Probably the result of yiayia's surveillance."

Mara giggles. Yiayia doing surveillance work. "Surely, she can't have alerted someone so soon."

"Believe me. She saw us coming long before we arrived. She probably started the warning when she saw Eleni and Lela." Mara covers her mouth. She doesn't want yiayia to hear her laughing. Nikolas joins in her amusement. It's much easier to walk on the cobblestone than it was trudging up the trail. Yiayia's house is a rectangle box. It's two stories and long with windows equally spaced. The second floor has a wooden veranda the entire length of the front. Yiayia is waiting for them to reach the front door. She already has it open waving them to come in.

"Hurry. It's cold." Yiayia places her scarf across her mouth. Her white hair has wisps flying in every direction on top of her head. Probably from being held down by a scarf. Yiayia pushes it back from her face. "Come. Back here where it's warm by the fire in the kitchen."

Mara scans the house while she walks down the hall to the rear. To her right are the stairs leading up to the second floor. They are wooden like the outside veranda. The second-floor landing is open and visible from below and has multiple rooms. It is separated by waist-high, wooden balustrades to match the staircase. It appears to run the length of the house. The walls are stone like the outside. To the right is a sitting room and formal dining room. She can't see it well because the light is beginning to dim as the evening progresses. The room ahead is full of the glow of candlelight or maybe the fireplace because it is the size of one wall. To the left is the kitchen area with a small table and chairs. The other side of the room is more to Mara's liking. A couch, two chairs, and a small table sitting in front. The couch is loaded with pillows of different sizes, different colors.

"*Katse*! *Katse*!" Yiayia motions with her hands and points to the couch. Mara raises a brow at Nikolas.

"Sit. She wants us to sit."

"No argument from me." Mara plops down. Every muscle in her body must be aching to make her so exhausted. "What happens now?" Nikolas sits down next to her removing any pillows in the way.

"Tomorrow I will have to meet with the Klepht captains and discuss my uncle's plans. Tonight, we will enjoy a well-deserved rest."

Yiayia slams her cupboards looking for something and then pulls out a bunch of dried herbs. She fills a pot with water and positions it over the fire to heat. Mara follows her every movement. She brings the dried bunch of grayish and yellow buds near to the fire and starts to break pieces into the pot beginning to boil. Mara is fascinated by the fire and the activity going on around it. Her attention jumps back to Nikolas. "Where are Eleni and Lela?"

"They're here. Probably already settled in their rooms. I brought them here before I returned to get you."

"Ah. Will they come down do you think?"

Nikolas' response is interrupted by a knock on the front door. Yiayia goes to open it. When she returns, an angular young man follows. He barely raises his eyes when he enters.

"Georgos!" Nikolas stands and steps around the small table in swift movements to grab hold and slugs him into a tight embrace. "It's good to see you. How's your mother?"

Georgos pulls back, still glancing in intervals to the floor. "Good."

"Come. Join us. Yiayia is pouring us tea."

"I would like to, but actually I was sent here to ask you to come to the *plateia*."

"Now?"

"Yes." Nikolas studies Georgos before answering.

"I'll come." Georgos points to Mara still sitting on the couch.

"They want her to come also."

"Mara?"

Now it's Mara's turn for confusion. "I'm sorry, you need me to go where?"

"It's all right. The *plateia* is the center of village. It's where the captains meet to discuss business."

"I don't understand what they could possibly want with me."

"We need to find out. Do you think you can manage it?"

"What kind of people are these Klephts? Don't they know the distance we've come?"

Nikolas waits. "We have to go. They don't summon at this time unless it's important."

"I will come. But I don't understand what is so important it can't wait until tomorrow. Can I at least drink my tea?"

Yiayia brings four metal cups filled with tea and a container with honey in the center. "*Katse!*" She sets the tray down on the small kitchen table, pulls out a chair, and motions for Georgos to sit.

"*Oxi, yiayia.*" Georgos is shaking his head. "Not now." Yiayia won't take no for an answer.

"*Katse!*"

Nikolas smiles and looks at Georgos. "I don't believe we have a choice in the matter. Let's have our tea and go."

Thankful for Yiayia's insistence, Mara sits at the table with Yiayia and the men, drips a heaping spoon of honey in her tea, and sips. Eleni and Lela join them and Yiayia insists they have some tea too.

"We really must go now. Mara, come." Nikolas stands to help her to her feet and navigate her out the door. Georgos follows.

Outside the sky is black with white diamonds laced in every direction. She stumbles trying to look at them and walk at the same time.

"They're beautiful, aren't they?" Nikolas stares up at them too.

"I have a sense I can touch them, they're so close. I've never seen stars so intense before."

Nikolas places his hand in the small of her back nudging her along faster than she wishes. Georgos is a good distance in front of them already. "We need to find out what's so urgent the captains sent for us."

"If you think it's that important." Mara isn't sure anything is more important than the magnificent view above them. Surely, whatever it is can wait until tomorrow morning. Voices ahead bring her back down to earth. Not talking voices. Singing voices. The closer they get the louder they are. Someone is playing the clarinet. Mara would recognize that instrument anywhere. And, a guitar? They reach the circle of the *plateia* where square, wooden tables line the edge. A tall, dark-haired man approaches, arms spread wide. "Nikolas! Welcome back!" Conversations quiet, and the music stops. Everyone's attention is directed at them.

"Denni? Is that you?"

"Of course, it's me. Who else but me can give you a proper homecoming?" Denni pulls Nikolas hard against his chest, slaps him on his back, and plants hard, masculine kisses on each cheek. Denni matches Nikolas in height and his dimpled smile spreads wide across his face. Nikolas regains his balance only for a minute before other men approach him and greet him in the same intense, warm manner.

Denni turns his attention to Mara. "And this lovely lady is the one, no doubt?"

"I'm sorry, the one?" Nikolas turns a confused expression over his shoulder at Mara. "I'm not sure I know what you mean."

Denni looks at Nikolas, at Mara, and back at Nikolas. "Of course, you are to be married, yes?"

Mara opens her mouth to respond, but Nikolas responds first. "Where did you hear this from?" Mara's stomach zings to her feet. "I assure you my mission is to escort Mara, ah, Miss Wingrove safely to Kerkyra per the instruction of her father, Sir Conrad Wingrove."

Denni rolls back his laugh. "So you haven't spent the night together for the last, how many days is it, now?"

Mara can't make one word come out of her mouth. She stares at Nikolas. He raises his hand to silence them all. "Denni, let me be clear. Nothing has happened." The zing now moves to Mara's throat. How can he say nothing has happened?

"So, reports I've heard are not true?"

"It depends on what reports you are referring to, but Mara and I will not be getting married."

"And, where will she be staying."

"Of course, she will stay with yiayia."

"Not if you want the rumors to stop. She is more than welcome to stay with me and Irene."

Mara's mouth loosens. "I see no reason to stay anywhere but where I am." She looks at Nikolas. Nikolas doesn't respond immediately.

"Denni is right. It would probably be better to stay with them." Mara's heart starts racing. Fear begins to overcome her reason. She doesn't want to be left anywhere, but near Nikolas.

He's the one who has kept her safe. He's the one she trusts. Not Denni. Not anyone. Nikolas pulls her away to speak with her privately. "What is it? What are you thinking?"

"What am I thinking?" Tears are pushing against her eyes, trying to force their way out. She doesn't want to cry.

"Mara? Tell me."

"I don't want to be far from you. I'm afraid." She can't believe she said it. But, she did. Nikolas remains fixed on her. She won't meet his gaze. Instead, she watches her own hands playing with the fabric on the front of her dress. His hands are holding each of her elbows.

"Mara, it's all right. I've known Denni and Irene all my life. We're family. He's like a brother. I trust him." Mara can't put words to her feelings. The music starts again and she can hear the men singing. She looks up past Nikolas to see men and women dancing in a line, but in a circle.

"Why are they dancing and singing? Is this a celebration?"

Nikolas steps to the side and follows her line of sight. "Maybe. Come. Let's go and sit."

"No, I'd rather not." Denni comes to where they're standing.

"Come. It'll be fun. We can't let good friends, good food, and good dance go to waste. Can we?"

Mara studies him for a minute. His big brown eyes do not frighten her. His smile still spread across his face is pleasant. Maybe Nikolas is right. "All right, for a while." Mara allows the men to escort her to the table. Nikolas pulls her chair to allow her to sit. She turns to Denni and asks, "What are we celebrating?"

"Tonight? Tonight, we celebrate." He raises his glass in the air and shouts, "independence." Those around shout independence and drink. Denni drinks from his glass, raises it again, and shouts, "And safe homecomings." Everyone drinks and Denni pulls Nikolas to the center of the *plateia*. The music begins again. This time it's different. Only Denni and Nikolas dance in the center. Each man moves with the music. Their arms are raised above their heads while they weave around in circles on their heels. They swoop low and whirl to the music almost losing their balance, but don't. Mara is focused on Nikolas. His dance is strong. She has heard of this dance that men do on Cerigo, but never witnessed it. He is agile. His moves are firm and relaxed. The music is similar to her dancing music. The clarinet whines and asks her to join them, but she doesn't. Not until Nikolas reaches his hand out to her. She can't resist. She takes it. The music changes again. Nikolas kneels before her. Her body takes over and moves to the moan of the clarinet. A drumbeat joins and her hips begin the familiar sequence.

THE DRUM'S RHYTHMIC beat matches the beat in Nikolas' chest. Mara is dancing for him. Her eyes find his each time she circles. All the times before, it was for someone else. But, not now. He will not remove his gaze from the flow of her arms above her head to the pop of each hip swirling in half circles in front of him. The clothes Rachel gave her do not reveal the same amount of skin, but it doesn't stop the seductive shimmy of her hips. He can still enjoy her plump flesh overflowing from the tunic she wears. She kicks one leg to the front then points her toe to the ground while arching her back to allow her hair to hang free behind her. She shakes her bosom while rising. The men watching cheer and he wants to throttle them all. The loud cries muddle her rhythm, but Mara's eyes find his again, restoring their connection. She circles around him and stops behind his back and the music stops. Nikolas stands up and faces her, taking her hands in his.

"Mara, your dancing is outstanding. I cannot find the words to tell you how I..."

A hard slap on his back reveals Denni's smiling face. "Very good!" He places his hand on Mara's shoulder to pull them together for a three-person hug. Mara shirks back. Denni keeps his arms on their shoulders. "Come. I want you to meet Irene. I know you will enjoy her company. She's also *ksenoi*."

"*Ksenoi*?" Mara's voice is a whisper and she is pale from the exertion of the dance. Nikolas backs away, keeping her close to him in the process. He directs her to their table to sit. Denni joins them and pours them all a glass of retsina from the decanter sitting in the center.

Denni answers her question while pouring. "You know, foreign. Not from Morea."

Mara sips and licks her lips. She studies the glass and its contents then gulps down the remaining. "Oh. Where is she from?" Denni refills her glass.

"She's from South Africa."

"South Africa? Is she a negro?"

"Mara!" Nikolas is stunned. What has gotten into her? Too much wine. He tries to take the current glass she is drinking, but Mara cradles it close to her chest.

Denni's hearty laugh is more robust than all the night's revelry. "Don't worry, my friend. If you only knew how many ask me if she's black the minute I mention she's from South Africa." Denni settles and focuses his attention on Mara. "There are whites too in Africa, you know. And, no, she is not black." Denni smiles and pats Mara's hand. "Here she is." Denni stands up and gives Irene a hug that lifts her off the ground.

"Denni, please. You don't need to sweep me off my feet again. You know I'm yours." Irene smiles at Denni then looks at Nikolas and Mara. She breaks free of Denni's embrace to give Nikolas a hug of his own. "Nikolas! When I heard you were back, I was so happy. Do you like our little setup?"

"It's good to see you too, Irene. And, yes. It is very nice. Do we have you to thank?"

Denni answers for her. "Of course. Who else? My Irene knows how to put together such a celebration, eh?"

Irene slaps Denni on the forearm. "Husband, you very well know all of us are quite capable."

"Can't a husband be proud of his wife?" Denni smacks his wife with a kiss on the mouth before she can respond. Nikolas looks at Mara, who has finished another glass of retsina.

"Look, Nikolas. You must have Mara stay with us." Irene then switches her attention to Mara and holds out her hand. "I'm Irene. Some call me Rena." Mara shakes her hand, but doesn't say anything. This is the first he's seen Mara so quiet. "It really is best if you stay with us rather than Nikolas' yiayia."

Mara shrugs her shoulders. Her answer is low and quiet. "I don't understand what it matters now. After all, my father did put Nikolas in charge of my safe arrival to Kerkyra. With everything that's happened so far..."

"Tsk. Tsk. Tsk. No, you're wrong. Here in the village, it does matter. Are you betrothed?"

Mara's face flashes red splotches from her neck to her forehead. She looks at Nikolas and then back to Irene. "No, we are not."

"Well then. You cannot stay at yiayia's. You must stay with us."

"But, Eleni and Lela are there with us. And I saw many rooms at yiayia's. Surely, as long as we are separated."

Mara's silent pleas cannot be acknowledged. There is nothing Nikolas can do. Denni is right. The village will not approve of them staying in the same house. And, Denni being one of the Klepht captains will not go against village law. Nikolas scoots his chair closer to Mara and forces her to face him. "Mara, I know you may be nervous staying in a house with people you only just met. I assure you, I've known Denni all my life. We grew up together. You can trust him."

Mara looks down at her lap and then looks to the sky before releasing a long breath. "All right. But, please do not leave me. I don't want to stay here. I want to go to my father and Nana. I need to make sure Nana has arrived in Kerkyra unharmed. I must know this, Nikolas."

"I promise I will do everything in my power to see this happens."

Irene rests her hand on Mara's shoulder. "Come. Let's get you settled and maybe we can come back if it isn't too late. Our house is just over there behind those spruce trees."

Nikolas watches them leave. Mara looks back at him over her shoulder and he waves her good night. What he really wants to give her is more than a wave. She's right. After all they have been through, it seems odd to be required to stay at separate lodgings. He also knows it will be difficult if not impossible for him to keep his promise. Although, he did say everything in his power for a reason. It may not be in his power to keep her with him. He needs to meet with the Klepht captains and let them know what his uncle requires. "So, Denni. I need to speak with the captains. I have orders from my uncle. When can we meet?"

"Now is as good as any time."

"Now?"

"Why not? Everyone is here. We're all anxious to hear news anyway." Denni takes a deep breath, curls his tongue behind his teeth releasing the high tone of his whistle. Men dancing, stop. Ladies' discussions are silenced. The music continues, but the men crowd around Denni and Nikolas, pulling chairs close around the table.

Denni begins. "Nikolas brings us orders from Kolokotronis we need to hear." Denni takes note of them all one by one. "Everyone is accounted for. Tell us."

Nikolas clears his throat and repeats his uncle's instructions. No one speaks. The music overcasts all conversation. Denni replies first. "When will you be leaving? You will need to leave Mara here of course."

"Yes. Mara must be left here. I cannot take charge of her and Benderli at the same time. Not after what that man did to her."

"And, do you know where Ali Pasha is now?"

"Yes. He's camped not far from Navarino Bay."

"Who will you take with you?"

"Souli and Spero are still with Benderli at Hydra's Peak. They can come with me and the three of us should be able to manage him."

"Good. You will need to leave first light tomorrow."

IRENE'S HOUSE IS ALSO made of stone, but square not rectangular like yiayia's. The door is red. Its bold color is visible even in the dark night. Mara begins to feel more chilled. Small puffs of breath float between her lips when she exhales.

"How many days have you been traveling?"

Mara hears Irene's question, but the answer doesn't immediately form words into a response. She doesn't know how many days, exactly. From almost the moment she left their manor house on Cerigo, she has faced trials she never imagined possible in her life. She's tired and broken. Now she must endure more in this village, away from Nikolas who gave her the strength when she needed it. Now, he's leaving her here, with strangers. "Honestly, I have not counted. It has been many days since I've actually slept inside a house."

Irene pulls some linens from a closet in the hall. "Come with me. Let's get you set up. I hope you sleep well in our guest room." Mara follows her to a back room off the kitchen. It faces the back of the house. Cold air wallops them in the face. Irene changes the pillowcase and starts a fire in the small fireplace in the corner of the room. Mara joins her and begins to warm her hands. "If you need anything, let us know. Denni will probably be back much later. I don't plan to wait up for him. We'll see you in the morning."

Irene closes the door behind her. Mara stands longer in front of the fire to allow it to warm her through. At least tonight she will sleep in an actual bed. Mara removes all her clothing except for the tunic, then pulls down the coverlet to hop in. A knock at the door surprises her and she hurries to cover herself. "Yes, come in?"

Irene walks in and places a pile of clothing on the dresser in front of a mirror. "I realized you probably don't have any other clothes to wear so I brought you a nightgown and something to put on tomorrow while we get your clothes washed. You and I are about the same size, these should fit you nicely." Irene is smiling at her, waiting. Then adds, "you can put them in the drawers if you want. Most of them are empty." Irene pulls one drawer then the other while she speaks.

"Thank you, Irene, I'm sure they'll be fine."

"I'll be up early tomorrow so get some rest, sleep late if you like. We'll talk more tomorrow." Irene leaves and the door clicks. Mara sits for a minute staring at the door. Did Irene just lock the door? What does she think? She'll sneak out to find Nikolas? Mara steps out to change into the nightgown Irene brought. It is nice to wear something clean again. If only she could wash up first. She opens the top drawer and places the extra clothing in and catches sight of herself in the mirror. The woman staring back at her looks ten years older than the one she left at Cerigo only a few days ago. Mara leans forward to look closer at her reflection and sees a piece of crumpled up paper under the bed. She reaches under and picks it up. It's a letter. A letter addressed to her. How is this possible? She recognizes the handwriting. Nana! Thoughts are swimming wild in Mara's head. Nana is here. Where? She skims the words on the paper. It doesn't make sense. Nana writes everything is all right. She's in Kerkyra. How did this letter find its way here? Mara can't wait until morning. She must ask Irene now. The door won't open. Why won't it open? Mara shakes it, bangs her fist hard on the wood. Nothing. Anger and frustration cut through her peace. Mara plops herself on the bed and stares at the floor. Tears well in her eyes. Why would Irene lock her in?

BIRDS. THE TRILL OF their song is not pleasant. It's too early. Mara folds the pillow around her head covering her ears. The sun hasn't even made its way above the horizon. It's still dark in her room. Falling asleep last night proved to be more difficult than she anticipated regardless of the comfort of the bed. The fire is out. The room is nippy. Mara doesn't want to get up in this chill, but she wants answers. She needs a fire to get the chill out. No maids here. It's good Nana made her learn. *"You can't always depend on someone else."* Nana's words echo in her ears. Nana. How early did Irene get up? Would she be up now? No matter. Mara needs answers. She bangs on the door. She'll bang until her fists are raw if she must. Finally, there's metal to metal clanging. A key jiggles on the other side. The door opens and Irene stands there with a candle in her hand.

"Mara, please be still. It's still very early."

"I don't care what time it is. I want to know why you've locked me in and I want you to explain this." Mara pitches the letter at Irene who catches it against her chest. She shakes it straight and holds it out in front allowing the light from the candle to shine on the paper.

"Oh. I see." The tight line of Irene's lips is all that is visible on her mouth. "You'll need to discuss this with Denni."

"Denni? Well let's get him up then. I must know. This letter says Lovina is in Kerkyra. I want to know why it's here. Where is she?"

"Mara. Calm down. Denni will answer all your questions when he returns."

"Returns? He's not here?"

"No. He's gone on business. I'm not sure when he'll be back."

"No. He can't be gone on business."

"He is. It's the way of the Klephts. They go where they are needed, where they are told, and when. Come. Let's get some breakfast."

"I don't want breakfast. I want to know where Lovina is."

"Well then, rest and I will bring a tray to you." Irene closes the door. Click. Click. Again. Locked in, again. Mara is not about to lay down.

Mara dresses quickly in her own clothes and leaves Irene's neatly folded on the dresser. She takes the letter and stuffs it in the pocket of her yelek. She pulls back the curtains and inspects the window. Filtered sunlight enters the room. Good. No bars and the clasp is locked from the inside. And she's on the first floor. Mara opens the window and climbs out onto a small stone patio ending at the base of the mountain. She looks both ways. No one. Now where? Mara picks a direction and creeps along the edge of the mountain looking down in between each house she passes. She decides on one and walks the path toward the *plateia* at the center of the village. She can hear the crow of the roosters in the distance. People will be up and moving about their morning chores soon. Mara doesn't know where to start. One thing she does know. She will not be kept locked in a room. Not ever again. Benderli forced her to his will, she will not allow another to do the same.

"Mara!" No. It can't be. "You're up early. I would have thought you might want to sleep late into the morning, catch up on your rest."

Mara has no choice but to turn and face Denni. "Is that why you had Irene lock me in my room?"

"Ah. That." Denni looks at the ground. "I apologize. I didn't want to do it, but it had to be done."

"What do you mean? How is locking me in my room something that had to be done?" Mara's voice raises a pitch. How can he stand there full of pleasantries and say that?

"Listen. I'll explain. First, let's go and have something to eat. We can talk."

"I don't want to eat. I already told Irene. I want answers."

"It's really quite simple and here is not the place."

"Tell me about this." Mara pulls out Lovina's letter and hands it to him.

"Where did you get this?"

"I found it in the cell you locked me in."

"Mara, it is hardly a cell. Nikolas would skin me alive if he thought I locked you in a cell."

"Enjoy your skin while you have it. If you think I will not tell him, you are mistaken."

Denni stands silent, his brows are scrunched together. "Fine. Come. I will explain everything."

Denni directs her to follow him across the *plateia* and between two more houses before they reach a small house made of the same stone. The veranda is clothed with blankets stretched across the rails to air out from the night's slumber. All the windows are open. Even the windows have blankets hung out. The sun shows bright now. Denni knocks on the door. A young woman answers.

"Denni. I thought you'd be gone by now." The woman brushes tight curls back from her face and turns them behind each ear.

"Not yet. Soon."

"And who's this?" She places her hands on her hips and studies Mara.

"This is Mara."

"Mara?"

"Yes. We need her to meet with your guest."

"Oh. Of course, come in, I'm Vanessa." Vanessa steps aside to allow them to enter. Vanessa's house is similar to the others she has seen, most of the interior is stone like outside. Mara and Denni follow Vanessa to the kitchen.

"This is my sister, Kiki." Kiki nods downward with a closed-lip smile, her eyes intent on the knitting in her lap. Kiki mouths counted stitches along one side of the needle. The wool is dark, but not black. Burgundy.

Mara is fascinated. Kiki's fingers move swift and constant. "What are you knitting?"

Kiki stops the click-click and rests her hands in her lap. "It's a sweater for one of the captains."

Vanessa chimes in. "One of the unmarried captains."

"Vanessa, please." Denni's words prompt silence between the sisters. "May I show Mara to her room?"

"Yes, come with me." Vanessa walks around the table and back out the door. Denni and Mara follow her up the stone staircase to the second floor. Vanessa stops in front of a door and fiddles with her keys to unlock it. They walk into a large well-lit sitting room with a window facing the street. Doors leading to the veranda are open. Wind blows white lace curtains back and forth. The person on the veranda pulls the lace to the side and steps in. Mara recognizes the woman instantly.

"Nana!"

"Mara! Is it really you?" Mara races to Lovina and wraps her arms around her neck pulling her into a tight hug.

"I have been so worried. Nikolas assured me Georgi would keep you safe, but I couldn't believe it until I saw you." Lovina leans back and brushes Mara's hair away from her face. "I know I must be a sight."

"You are a beautiful sight, my girl." Lovina takes Mara's hand and gathers her near the couch by the fireplace. The warmth is welcome. Mara surveys the room behind her. Denni and Vanessa are gone. The door is closed behind them.

"Nana, what happened? How did you end up here? You know they locked me in their guest room last night. And, again this morning, but I climbed out the window only to run into Denni."

Lovina laughs. "You never allow anyone to force you to do anything." Mara's eyes fill with tears. She wipes them before they fall. "What is it, child?"

"There's so much that has happened since we parted in Cerigo. I don't know where to start." Mara is crying full force and falls into Lovina's embrace. "I'm so happy you're alive. I was so worried. I saw you were shot."

"Shh. Calm yourself." Lovina rocks her back and forth. "It's all right. I'm all right, child." Mara's sobs are replaced by her even breathing. "There, now. When you can talk about it, you will."

"I don't believe it's a matter of when, but rather a must."

Lovina nods. "Go on, then."

Mara spills everything about the trip, starting with their trek across the sea on Rachel's ship to the point where Nikolas rescues her from Benderli before cracking once more into silence. "I'm not sure what would have happened if Nikolas hadn't come when he did."

"You would rise above it. Like you are going to do now. I know you, Mara. You have strong will. Refuse to let this break you. Benderli will be dealt with."

Mara sniffs and raises her eyes to Lovina's. "How do you know? I imagine how much I want to dagger him in his chest. The Klephts plan to deliver him to Ali Pasha. What good will that do?"

"My advice right now is to let him be. Don't allow him to control you with worry and a desire for vengeance. His time will come. You must believe that."

Mara isn't sure if she does believe it, but one thing is certain. She hates the idea of his actions having control over her. Maybe letting it go will free her from the turmoil he has caused her inside. Mara closes her eyes, breaths deep and exhales. She does this a few times until she is calmer. Her focus must be on her Nana and the joy of their reunion. Mara opens her eyes. "I don't know if I will be able to, but I will try. Now, you must tell me why you are here?"

"There isn't much you don't already know. That Georgi saved my life. After being shot I lost consciousness and succumbed to fever. I recall blurred moments of the journey that ended here in this apartment." Mara's eyes gloss over. "*Nooo*. No more of that. I have recovered."

"But, Nana, you were shot. Surely, it hasn't healed completely. Let me see."

"No, no. They come daily to change the dressing. It's healing. The apothecary here is exceptional. He knows the herbs in the area and is able to use them most effectively."

"Does it hurt?"

"Sometimes. Stitches will come out in a couple more days."

"Have they allowed you outside this apartment?"

Lovina looks down at her lap and twists the fabric of her dress between her fingers. "No."

"I don't understand. Why have they locked us here? Are we prisoners?" Mara gets up to check the door. Locked. She slams her hand against the center. "Ugh! They can't do this."

"Come back, Mara. It's no use." Mara walks to the veranda doors still open wide. She shoves the blowing lace to the side and walks out. She surveys the area. The veranda is the length of the back. All the windows open to the veranda. The closest house is a good distance away. Nothing is close. Mara leans over to look down. A stone patio lies below. It's lined with planters filled with new sprigs of red, pink, and white flowers. Probably geraniums. It's too high to jump. Nana will never make it in her condition even if she tries.

"I know you're looking for a way down."

"Of course. We need to get out of here."

"It's no use. Mara, I think it's best we stay. They have not mistreated us in any way."

"Not mistreated us? What do you call locking us in a room?"

"But, they have kept us in very comfortable accommodations. Look. I have the entire apartment." Lovina takes Mara back inside and gives her the tour. "The bed is very comfortable. And they come each day and see to the fire. The food is also quite good. Vanessa makes the best Moussaka. And, last night, *stifatho*."

"*Stifatho*? Really, I refuse to allow them to appease their consciences with lamb stew."

"No, of course not. I only want you to see it could be much worse."

"But, why, Nana? Do you know why they're holding us captive?"

Lovina returns to her place in front of the fire and Mara joins her. "I did overhear some men talking on the patio. Or, maybe it was when I was with fever. "

"And?"

"I believe they wish to hold us for leverage to force Maitland to join the Greeks in their attempts to gain independence from the Turks."

"What? Lord High Commissioner of the Ionian Islands? How could they think such a plan would work?"

Lovina remains silent.

"Nana?"

"I don't know, child." Lovina's voice is barely a whisper. "Your father is a peer. And you are British. Maybe they think holding his daughter will give them notice."

Mara sits back, arms crossed in front of her chest. "I can't believe Nikolas would allow this."

"Maybe it was his plan all along."

CHAPTER TWELVE

IT'S EARLY. SO EARLY the roosters aren't awake. Nikolas hitches two horses to the front of the cart and ties two to the back to follow. It's going to be a long way down around the mountain. He will need to take the long way back to Hydra's Peak with the cart and horses. Pano helps load it with provisions to replace those used in the cellar. "Do you think feta is a good idea?"

Pano smiles while he loads the barrel containing the cheese in the back of the cart. "Feta is always a good idea."

"I'm not sure. Will it keep?"

"It keeps in the barrel here, doesn't it? The cellar is big enough. Put it to the side. The top isn't sealed. All you need to do is reach in to get what you want."

Nikolas' stomach rumbles. Pano laughs. "Stop at the wife's on the way out. She'll take care of you. Just pulled loaves from the oven before I left." Fresh bread and feta sprinkled with olive oil and oregano. That will put him right for the journey ahead.

"That I will do, thank you, my friend." Pano continues to load the cart with more nuts, dried fruit and *hilopites* ending with a container of olive oil. "And, *hilopites?*"

"It's what we have. Here take these too. You'll need them." Pano hands him a cast iron hanging pot and utensils. Nikolas tosses them into the cart and heads to the front. "Take more flint. Can't have enough." Nikolas places the bag in his pocket and steps up into the cart.

"Safe travels."

"Thanks, Pano."

Nikolas winds his way slowly through the village. He takes Pano's advice and stops at his house. Calli does just as Pano said she would. Fresh bread and feta. Superb. The bread is still hot and the salty feta with olive oil opens his appetite. Calli smiles. "Here. Have more. Eat while I make you some eggs. "

"No, no. I need to get moving. I'll have to take the long way down."

"Sit. You need strength and it will only take a few minutes. The eggs are fresh too." She pulls out a chair and points for him to sit. Nikolas does as he is told. Calli cracks the eggs and scrambles them with tomato paste adding more feta at the end. In minutes Nikolas has the plate clean.

"That was amazing. It has been so long since I had *kagianas*."

"See? I told you. Now, you can leave with a full stomach. And, take this." Calli hands him a *briki* and a sack of coffee. "Put it in the cellar."

"Word seems to travel fast. One comment. I made one comment to Denni about lacking provisions at the Peaks."

"We want our men to be taken care of when we aren't there to do it."

Nikolas steps up and takes the reins after placing the coffee in the corner in the back of the cart. He waves to Calli and slaps the reins, thankful for her insistence. A full stomach will make the drive less tiresome.

"*Ai sto diaolo.*" Nikolas reaches Hydra's Peak at almost sunset. "What happened to him?"

Nikolas jumps down from the cart and walks to Benderli, who's still tied to the same tree. His head hangs down. Nikolas kneels to inspect his face. He turns it from one side to the other. Eyes swollen shut move in the same direction. Red gashes above his brows and across his cheek ooze. Spero kneels next to Nikolas. "We decided to give him back some of what he's been giving."

"Spero, you know better. This is not our way."

"Well, it should be."

Nikolas stands up. "Listen. I know we're at war, but the captains will not be pleased."

"Won't they?" Spero turns and heads back to the cart to begin the process of unloading. "Who do you think took the first swing?" Nikolas doesn't need to answer. His uncle all but told him he was headed here to do just this very thing.

Nikolas grabs a jug and heads into the cave following Spero. "How does he expect us to turn him over to Ali Pasha in this state?"

"He's your uncle. I'm not about to question him on it." Spero grabs another sack to take to the cellar. "*Hilopites*? It feels like months since I've enjoyed a hot plate. And, olive oil. They really loaded up this time."

"Apparently, the women want their men cared for."

"Probably Calli. She's going to have Pano unfit for duty soon."

They crisscross back and forth until they're finished unloading the cart. Nikolas sets the horses to feed in some grass near where Benderli is tied. The grass won't be enough. It's good Pano added a bag of feed to the stockpile.

"Where is Souli? Of course, he's not here when there is work to do."

"I wasn't sure when you would be back. I sent him to hunt something for dinner."

"He should be back soon. It's almost dark." Nikolas grabs the flint and plops it in with what is left in the cave. The fire still burns hot but needs more wood for flames strong enough to bring water to boil. Souli returns with nothing.

"Buck up! Tonight's dinner is compliments of Calli."

"Calli?" Souli heads to the fire and lifts the lid, burning his hand in the process. He shakes it out and joins the other two where they lounge against the rocks of the cave. "So, we're really sending the bastard to Ali Pasha?"

"Relax. Ali Pasha is not happy with him. I doubt it will be a pleasant reunion for the two."

"And we're just going to hand him over? I say he should meet with an accident before we get there."

"I'm sure my uncle knows what he is doing."

"Right."

Nikolas isn't sure that's an agreement or not.

NIKOLAS SNAPS THE SPYGLASS shut and hands it back to Spero. Turks.

"Let me see." Spero extends the lens and looks. "What do you think they're doing?"

"I think they're gathering for battle."

"Should we let the other Captains know?"

"Yes. Send Souli back with the news. I'll take Benderli."

Nikolas mounts the rouncey Pano gave him and winds his way down to the beach. It's almost the same spot Rachel dropped them. Spero catches up with Benderli in tow. Nikolas dismounts and waves his hands in crisscross movements over his head. He pulls Benderli to his side. He looks through the spyglass. His signal worked. A dinghy is lowered. Two men row the boat to shore. Another is perched at the stern. Nikolas adjusts his pistol behind him and waits. The men jump out and splash to the shore, dragging their burden with them.

Benderli runs to them yelling, "Arrest these loons at once!" Nikolas yanks the rope, flopping Benderli to his knees. Another pull and he's face down in the sand. Nikolas clicks his pistol to ready before any of the Turks can draw theirs, but one kilij manages to rest on his throat. Its owner being one step in front of him. Spero is nestled in a headlock while Benderli spits sand. "What are you waiting for? Take them out."

Nikolas doesn't move. His eyes focus on the man in front of him. He doesn't move. "I have orders to bring this animal to Ali Pasha."

Two bulging frog eyes widen in silence. "Infidel. You treat the Sultan's appointed with disrespect. I slit your throat where you stand."

"I think not." *Tick.*

The Turk presses his chest into the barrel of Nikolas' pistol. "You do not wish to do that." He snaps his fingers.

Spero groans. The arms surrounding his neck tighten while Spero begins to sink to the ground. Benderli is standing again, swiping his palms together. His laugh squawks like a seagull hovering above them. Nikolas lowers his pistol and yanks again on the rope. Benderli flounders to stabilize his steps. "My orders come from Kolokotronis himself. He will not be pleased to see his men mistreated."

Benderli struggles to remove the rope binding his wrists. "*Pfft*. Kolokotronis. He is nothing. I serve the Sultan. You will obey me!" Benderli scuffs his way toward them but tangles his feet in the rope on his way. Prone once more his face fumes purple. Nikolas drops his pistol to his side.

"You will deliver us to Ali Pasha immediately." The kilij lowers and the chokehold on Spero is released. Nikolas replaces his pistol to its place in his belt. Benderli is upright once more.

"Remove these bonds at once!" Frog eyes replaces his kilij and complies in silence. Benderli waits while two sets of strong Turkish arms lock to form a seat, hoisting 'His Excellency' to the boat held by the third.

"Spero, take the horses and wait for my return. You know what to do if I'm not back in time." Spero takes the reins and nods. Nikolas follows the Turks to the boat. No armchair awaits for him. He sloshes aboard.

Benderli takes his seat at the stern. Frog eyes pushes off and leaps in. He shoves an oar into Nikolas' hand. No words. It will take the strength of all four to make it back to the ship rowing against the current. Slow and steady. Nikolas' arms burn. Frog eyes stops first. The frigate rests behind them. A rope ladder falls over the side. Frog eyes casts the rope to the deck hands leaning over the side. Unbelievable. A hanging throne is lowered for Benderli to perch himself on. How many of them does it take to haul him aboard? After Benderli's sneering face passes over the side, one by one the rest board. Nikolas has never been on a Turkish frigate before. It's not much different from Rachel's. More curves to the architecture, but similar. Benderli is nowhere. Frog eyes pushes him forward. His legs are weak, but his arms are weaker. Water. He needs water. They pass through a small corridor before passing through an elaborate door in gold, red and purple. It's decorated with Turkish war emblems. Captain's quarters.

"Ah. Nikitaras? Yes?" Ibrahim Pasha is reclining against a floor lined with pillows. This room is very different from Rachel's. Nikolas just walked into a Turkish Palace of gold, silver, and gems.

"No. Nikitaras is my father. I am Nikolas."

Ibrahim circles his hand around empty space. "Nikitaras, Nikolas, the same no?"

"No, it's not the same." Ibrahim frowns and lays one arm across his bended knee and scratches his chin with the other.

"Hm. Nik. It's Nik then."

Vlakas. He doesn't care what the insurgent calls him. "Where is Ali Pasha?"

"He's not here." Ibrahim's dark eyes peel into Nikolas. He offers no further explanation.

"I will need to take Benderli back and continue on until I find him."

Nikolas' bluff doesn't work. "I'm afraid that's not possible."

"I am under orders to deliver Benderli to Ali Pasha. This arrangement was agreed to by the Pasha himself."

"I'm afraid it's not possible. I know of no such instructions. I myself have orders."

"Oh?" Here it comes. Ibrahim stands to address Nikolas within five inches of his face. Ibrahim's stench is warm on his skin when he speaks.

"You will be detained here as well, my Klepht Captain. The Sultan will require answers. You will provide these answers."

"I'm sure I don't have any answers of use to you or your Sultan."

"I disagree. You are son of Nikitaras. Kolokotronis is your uncle. I doubt you are not informed of the rebellions happening in Kalamata and uprisings in surrounding areas."

"You are mistaken. I have been in Cerigo and have had no contact with my uncle or my father for some time."

"*Hmpf.*" Ibrahim returns to his place on the cushions. "You will accompany us to Navarino Bay. Ali Pasha can decide."

"You said you didn't know where Ali Pasha was."

Ibrahim waves his hand in the air while putting an olive in his mouth. Frog eyes again. He grabs Nikolas' elbow to drag him to the door. Nikolas shakes free and stares at Ibrahim.

"I lied."

CHAPTER THIRTEEN

Somewhere Near Pylos

WATER. NIKOLAS' TONGUE sticks to the roof of his mouth. Words form. Voice fails. *Anathema tous.* How long will they keep him dehydrated? Nikolas' cheeks are pressed against the wooden planks of the cabin floor they threw him in. How many days has it been? He can't remember. Nikolas decides then and there. He's going to dagger the Turk at first chance. His father and uncle will hear of his treatment. They will not be pleased. The lock on the door jiggles. He sits up. It's frog eyes.

"Get up." The Turk doesn't wait. He bends over, grabs Nikolas by the wrist and hauls him to his feet. Nikolas sways. He can barely stand. Frog eyes pushes and he stumbles forward grasping the wall to steady his step.

"Where?" Frog eyes pushes him out the door. Silence. Nikolas stumbles up the stairs to the quarterdeck. The sea air fills his lungs. It's refreshing, but he needs water. Ibrahim turns around. His gold and green turbaned head sparkles in the sun. The glare is almost blinding. His indigo kaftan reaches his ankles. Does he believe he's the Sultan himself?

"It's time you take your leave." Ibrahim's dismissal is brief. Before Nikolas can respond, frog eyes drags him away. Benderli's 'throne' is again in the process of being lowered to the boat already in place below.

"Over." Frog eyes points to the ladder hanging over the side. Nikolas slides himself over the side. He barely has the strength to descend. Frog eyes and his men join them. The way to shore is much easier. Good, because there is no way he has any strength to row this time. Nikolas' hands are bound with rope in the front.

Navarino Bay. He recognizes the landscape. So, Ali Pasha has set up camp here. That is, if Ibrahim is truly taking them to Ali Pasha. He's less than honorable. Benderli is oddly silent. Smug, and silent. It's clear he has not met with the same treatment doled out to Nikolas. His clothes are almost as extravagant as Ibrahim's. Probably are Ibrahim's. Frog eyes' men repeat the same routine for Benderli's removal to dry land. Nikolas' exit is also repeated. Now what? He stands in place barely able to stay upright. Frog eyes pushes. "Move." Nikolas is going to 'move' frog eyes once and for all when strength is returned to his limbs.

They begin to move forward. "How far is it to the camp?" Benderli's conceit when he speaks spurs Nikolas' determination to end him.

"Almost 5,000 ayak."

Benderli shakes his head. "No. You will carry me."

Nikolas can't help the garble of laughter. He coughs to cover the sound. Frog eyes squints in his direction before nodding in the direction of his men to accommodate the command. At least their pace has slowed and he can keep up. The exertion is almost too much. Nikolas looks in the distance and sees smoke rising above a small hill. It must be the camp they are heading for. Benderli complains for the duration of the trek. Frog eyes and his men have no reaction. They keep moving forward, drenched in sweat from their own exertion. They reach the entrance of the camp and frog eyes speaks with the guard. Nikolas cannot understand what's being said. Benderli is lowered from the back of one of the men. The man loses his balance, and Benderli falls back. Frog eyes reaches down to help him up. He stands, slaps his arm away, and grabs the kilij fastened to his waist. Frog eyes doesn't move to stop him. Benderli walks to face the man who dropped him and slays the blade across his face twice. "Insolence." The man crouches on his knees holding his face as blood trickles through long fingers. No one moves to help. All eyes stare at the ground. Nikolas can do nothing.

"Move."

More of the same conceited entitlement emanates with each of Benderli's steps. The camp is lined with rows of tents and fires for warmth and cooking. At what must be the center, a large circular tent is guarded by two men. Frog eyes stands tall to address the guards. One of them flips the cloth door open and enters. He returns holding the cloth to the side allowing them to pass. Benderli goes first. Frog eyes pushes Nikolas in and presses his shoulder until he's on his knees on the carpeted ground of the tent.

Ali Pasha reclines on a bed of cushions, Kyria Vasiliki at his side. "What's this? Benderli, why is this man bound and famished?"

Nikolas raises his head and frog eyes slaps the back of his head, causing him to bow forward.

"Enough." Ali Pasha points to frog eyes. "You, unbind him and fetch him some water to drink."

Benderli interrupts. "My liege, I assure you it was necessary."

Ali Pasha's puffy cheeks harden. "You, do as I say. He is the nephew of Kolokotronis. I wish his person be tended to immediately."

Frog eyes leaves and returns with a dried-out gourd filled with water. Nikolas raises it to his mouth and drinks all the water contained inside. He wants more. He hands it back to frog eyes. "More." He can still only say one-word sentences, but the re-hydration of his tongue is pleasant.

Benderli continues his rant. "He is a Klepht captain."

Ali Pasha takes a sip from the cup offered to him by his wife. "And?"

"The rebels? You are aware the Klephts are involved?"

"I am. I am also aware they are useful to keeping the people compliant. I do not wish to have the nephew of one of their most resourceful Klephts mishandled."

"Mishandled? You have not yet heard the handling against his Excellency's appointed Grand Vizier."

"I do not wish to hear of it. The Sultan has made his wishes clear. You are to make an appearance before the Sultan immediately."

"What is this you speak of?"

"You shall know soon enough." Ali Pasha nods to his men. Benderli is escorted out.

Ali Pasha directs his attention to Nikolas. "So. You have relinquished your English attire. Much more true to form." He inhales the smoke from the burning nargile. He exhales his next words. "You are of the Klephts. Does Wingrove know? Does the British Resident know?"

Nikolas tries to answer, but his throat sticks still. He drinks from the refilled gourd and begins his sentence again. "You are aware. I don't know if Heathcote is aware or not."

Kyria Vasiliki hands him a tray of figs. "Here, eat. You are drained." Ali Pasha turns on his wife. His tight cheeks reveal the displeasure of her interruption. She sinks back.

Nikolas chews and swallows the handful he grabbed from the tray, thankful for her interruption. These will help him regain energy. He needs more.

Ali Pasha squints his next question. "Your uncle. Where is he now?"

Nikolas raises his head and sits back, crisscrossing his legs with an arm over each knee. "I don't know. He doesn't tell everyone what his plans are."

"Ah." Ali Pasha relaxes back into his padded nest. "So, you were unaware of the uprising?"

"I knew it happened. I was in Cerigo as you well know. But, I was not advised of plans for it, if that is what you are asking. I am surprised to find you here. I was under the impression you and Ibrahim were to remain in neutral zones."

Ali Pasha sucks deep, looks up, and exhales. "It was the initial plan, yes. But, on further consideration I will not cower to the infidels. I am confident we can reassert our position in this region."

"And Ibrahim?"

"Ibrahim and I are in agreement on this point. But he should not have detained you. For that, he will be dealt with."

"And Benderli?"

"What do you imply?"

193

"With respect, I am not implying anything. The man is retched. His actions must be addressed."

"What actions are those, specifically?"

Nikolas wants to wallop the man where he sits. "You must know of his mistreatment of those in his charge."

Ali Pasha does not respond. Kyria Vasiliki hands him the tray of figs and nuts. Ali Pasha's eyes are still and locked on Nikolas. He chews a handful of nuts. "Mistreatment. Yes, indeed."

"Do you approve of it?"

"Benderli has garnered the disfavor of the Sultan for other reasons. He will be exiled. You need not be concerned with him."

"Exiled? The man should be daggered slowly." The thought of an Ottoman mistreating his own mother the same way churns the emptiness in his burning stomach.

"Ha. You. Your self-righteous pleas. Do you believe him the only man guilty of this? Greek warriors. Do they not do the same to their captives? You are a fool if you say otherwise." Ali Pasha turns his face to the side and sits. Silent. Nikolas wants to vomit. Klephts are honorable. Such conduct is not tolerated. Kyria Vasiliki stands and leaves the tent.

"She does not wish to listen to such topics."

"Forgive me." Nikolas lowers his head.

"I do not condone these actions of a few. Wingrove's child. She is safe?"

"She is with my clan. I have been charged to get her safely to Kerkyra."

"Hmm." Ali Pasha leaves the nargile in his mouth then inhales again. "You will remain here until you are strengthened. I give you leave to move her to Kerkyra."

"Thank you."

"I will require your services in the future. You will aid me in the way your uncle aids me. Yes?" The smoke from the nargile floats in waves of gray throughout the tent. There is no choice.

"Agreed."

CHAPTER FOURTEEN

Katafigio

HOW MANY MORE DAYS must they continue locked in this apartment? Mara is ready to make the jump from the second-floor veranda. Lovina is not as agitated. She spends her days mending clothes provided to her by Vanessa and Kiki. The keys jiggle in the door. Warm and spicy aromas fill the air when it opens.

"Come, ladies." Vanessa scans the room. Her smile widens when her eyes meet Mara. "We have guests for dinner. You may join us in the dining hall."

Dining hall? They have a dining hall? Lovina stands. Mara follows. "Thank you, Vanessa. Mara and I will be glad to join you."

"As if we have a choice in anything we do." Mara crosses her arms across her chest. Vanessa's smile sags.

"Mara." Lovina takes her hand, to loosen their hold.

Lovina's polite reprimand will not work this time. "Nana, it's true."

"I did not teach you to be unkind. Yes, we are restricted, but well cared for." Lovina nods at Vanessa. She tightens her grip on Mara's hand.

"Never mind." Vanessa motions them to follow her out the door. "Maybe the lemon chicken will calm your nerves."

"I'm sure my nerves have nothing to do with it." Lovina squeezes again. She can feel Nana's glare, but refuses to look. They follow Vanessa down the stairs and into a larger room previously closed off behind the stairs. Hm. There is a small dining hall. Cloth covered chairs surround a long wooden table. Denni and Irene are seated at one end. Spero and Georgi are on one side.

"Ladies, welcome." Denni raises his glass to salute them. Vanessa motions them to sit next to Irene.

"It's not as if we have a choice."

Vanessa takes a seat next to Georgi.

"Yes, but I am sure you will want to hear the news."

"Do you mean to allow us the freedom to leave?" Mara continues to ignore the constant pressure pinching her left arm each time she speaks. She is angry and will not sit still waiting to be told when she may do as she wishes.

"Ah, not exactly." Denni drinks from his wine and Kiki begins to serve the food.

"Then I have no use for any other news."

"I believe you do. Spero?"

Spero clears his throat. "We delivered Benderli to Ali Pasha at the harbor as directed—"

"What?" Mara chokes on the water she was sipping. Lovina hands her a napkin to wipe her mouth. "You delivered him to Ali Pasha? So, he's not to be punished for anything?"

Denni raises his hand to silence her. "Just wait. Spero, continue."

"When Nikolas didn't return from the frigate, I tracked them along the coast until they dropped anchor in Navarino Bay. It turns out the frigate was captained by Ibrahim Pasha. They brought Benderli and Nikolas to a camp where Ali Pasha resides."

"Ibrahim Pasha? Ali Pasha? I don't understand." What are they doing in Morea? The whole point of her being sent to Kerkyra was in response to the Pashas using Cerigo as a safe haven.

"Mara." Denni's voice is kind. She still doesn't trust him. "Did you overhear anything about their plans?"

"Their plans? How would I know? We were sent away to Kerkyra with Nikolas in attempt to secure our safety. You can see how well that turned out."

"And you, Ms. Aponsuwa. Have you any information you can provide us?" Mara looks at Lovina. How much information about them has she already shared with their captors?

Lovina continues to look at her plate. She doesn't raise her head when she answers. "I have no more information than Mara. Such information is not discussed in our presence."

"This is absurd." Mara drinks the wine in her glass in one gulp. "You should be more concerned with Nikolas' rescue instead of sitting here questioning us about things we clearly have no insight into."

Denni cuts a piece of the food on his plate and chews. Fork in one hand, knife in the other he looks around the table and cuts another piece.

"Well, are you?"

"I'm sorry?" More chewing. "Was there a question?"

Mara stares at the mirror hanging on the wall just above his head. She wants to shatter it. "Nikolas. How will you get him from Ali Pasha?"

"Oh. We're not."

"What?" Mara stands and throws her napkin across the plate of food she hasn't touched. "You can't leave him."

Lovina's hand caresses her palm. "Mara, please child. Sit. Finish your food." Mara looks down at Lovina. Her forehead is creased with lines she never noticed before. Mara grunts a deep breath and sits. She places her napkin back on her lap and stares at Denni. He continues to eat. She looks at Georgi. Eating. Spero. He's staring at his plate. Not eating.

Denni stops and looks around the table before scooping another bite from his plate. "We're confident he will not be harmed."

"And what makes you so confident?"

Denni pauses before answering. "The Pashas use the Klephts. They believe the Klephts help them to keep order among the people. He'll not be harmed."

"But, how can you be sure? The rebellion. They've started a war of independence."

"True. He's also Kolokotronis' nephew. They won't touch him."

"But—"

"Mara." Lovina doesn't have to say more. Her hand rests on her knee. She wants her to stop. But she can't. She looks at Spero. Still not eating. "You have to get him out."

"MARA, PLEASE. DON'T do this." Lovina is using her best pleading voice. It's not going to work. She must find a way to free Nikolas. All he has done for her. She will not leave him to the Turks. "They have stopped locking the door. I don't want to risk being locked in again."

"Whether they lock the door or not, we are still prisoners. There is only one way out and they have posted guards. They know the mountainous regions surround us. There is nowhere to go but down the paths they guard."

"Mara, you will get lost. Or worse. Be found by these savages, again." Mara looks at Lovina sitting at the edge of her seat in their small accommodations. She kneels before her. "You don't understand. I can't leave him. He saved my life, Nana. Besides, I intend to enlist some help."

"Help?"

"Yes. I'm quite sure Spero agrees with me. I'm going out to find him."

"Have you thought about me? I shall have no choice, but to stay here."

"I know. I also know they will not harm you. I don't believe they'll harm us. Besides, they want us for ransom, right? We're no use to them otherwise."

"Mara! How can you say such things?"

"I'm sorry, but it's true. Trust me." Those are the words Nikolas said to her only days ago. Lovina pats Mara's hands resting on her knees.

"Promise me you will come back."

Mara kisses Lovina's fingers. "I will." She stands and swings a small cloth satchel of rummaged supplies over her shoulder. The door closes behind her.

Spero isn't difficult to find. The village stables house the horses used by the Klephts. Horses strong and trained to endure the mountain terrain. There. By the black rouncey. Mara has seen him riding this one many times. She walks up to him, runs her fingers through the horse's forelock. He stomps and bobs his head.

"Shh. That's a good boy." Spero rounds his flank.

"I wouldn't get too close. He can be unpredictable." Mara steps back. "He must fit in well around here."

Spero's tight-lipped smile runs taut across his face. He slicks the horse's fur with a body brush. "That he does."

"What's his name?"

"Notos."

"Interesting name." Spero stops brushing and leans against the horse's back, placing his other hand on his hip. "It fits him. What brings you here, miss?"

Mara stares at Spero. Now what? He must suspect something. "I think you know what. I intend to rescue Nikolas."

Spero walks to the corner to grab a saddle. He flings it over a rail. "Thought as much." He pulls a small cart and hitches it to Notos. Mara watches him continue to load the cart. He throws the saddle in and other things of which she's not sure what they are and slings a canvas over them. Spero ties two more horses to the back of the cart then lifts the canvas. "Get in."

"What?"

"Get in. How do you think you'll get past the guards?" Mara stares at Spero. His tight-lipped smile has turned serious. He's going to help her.

She climbs in and he covers her body with the cloth. A vile stench invades her nostrils. Her stomach churns. The cart rolls. She turns one way then the other. No use. It's overwhelming. Her head slams against the back of the cart. She lays still while the cart jostles. Muffled voices are on top of her. A welcome slit of fresh air invades her space. For a second.

"Ugh." A man turns away and covers his face with his forearm. Spero flaps the tarp closed. Mara holds her breath, but not for long. The cart moves again. How much more can she take? She doesn't care. Enough. She shoves the tarp up and open. Clean, fresh, air. Spero is laughing.

"It's a good thing we've passed down over the hill. If Menio saw you, we'd be cooked."

Mara covers her nose and mouth with the back of her hand. "What is this stuff?"

"Fertilizer."

"I've never smelled anything so horrid."

"That's the point. It worked didn't it?"

"If you say so."

"It certainly put Menio in his place."

"True." Mara steps over the back to sit next to Spero on the bench. "What are we going to do with it? You don't mean to take it with us?" She coughs.

"No. I'll leave it in the fields on our way down. It needs to be worked in the soil anyway."

"Good."

"I doubt we'll have to worry you'll be abducted now."

Mara turns to look at Spero. The side of his smile quirks his cheek to reveal one dimple. Notos kicks at the reins slapping his backside. "Do I want to ask?"

"Probably not."

CHAPTER FIFTEEN

Somewhere Near Pylos

"ALI PASHA WILL NOT be pleased." Ibrahim walks around Nikolas with his hands folded behind his back. Ibrahim's men surround them. Ibrahim slaps one hand on top of the other still clasped behind him. He stops in front of Nikolas.

"When Ilyas told me of your release I was not pleased."

"Ilyas?"

"He is my...what do you call them? Quartermaster, is it?" Ibrahim motions the man to step forward. Frog eyes. Now he knows the name of the man. Ilyas moves to the center where Nikolas and Ibrahim are. "Bind his hands. We will bring him with us. No one will miss him."

Frog eyes, that is Ilyas, begins to bind Nikolas' hands. Nikolas swings one hand free. More men step forward and converge on Nikolas. "You can't do this. I've done nothing wrong and Ali Pasha released me."

"Yes. That is a problem. It doesn't matter. I can and I will keep you. You will prove useful in my negotiations." Nikolas struggles to keep his hands free. He punches Ilyas. His frog eyes widen but his face doesn't move. Great. Ilyas punches him in the gut. Nikolas wants to spit in his face, but his face is shoved to the ground. One arm is pulled back and then the other. The rope is taut around his wrists. They yank him straight and Ilyas returns a blow to Nikolas' left jaw. The sting knocks his head to the side. Inside, parts of his head crash together and his teeth slash his tongue. Salted metal flavors the spit dripping from his mouth. Nikolas takes one shot and hits his mark. Red drool slides down Ilyas' cheek. Another blow to Nikolas' groin bends him in half. Pain zings through the back of his head and dark splotches of fog appear in front of his eyes as pressure in his head pushes forward into complete darkness.

"WE HAVE TO HELP HIM."

Mara hands the spyglass to Spero. He perches himself on a boulder and squints through the lens and adjusts the scope. Mara raises herself to creep closer. Spero pushes her shoulder down. "We can't help him now."

"There are too many. Here, take a look." Spero hands the spyglass back to Mara. "They're surrounding him. We wouldn't stand a chance. We need to wait until there are less of them."

"But if they get him to their ship, we've lost him."

Spero holds his hand out. "Let me see." He takes the scope and scans the area. "I don't think they're taking him to the ship. They're setting up camp. Have a look."

Spero points out to the open water. Mara directs the spyglass in the direction he indicates. Four boats are en route to the shore loaded with crates and tarps. "What do you suggest? We can't just leave him."

"For now, we have to."

Mara continues to watch the largest Turk there slam Nikolas with the butt of his yatagan. Nikolas falls to the ground. Her insides tighten from the pit of her stomach to the knot in her throat. How can Spero sit and do nothing? Anger roars inside, clawing to get out. "I can't." Mara crawls forward to escape the hands reaching to stop her. She heads straight to the shore. Before she reaches the clearing where Nikolas is laying, she is thrust back. One strong arm around her waist and one large hand across her mouth.

The heavy whisper of Spero's voice burns her ear. "Now is not the time. I'm sure you don't want a repeat of what you experienced with Benderli." Mara's eyes burn wet. No. She doesn't. "I'm going to release you and we have to back off slowly. Do you understand?" Mara's vision blurs. She watches Nikolas' still form distancing itself from her. The strength holding her in place slowly releases her. Spero turns her to face him. "Believe me. I don't want to leave him either, but we have to. Come. I have an idea."

Mara reaches out to take the hand Spero extends her. "Where are we going?" Spero doesn't answer. He drags them through the woodlands. Mara trips and yanks his arm, forcing him to stop. "I want to know where we're going."

He comes closer and speaks low. "I'll tell you. But, we need distance from the Turks."

Mara bends over with one hand on each knee. "Fine. But wait two minutes please, while I catch my breath."

"One minute."

Mara looks up. "I'll take as long as I need. Leave if you want." Spero shifts his weight to one side and waits. "That's what I thought."

"We're not far enough yet. They're setting up camp. This area will be full of Turks scouring for wood for their fires. I suggest you take less than you need."

Mara looks up. "Fine. Let's go, but I will keep my hand to myself, thank you." Spero turns and continues to march them forward. She struggles to keep up. At least now she's not tripping from being dragged behind. Spero keeps a steady pace. He's not even sweating. What is it with the Klephts? "Are we almost there?"

"Yes." Spero stops and waits for her to close the gap between them. They're at the edge looking down into an open expanse filled with tents. "We're here."

"Where exactly are we?"

"Ali Pasha's camp."

"What? Why would you take us here? What can you possibly hope to accomplish?"

"Not me, you."

The man's gone mad. "You cannot expect me to do anything."

"As a matter of fact, I can. Your father is his Dragoman, no?"

"Yes. But it doesn't mean he's not a Turk."

"Well, you know him and we need to find out how Nikolas ended up with Ibrahim."

Spero is not wrong. But, still. Ali Pasha? He'll want to know why she's not at Kerkyra, if he even knows her father's plans. What if he decides to keep her with him? Add her to his harem. So many things could go wrong. Speaking with Vaso is much more preferable than her husband. "I have a better idea. We need to find Vaso. She'll know what we need to find out and I have a better chance of getting out if we, or I, approach her."

"Vaso?"

"Kyria Vasiliki."

"The Pasha's wife?"

"Don't ask. They stayed at our manor house on Cerigo. He and Ibrahim were there."

"You didn't think this might be important information for me to know?"

"I didn't think about it until now."

"So, Ali Pasha and Ibrahim Pasha were there."

"Yes. My understanding is they were supposed to remain there on neutral ground after the rebellion at Kalamata."

"Obviously, they didn't. Are you sure Kyria Vasiliki will help you?"

"No. But, we have no choice. So, what's the plan?"

MARA TRIES TO CALM the pounding in her chest. Deep breath in, deep breath out. One misstep will get her discovered. She crouches behind the tent Spero claims is Vaso's. What if he's wrong and she slips under to find a tent full of Turks? Not helping. More pounding explodes in her head now. There's no choice. She has to believe Spero is right. One minute more and she flips the tarp and rolls under. Empty. She waited too long. Now what?

The cloth covering the entrance flips open. A veiled woman enters and swirls, removing it from her head. She plops down on the cushions lining the carpeted ground. Mara crawls slow. She doesn't want to startle her. She starts to whisper and Vaso screams.

"Please, wait. Don't call your guards, please."

"Mara?"

"Yes, it's me."

"What are you doing here? And why are you dressed like this?"

"I can explain everything, please wait and hear my story."

"Quick, get behind me and the cushions." Vaso lifts the cushions and Mara lies flat on her stomach. Vaso repositions the mounds on top of her.

Vaso speaks first. "I am fine. It is nothing."

"I heard a scream."

"I know." The weight of Vaso leaning against Mara stifles her breath. "It was a bug."

"A bug?"

"Yes. You know how I hate them. I took care of it. It is gone now." There is no sound or movement. "What are you waiting for? I said I am fine. You may leave now."

Another few moments pass before Vaso leans forward and lifts the cushions.

"He is gone. It is safe." Mara breathes.

"I need your help."

"Hmm... What can I do?"

"Nikolas is in trouble."

"How is this? He was here. Pasha sent him on his way."

"What do you mean? He was a prisoner?"

"No. He is Klepht. His uncle is Kolokotronis. Pasha needs him."

"So he left on his own?"

"Of course. What has happened?"

"It's Ibrahim." Mara's tears threaten to fall again. "Ibrahim has him. I don't even know if he is still alive."

"Ibrahim? The Pasha will not be pleased. But I don't think he will be killed. Ibrahim knows better. I don't believe Nikolas will harmed. He is too valuable and Ibrahim knows it."

"Valuable?"

"Yes. Some Klephts are useful to help keep the people in line. Nikolas is considered useful."

"How do you know these things?"

"*Koritsi,* I know many things. The Pasha and I, we are not separated. I am present at many introductions and many political affairs."

"Political affairs?"

"Of course, it is government, is it not?" Vaso is calm and relaxed, watching her as she speaks. "What is it you would like me to do for you?"

"I need the Pasha's help to get Nikolas back. But I do not wish to make myself known to Pasha. Is there a way?"

"And why is this?"

"I don't want to return to Cerigo, and I don't want to be sent to Kerkyra yet."

"You will tell me why?" Mara isn't sure she should be telling Vaso the entire story, but there is no way around it.

"The Klephts. They have Lovina. They're holding her there to make Maitland support their cause. I was held also until I escaped to help Nikolas. We thought he was held captive here until we came across Ibrahim. He's making camp near the shore not far from here."

"This is insane. Sultan will not succumb to their threats."

"I don't know what they think. I'm not sure I care. I know Nikolas did not know the entirety of the Klephts' plans. He saved my life. I need to help him. And, I need to get back to Lovina."

"This is complicated. Let me think."

HOW DID SHE LET VASO talk her into such nonsense? "Here. Put this on. These clothes you are wearing should be burned. The stench will never come out." Vaso helps Mara pull off the yelek. "Hopefully it's not on your skin. I will have my hand servant wash these."

"No."

"No?"

"We won't have time for them to dry. As soon as we are done with this, this..." Mara flaps her hands in front of her. "...whatever I'm doing, I will need to leave."

Vaso places her hands on her hips. "What you are doing is putting the Pasha in a mood to grant your request."

"You're sure this will work?"

"No. But, it hasn't failed me yet. It's how he is. We do what we must." Vaso circles her hand above her head and turns around to look for something in a box on a low standing cabinet. "Here it is. Put this on."

"What is it?"

"It's a tikki. What do you think?"

"I can't wear that."

"Trust me. Pasha will like it." Mara takes the jewel. The diamonds and emeralds dangle from her fingertips. Vaso spins her around, pushes her to her knees, takes the tikki, and pins it in place. "Your hair is thick. It will stay on." Vaso places a hand mirror in front of Mara. "See?"

Mara takes the mirror. She barely recognizes the woman staring back at her.

"It's time. Stand up." Vaso claps her hands together twice. "One more thing." Vaso places a jeweled pendant around Mara's neck. "I want you to wear this too."

It's exquisite. The gold colored diamond is shaped like a drop and is surrounded by smaller diamonds all the way around. "I can't wear this. It's too large. And, too beautiful." Mara begins to remove it. "Please, take it back."

Vaso stops her. "No. Leave it. Ali will like it. It's my best piece, the Spoonmaker's Diamond."

Mara runs her thumb across the large diamond shaped like a spoon now fastened around her neck. "It is too much."

"Ah. It is more than too much. Priceless."

"Why is it called the Spoonmaker's Diamond?"

"Does it not resemble the bowl of a spoon? Come. We must go." Vaso pushes Mara out of the tent.

The drum beats amid the sound of a single lute whining its tune. Ali Pasha's outdoor entertainments are lavish in color. Men recline against large pillows placed upon thick floral carpets in a large circle, nargiles centered between them. The weight of their leers shoot daggers to the pit of Mara's stomach. Not again. She hasn't danced in this way since Benderli. The thought of that man's eyes, his touch, his voice draws up the burning juice from her stomach to her throat. Mara turns to Vaso. "I can't do this."

"Shh. Child, you must. It will be offensive if you back out now. He has already taken sight of you. You must dance. Dance like you did that evening we stayed at your house. Remember?"

Mara remembers. Vaso doesn't know. Vaso doesn't know how many times Benderli forced her to dance. Vaso doesn't know Benderli's touches. His evil eyes. The grunt in his voice. If it wasn't for Nikolas. Nikolas. She must do this for Nikolas. Mara closes her eyes to picture his face. To remember the night at Hydra's Peak. Anything to push away the evil thoughts. The music begins to mold its protection around her. The drumbeats pop. The lute strings whine their lonely melody. Mara takes a deep breath, holds it, and exhales before stepping into the center for her dance. Vaso takes a seat beside Ali Pasha and whispers in his ear. The veil covering Mara's face protects her, some. Pasha wraps his smile around the tip of the nargile and sucks in its smoke. Her dance begins.

The slow beat of a racing heart. Each beat is met with the pop of her hip. Swirls and circles guide her entwining arms and hands above her head, then come the waves of soft rolls at waist level. Mara hovers in front of her target to allow him full view of the gyrations of her belly. Solid. Focused. Sensuous. Mara's strong and trained movements entice him at each stage of the execution. Vaso nods her encouragement. Mara shimmies her chest and bends back while twisting and stretching her arms above her bent torso to climb the invisible rope leading her to safety. The music begins to intensify, less lonely. Mara's movements match this beat, ever in sync with its spell. The dance, the music, the rhythm become her soul until it slows to a full stop. Mara sinks to the ground and drops to the side, dead on the last tap of the drum.

IT'S OVER. DEEP BREATHS of oxygen fill Mara's lungs. She doesn't move immediately. She can't. The exhaustion of the dance, the beads of sweat covering her body, the chill of the air wafting across her skin. The masculine voice calls out. "Come to me." It's him. Ali Pasha. Mara looks up to see his mace pointing to her. Vaso relaxes, pleasant and calm at his side, twirling a swatch of her dark hair between two fingers. Mara crosses her legs at her ankles and rises up to approach him, keeping her eyes cast to the ground. Did it work? Will he help her? "Come closer. I see you have gained the favor of my wife. She has bestowed upon you her favorite jewels. Your dance pleases me. What can I do for you?"

Mara does not look up. Her heartbeat still races. How can she make her request and remain hidden? Should she stay hidden? She remembers this man from the dining hall of their manor house on Cerigo. Days have past, but it feels like months. Best to remain as she is. Hidden. Mara kneels before him. "I seek your assistance for my friend. He is being held captive by another of the Sultan's representatives."

"And what has this friend done to earn this Pasha's disfavor?"

"He has done nothing your Excellency." Mara's eyes remain fixed on Ali Pasha's feet. She does not move, but waits. He nods to the musicians to begin another song. This time vocals are added.

"Come sit by me and we shall discuss it." Mara peeks up to see Vaso smile and nod. Ali Pasha pats the cushion on his other side. She will have to endure it. Being treated like his pet. The only thing missing is a camel harness. "Tell me. Does your father know of your talents?"

"My father?"

Ali Pasha grinds his teeth on the tip of the Nargile. "It is no use pretending. I know you are my Dragoman's daughter. Vaso could not keep such information from my knowledge."

"He is aware I dance. He does not know the extent of my experience, no."

"Experience. Yes. That is the way to put it."

How else shall it be put? Lovina warned her. Men do not always think with their heads. Ali Pasha's hand is cold when he places it on top of hers. "Tell me, child. Who is your 'friend' and who is this Pasha?"

"Ibrahim Pasha." Mara wants to put his hand back in its place, but he removes it himself. He turns to face her. "And who did he capture, hmm?"

"Nikolas. Nikolas Stamatelopoulos. You may recall a brief introduction from your evening at the manor house."

The Pasha's brows converge in the space above his nose. "Yes, I know of who you speak. He is the one your father entrusted with your safe removal from Cerigo, is he not?"

"Yes."

Ali Pasha sucks deep on the nargile. He does not speak, but instead leans back on the cushion exhaling the smoke up. Mara waits. He says nothing. He smokes. She waits. "I shall send some men with you to get him back."

Relief overwhelms her. She puffs out a long-held breath. Music and dance continue while Mara sits at the Pasha's side. How long will she be required to remain? She peers over at Vaso who's still playing with strands of her hair. Should she try to make conversation? They can't possibly expect her to sit this entire time and not speak. Polite conversation is expected. Isn't it? "I was surprised to learn you were here. Were you not to remain in Cerigo while this conflict was sorted out?"

Vaso stops twisting the ends of her hair and widens her eyes at Mara. A slight twitch of her head makes it clear she made a misstep. A low rumble sounds before the burst of harsh words explodes from his mouth. "Who are you to be surprised? It is not for you to interpret the intricacies of government. Cowardice is not rewarded. I will be where I need to be." He looks at his wife, who does not meet his stare. "Remove yourselves from my presence before I decide to change my mind."

Vaso pulls Mara to her feet and they rush to her tent before more words can be exchanged. She flaps the door open and moves her inside. "That was not wise."

"I don't even know what I did." Vaso stares at her.

"Sit. We will have to wait until he sends for us."

"But, what did I do?" The pit of her stomach is quaking with fear.

"What didn't you do? First you speak when he hasn't spoken to you. Then you question his judgment. What did you expect?"

"I only did what we always do in the presence of company."

"Your ways are not our ways. You must remember that."

"How can I apologize?"

"You don't. You wait for him to allow you mercy, which I believe he will do. He didn't lash out as hard as I have seen him do for lesser transgressions." Transgressions. How does her father deal with such men on a regular basis? "Are you hungry?"

"No." Mara's stomach growls. Vaso hands her a plate with dried fruit, feta cheese, and bread.

"Your body disagrees. Eat. You need to keep your strength."

Mara looks at the plate, begins to eat, but her thoughts are on Nikolas. Will Ibrahim feed him? And, Spero. Is he still on lookout? The bread is stale, but the feta masks its taste. She is hungry. Mara eats it all, then sits back placing her hand across her forehead. The jewels. She unpins it and returns it to Vaso. "Thank you."

Vaso smiles and examines them dangling from her fingertips before returning them to their place in the box. Shuffling noises and male voices buzz outside the tent. Vaso opens the flap and a Turkish solder summons them to Ali Pasha.

It's almost dark and torches are lit along the path back to the center of the camp. Mara sees Ali Pasha's round form enlarge the closer they get. She makes sure the veil is fastened securely across her face. Another form is slumped in front of the Pasha. Spero.

"He is yours?"

"Yes. I mean, no." Pasha stares at her. "I mean yes, he is with me and here to help get Nikolas."

Pasha nods to the guard. "Release him." Spero's lip is bloody.

"You beat him?" Vaso grabs her hand and gives it a shake. She lowers her eyes. "I'm sorry. I mean thank you for allowing him to join us here."

Ali Pasha studies the two women standing before him. "Vaso, you will take care of this one. I will make arrangements for the other one. It is too dark to go tonight. I will send a group of men to assist you and include my decree to Ibrahim. If he refuses, my men will have their instructions."

"We can't go tonight?" Vaso yanks Mara's hand again, sending a stab of pain all the way up to her shoulder, then pulls her back to return to her tent for the evening.

NIKOLAS OPENS HIS EYES. Blurs of color surround him. His hands are pulled taut behind him. The wooden post holding him up pinches his spine down the center. He pulls at the restraints and receives pinches in return. No use. They're too tight. How long has he been in here? Muffled voices surround him. The door flap flips open. Frog eyes. Again.

Ilyas circles and taunts before pulling his yatagan from his waist. Nikolas struggles, pulling at the restraints once more. He refuses to let the Turk slit his throat without a fight. He kicks and misses. Ilyas laughs and backhands him across the face before kneeling on top of his legs. Ilyas places the blade to Nikolas' neck. "You are fortunate your fate does not lie in my hands." Nikolas grapples, one more attempt to tug his arms free, before Ilyas reaches around him and, instead, places the blade between Nikolas' wrists and cuts the rope. Nikolas doesn't waste time. He shoves the Turk with all his strength, sending him backward on the floor. Both men jolt up and the point of Ilyas' blade is once again searing a line across his neck. "Don't."

"Fight me with your hands." Nikolas isn't going to let them take him easy. Ilyas growls and drops the blade. Nikolas throws his hardest right swing, but his fist is swallowed by his opponent's halfway to its target.

"This we will finish another day." Ilyas jerks his arm down and curls it hard behind him, twisting him face forward. Ilyas shoves him forward out the door. Pain surges through his shoulder when Ilyas tightens his grip on the arm held behind his back. Two familiar faces appear behind Ibrahim. Ilyas shoves Nikolas to the ground. He looks up to see Ibrahim standing over him.

"*Tsk. Tsk.*" Ibrahim shakes his turbaned head. Is that a feather on the back of it? Ibrahim tilts his head to the side. "It seems we will have to forgo our arrangements, hmm? You seem to have gained the favor of Ali Pasha. Your friends have come to collect you." Ibrahim nods to Ilyas who immediately pulls him upright. "See that there is no hard feelings, hmm?" Ibrahim turns and leaves. Ilyas follows. Mara runs forward and wraps her arms around Nikolas' neck. "I was so afraid we were too late."

CHAPTER SIXTEEN

Katafigio

MARA'S ARMS ARE TIGHT around Nikolas' neck. He wraps his arms around her waist and matches her strength. He buries his head in her neck while her hair teases the side of his face. Mara's body molds to his. Her warmth envelopes him. He doesn't want to let her go. Ever.

Heavy coughs break the silence. Spero.

"We need to move."

Mara pulls away and swipes her hands down the front of her thighs. "Yes. We need to get back. Lovina will be worried." She takes his hand in hers and pulls him in the direction Spero leads. Nikolas holds the back of his other hand below his nose. Where is that smell coming from? He looks at Mara leading the way. Wait.

"Lovina?" Nikolas forces her to a halt. Mara peers over her shoulder at him. It's only been a few days, but how he has missed her eyes. How they question him. Mold him. Move him.

"I'll tell you more about it on the way. Come. We must hurry."

The more Mara tells him the details of what has happened, the more Nikolas seethes anger. Denni is going to regret they ever met. How can he take them prisoners? What possible motive is there? Maitland will never cower to their demands. Of course, they are British citizens. But. They have no influence over anyone or anything. Do they? Nikolas studies Mara. Her steady pace, her steady motion, her steady breathing. Her endurance has improved since the last time they trekked this region together. She's focused, driven. Something is different about the way she carries herself. Hydra's Peak is not far now and it's still mid-morning. With Ali Pasha's men on their way back to Pasha's camp, they may be able to make it back to the Klepht village by nightfall if they keep this pace. No doubt that is Mara's goal. What else could it be?

THE AFTERNOON SUN IS warm. Hydra's Peak is behind them and the next stop is the caverns. Nikolas slows to match stride with Mara. "You know the caverns will be the next stop."

"I remember."

Mara doesn't take her eyes from the ground. Curious. How might he address the issue? "You know there's the warm waters of the bath inside."

"Yes, I'm aware." Mara continues her trek forward with determined steps.

Nikolas inhales intense and deep through his nose and almost gags. "Might it be a good opportunity?"

"Opportunity?"

Nikolas clears his throat. "For a wash. It might be a good opportunity for a wash."

"A wash?" Mara spits her words out. She stops walking and Nikolas turns to face her. "Yes, of course you would like a wash. Who wouldn't be in need of one after all you've been through?"

"Me?" Nikolas curls his upper lip and then rolls them both in a tight line across his face. "Yes. You're right. We'll stop over in the caverns."

"So, you can have a wash." She turns her wide grin at him. Their pace returns to the original stride. She covers her mouth with her fingers and turns away. Her shoulders ripple. The sound of uncontrolled laughter squeals from her mouth.

"What the devil is so funny?"

"You." She manages to sputter out. "Why don't you just tell me I smell of horse shit?"

"Tell you? How does one tell a lady they..." Nikolas clears his throat again. "...smell?"

"Why not ask Spero? He's the one who shoved me in the wagon with sacks full of horse sh—"

"Fertilizer! It was fertilizer for the crops." Spero yells back over his shoulder at them. "It was the only way to get her out of the village. The guards barely lifted the cover from the smell."

"So, there you have it." Mara continues to blaze forward. "And to put your mind at rest, I will have a bath when we get to the caverns."

"Well, then." Managing his thoughts on the subject soon proves to be more challenging the closer they get to the caverns.

SIT. SHE MUST SIT. But, she will not. Mara can see the caverns in the distance. The weight of her legs and feet are heavy. Mara's muscles burn to get to the top. She refuses to let Nikolas and Spero know how intense the pain is. She urged Spero to help her get Nikolas at the start. It will not do for her to show weakness. And, Nikolas. How much he endured with

Benderli and Ibrahim Pasha certainly doesn't compare to her pain. And, laughing? What on earth caused that? She must be exhausted. Nervous. Afraid. Yes. All of those things. Mara will not stop until they reach the caverns.

The warm water of the spring soothes the muscles aching to recover. Naked and alone in the caverns with Nikolas and Spero keeping guard gives her pause. No matter. Mara puts it out of her mind. She swims lengthwise across the pool of water. It's not very long, but she is able to get in about five strokes before turning in the other direction, floating on her back and counting each back stroke to avoid cracking her head on the rocks. Her ears are below water. Whooshing pulses and the dull splash of the backstroke calm her insides. She stops to hover in one spot, floating on her back, listening. The soft tickle of algae wisps around her ankles. Wait. It's not algae. It's moving! Mara jumps up and out of the water screaming.

"An eel!"

Nikolas runs into the cavern, sliding on the dirt as he stops in front of her. All of her. From top to bottom-all of her. He looks to the ground then raises his head to the top, landing on her eyes. Mara stands completely still. Frozen. Nikolas' face has no expression. She crosses her arms in front of her chest and squats to the ground. Nikolas swivels around so his back is to her. His voice is brusque. "What exactly happened?"

"An eel." Mara's voice is gone, more of a breathless whisper.

"An eel?" Nikolas' face turns sideways so only his profile shows.

"No! Don't turn around." Mara crouches in a tighter ball. "Can you get me my clothes?"

"Um. No."

"What do you mean, no?"

"I sent Spero to the village to get you some clean ones."

"So, I have nothing to put on? I can't even get back into the water."

"Mara, I assure you there are no eels. We've been bathing here for years and there has never been any sight of one. I'm sure it's the algae."

"Stop turning your head to talk." Mara moves so she is more directly behind him. "What should I do now? How long will he take?"

"It shouldn't be long. You could dip back into the water?"

"Are you laughing?"

"No." His shoulders are shaking.

"You *are* laughing!" Mara picks up a handful of dirt and whizzes it through the air. Nikolas hunches over and turns around with his arm covering his head to block more of her attack.

Mara grabs more dirt and keeps throwing. Nikolas blocks his eyes to protect them from the onslaught while moving in her direction. Mara screams when Nikolas grabs her up and pulls her tight against him. Any further sound is muffled when he covers her mouth with his.

ACH! AUTO TO KORITSI! Tangled tongues send zings of sensation through Nikolas' body. He's careful to keep her tight against him, not the time nor place for anything other than kisses. Spero could be back any time. Nikolas moves Mara deeper into the cavern. His lips spar with hers as they walk back. The palm of his hand splays across the small of her back, threatening to move lower. His other hand holds her entwined fingers against his chest like a dance. Thoughts of Spero long gone, he makes the move to lower his hand. But, a sudden jolt sideways, a strong shove back, and instead he's grasping at air before he lands in the warmth of the water, soaked. He can't touch the bottom and all he sees is a dark shadow of Mara crouching near the edge.

"I think you'll agree we needed that?"

"What? You think *I* needed to be doused in full clothing?"

"Well, didn't you?" The shadow of a smile widens across Mara's face.

"Not in the least." He lies. Nikolas forgot how difficult it is to tread water fully dressed and with boots on. He swims forward toward the edge and Mara backs up.

"Stop! What are you doing?"

"You can't expect me to stay in here with all my clothes, do you? Not to mention my boots, now ruined."

She backs up further almost behind some rocks jutting out on the side. "You did say Spero would be here soon, did you not?"

"Yes, but in actuality, who knows how long he will take."

"Ah. So, there you have it." Mara is barely visible huddled next to the rocks.

Nikolas lifts himself out of the water, it weighs him down. He kicks one booted foot against his opposite ankle and then the other. Ruined. He shakes his head. Water flings everywhere. He looks straight ahead and walks out shaking his hands in the process. Maybe he did need a dip after all.

"WHERE ARE YOU GOING? You're leaving me in here? Alone?" For the first time, Mara hears herself echo through the caverns and shudders. It's cold. Damp. Dark.

"If you hadn't doused me into the pool, I might have come up with something. Here. See if this works." A lump of wet cloth flies through the air and lands a few feet ahead of where she sits.

"What is it?"

"Try it on and see if it fits. Or, at least covers you."

Mara walks over and picks up the wrinkled cloth. It's wet and covered in dirt. She shakes it out a few times, turning her head against the granules of dirt flitting through the air. Mara holds it up in the air. She flattens a men's, somewhat white tunic against her front, pulls it over her head, and lets it hang. It stops above her knees. She walks out to a shirtless Nikolas lounging, legs crossed, and arms folded above his head.

Nikolas stands up and throws a chewed piece of long grass from his mouth. Both turn in unison to the direction of steps approaching. Spero.

Spero stops in front of them. Silent. He looks from one to the other. He places folded clothes and a pair of shoes on the rocks next to them, shakes his head, and returns in the direction he came.

CHAPTER SEVENTEEN

"YOU COMPROMISED HER!" Nikitaras Stamatelopoulos slams his fist onto the table he was standing beside.

Nikolas matches his father's tenor and slams right back. "I did not, I tell you! Nothing happened!"

"Even if that is true, it doesn't matter. You walked back into the village in front of everyone dressed as you were, sopping wet with her by your side."

"She wasn't sopping wet."

"Don't speak to me in that tone. Spero was there. He knows."

"I don't know what you think Spero knows, but I assure you he saw nothing. And even if he did, he would not speak of it."

"So you admit something happened?"

"I admit nothing."

Nikolas' father moves closer, face to face, inches apart. "You may have ruined our chances with Maitland."

"Maitland. I brought her here to keep her safe. Not so you could leverage her with Maitland."

"The Klepht Captains knew you were too close. And now we know just how close."

Nikolas steps back from his father. "I was tasked to get her to Kerkyra safe. Her governess too. I intend to complete that task. Maitland will not be bullied to support Greek Independence. They are nothing to him."

"That is what he wants you to believe. We have learned otherwise."

"Learned otherwise?"

"It makes little difference now. You prove to be just like your mother." Nikitaras flicks his hand in the air and his face scrunches in disgust. He turns his back.

Nikolas grabs his arm and whirls him around. "And just how does this have anything to do with my mother?"

"You side with the enemy." Nikitaras frees his arm and glares back.

"The enemy? How is it my mother sided with the enemy? She had no control over what was done to her!" The man is *Hazo*. Crazy!

His father's eyes burn with rage. "That is what was agreed upon. We had plans for your future, your assignment. But, that is not what happened."

"What exactly are you telling me? She was a traitor? And, you let her live?"

"As far as I'm concerned she was a traitor. She *chose* the Ottoman. He did not force her."

Rage, fury, confusion, and resentment. All of those feelings gurgle in the pit of his stomach. "You're telling me the Turk who is my father did not force himself? It was consensual?"

"Hmpf. I did *not* consent to my wife being with another man. So, it was not consensual, as you put it."

Nikolas wants to punch the wall and cry at the same time, but does neither. The rage and fury bubble between his ribs and his fists tighten into balls at his sides. He can feel his nails cut into the palms of his hands. The years he's lived with the knowledge that his father, an Ottoman, forced himself on his mother. All the difficulties growing up, relentless teasing and poking fun. The worry he may be like his father. Lies. All of it.

Nikitaras is silent, scowling and mean. The door slams shut and Kolokotronis stands in front of them. His father's silence is broken. "What is it?"

"We're needed at Vanessa and Kiki's house."

"What happened?" Nikolas will not be kept in the dark again. "Is anyone hurt?"

Kolokotronis puts his hand on Nikolas' shoulder. "No. No one is hurt, but you need to stay here."

"I will not stay here. As I told my father only a moment ago, I will see those ladies safely to Kerkyra. I promised Wingrove."

"Things have changed. You will learn soon enough."

"What do you mean? What things have changed? I'll not be put off on this uncle!"

Kolokotronis places both hands on each of Nikolas' shoulders and looks him straight in the eye. "It needs to be this way. Now, sit. I'll let you know when we need you."

"PAPA?" MARA'S EYES connect with his the moment she enters Vanessa's and Kiki's house. "What are you doing here?" She quickens her step to reach him faster. He's sitting in a chair in the center of the room. She bends down to hug him. He doesn't hug her back. Mara scans the room. Lovina, Vanessa, Kiki, and Georgi. Something isn't right. She looks at her father. His face is bruised and his eye is swollen with a cut over his left brow. Mara steps back to take in the scene again. "What's happened? Tell me. Someone!" Kiki leaves the room. Lovina moves to Mara's side and places her hand on her shoulder.

"Come. Sit with me now."

"No!" Mara shakes her away. "Not until someone tells me what is going on." She looks at her father. "Papa? Why have these men brought you here? Are you to be held prisoner too? I don't understand. What do they possibly think to accomplish? Maitland will not cower to them. Or their demands."

"That is where you are wrong." A tall man enters the room. His eyes are murky black. His hat hangs to the side with a tassel over the shoulder. His voice threatens the air, daring a response. Mara stares back. He directs his next comment at Wingrove. "Are you going to tell her? Or shall I?" The stranger's lips are invisible under his full mustache. It only twitches when he talks.

"I will tell her." Wingrove raises his head up and stares daggers at this man.

"No." Lovina moves from her spot, closer to Wingrove and Mara. Her eyes mist over and her voice pleads. "Please, Conrad." The mustache lifts on each end. Is he smiling?

Wingrove places his hands, one on Lovina and one on Mara. He looks from one to the other and lands on Lovina. "It must be done. We have no choice. Better it come from me."

Mara stands up. "What? What is it?"

"Mara, my dear," Conrad stands up and takes both her hands in his. "You know I love you and I will always be a father to you."

"Of course." Mara hears Lovina sniff at her side. "Papa, you're scaring me." Lovina stares at the floor. "Nana?"

"No, no. Don't be scared and let me finish." Conrad pulls her to face him directly and rubs up and down the sides of her arms. "Listen to me. It was a long time ago. He needed you and your mother safe."

"What? Who needed us safe? I don't understand."

"Maitland. Sir Thomas Maitland is your father." Lovina breaks into a full out sob.

"What are you talking about?" Mara moves closer to Lovina. "Nana, please."

"I'm so sorry. For so long I've wanted you to know, wanted to tell you." Lovina hiccups. Mara is numb, her head swimming and a blank, hollowness radiates throughout her body. What will this mean? Sir Thomas Maitland. The Lord High Commissioner of the Ionian Islands. Her father.

"Are you going to tell her the rest?" The mustache speaks again. Their captor's voice infuriates Mara. Lovina places her head in her hands and is inconsolable.

Mara is done. She whirls around and shouts. She'll deal with her own feelings on the subject later. She will not allow them to cause Nana any more pain. "Haven't you done enough? You have your prisoners. Leave us now."

"No, Mara stop, please." Lovina reaches to grab her arm and pull her back, but Mara avoids her grasp.

"You should listen to your mother." The mustache roars back. Lovina falls back into her seat.

"What?" All sounds around Mara stop. She looks at Lovina and then at her father or at least the person she has called father all her life. "What is this...this..." Mara glowers at the mustache sitting on his upper lip "...hornblower talking about?"

Wingrove bores a void straight through the man. "Mara. It's true. Lovina is your mother."

The emotions filling her insides threaten to break free. She looks at Lovina sobbing on the chair. "Is it true?" Mara knows it is. Deep inside she's always known. She needs to hear the words from Nana herself, to make it so. But, Lovina doesn't move. Doesn't look up. Only cries, without letup. Mara returns her attention to Wingrove. The man who raised her. The man who's always been Papa. "I need to think." She heads for the hall to leave and Vanessa steps in front of her, gently blocking her way.

"Let her go." The voice of the mustache is less severe. "She will not go anywhere. Her family is here."

Vanessa moves to the side to allow her to pass. Mara's steps are strong, purposeful. The voices in the room behind her melt into silence when the door closes behind her.

NOT ONE MINUTE PASSES before Nikolas is out the door to the sisters' house. He will not stay and wait. He will not allow them to keep secrets on this. Not when it has to do with Mara. Or her family. Not again. His pace is fast. Moonlight irradiates the path. Crickets begin their song and a dog barks in the distance. He sees the shadow of a person leave the house and move in his direction. Mara. Something's wrong. He heads straight for her. "Mara?"

She stops and faces him. Her stare is distant, vacant. "Did you know?"

"Know what?" Nikolas places his hand on her elbow and directs her off the path to a stone block low enough for them to sit. Mara's level expression searches his face.

"About my father."

"Wingrove?"

"No. My real father." Mara's voice cracks and tears begin to trail down her cheek. Nikolas reaches to swipe them with his thumb. She holds his hand against her cheek.

"Mara, you're not making any sense. Tell me. What is it that has you so upset?" He wraps one arm around her shoulders. Mara chokes back a sob.

"Papa just told me he's not my father." Sobs break up her words. "Sir Thomas Maitland is." Her weeping is louder. Nikolas tightens his hold with both arms now and places his chin on the top of her head, rocking her.

"Wait." He leans back to look in her eyes. "Wingrove is here?" She nods. "This explains much."

Mara leans the side of her face against his shoulder. "What do you mean?"

Should he share with her his own revelations this evening? About the secret *his* father kept from him all these years? She may hear of it. Better she hear it from him.

"I, too, just discovered a secret my family kept from me."

Mara lifts her head to look at him. Nikolas can't face her. He stares at the darkness in front of him, it somehow makes it easier to talk about. "My mother wasn't forced. She was in love with the Ottoman."

Mara places a gentle hand along his jaw to coax him to face her. "Don't you see, this is good? She was in love with your father and there is no doubt she loved you."

Nikolas knows she's right. But, the years of torment, the ridicule. All he endured because of it. They sent him away. His father sent him away. Rather, his mother's husband. Questions streak through his mind like the fireflies flashing in the dark.

Does the Ottoman even know? And why did his uncle allow it? Surely, Kolokotronis could have fought to protect his sister and her newborn son? No matter the circumstances.

Instead, they send him away to be educated by British tutors and then assign him to Cerigo. His Klepht training begins to fill in the blanks. It all makes perfect sense. They needed him. They wanted eyes on the British. What better way than to embed him from a young age?

Cold night air attacks him from all directions. Inside and out. The only warmth keeping him alive is fastened close against his side. Mara's steady breathing regulates his heart pounding anxious through his chest. Everything is changing.

THE FAST PACE OF NIKOLAS' heart matches the turmoil beating inside Mara's own flesh. He doesn't even know the whole of her story. Yet. The night's revelations cut like the jagged edges of a coral reef upon her skin.

"I'm so angry. I want to punch someone."

Nikolas strokes the upper part of her shoulder. "I want to punch someone too. But it won't do any good."

"Isn't there anything we can do? Allow them to ransom us? How do we know they'll even keep their end of it? For all we know, they'll keep us here until the end of it all. Who knows how long that will be."

"First, I think we need to try and think clearly. I don't like the idea of you being ransomed, but I do know these people. They'll not harm you unless you pose a threat. I doubt you'll do that."

"It's true." Nana's been well cared for and Irene's accommodations were comfortable. "We haven't been mistreated other than keeping us here against our wishes."

"And no doubt security has been increased since your most recent flight from the premises."

"Flight? That's not what I would call it. More like an elimination." Mara's unintentional play on words does not go unnoticed. The smirk Nikolas reveals turns his dark outlines of sorrow into shades of escalating laughter. Mara nudges him on the arm before joining him. "I came back, didn't I? And *with* you, no less."

Nikolas quiets. Serious again. "It doesn't matter. They'll take steps to ensure it doesn't happen again. I've no doubt they have watchmen stationed strategically all around the village. Probably even watching us here."

"What?" Mara begins to pull away, but Nikolas doesn't allow it.

"It doesn't matter. They've already decided you're compromised."

"But, how—?"

"How?"

Even in the dark Mara can see the shadow of his smile return across his face.

"Of course I know how. I mean how do they *know*?"

Nikolas clears his throat. "Uh, that would be Spero."

"Spero? I thought he could be trusted." Mara crosses her arms in front of her chest.

Nikolas turns her body to face him. She can't look at him now. Instead she studies the shape of his boot. The one closest to her. He takes her chin in his hand and raises her face until she can see his eyes. "You *can* trust him. I do."

Mara stares into his eyes for a brief moment. "Why did he betray us?"

"*Agape mou.* I don't think he did, intentionally. My father is very good at getting information."

Mara's eyes focus on Nikolas' lips. Did he really just call her his love? The rest of his words are echoes in the night. All she's aware of next is her chin pulled to his and the kisses that follow. Mara kisses him back. Need. Want. Comfort. The warmth of his arms holding her tight around her waist is all of that.

The touch of his skin. The soft, wet feel of his tongue dancing with hers. He brushes her lips with his tongue and she flattens her palms hard against his chest, raises to wrap her arms around his neck, and pulls him so close there is no way he can stop. But he does.

"Mara." Nikolas reaches to unclasp her arms then stretches his head back so she can see him again. "I want nothing more than to take you wherever you want to go. But, we have to stop."

Nikolas is right. They do have to stop. "What are we going to do?"

"Go back to Ali Pasha. Ask for his help. I'm sure it's in his interest to dissuade them from using you to get Maitland and the British Empire involved."

Mara's head spins. She stands up. Nikolas grabs her hand and joins her. Words want to form, but nothing comes out. *She* wants to know what they're going to do about their compromising situation. *He* wants to know what they're going to do about Maitland and the Greeks. Mara does too. But not after he calls her his love. Not after the kisses. Not after the secrets they shared with each other. Mara sits back down. Nikolas sits next to her. Mara moves over.

"What is it? What's wrong?"

"Nothing. Everything." Mara covers her face with her hands and shakes her head. "I don't know what to do."

"You don't have to do anything alone." Nikolas removes her hands from her face. "We're going to find a way."

"There isn't one. I don't even know my own family anymore."

"Of course you do. "

"You don't understand. It's not only me they're using to get to Maitland."

"Your father?"

Mara shakes her head. "Lovina."

"What leverage could they possibly have regarding your governess?"

"She's my mother." Nikolas' silence is long. Is he going to say anything?

"Lovina has always been a mother to you." Tears form and Mara tries to hold them back. She covers her face again and Nikolas tugs each hand down to her lap, cradling them in his own.

"I know. That's the problem."

"What is?"

"Nana has always treated me as her daughter. How can I face her now? I'm compromised! After all she's taught me, I let her down. And, now she's my flesh and blood." More tears pool around the edges of her eyes. "That is what I don't know what to do about."

"Mara." Nikolas moves closer. He doesn't let go of her hands in the process. Tears fall and more follow. "Mara, shh...shh...listen." He positions himself on one knee in front her. "*Agape mou glikia.*" Nikolas wipes the tears from her cheeks. "I have known from the first night we spent together at Hydra's Peak I would marry you. Have my actions not shown you how much I love you?" He loves her? He loves her. Words hide from her mouth again. "Tamara. Mara. Will you marry me?"

CHAPTER EIGHTEEN

Somewhere Near Pylos

NIKOLAS HANDS THE SPYGLASS to Mara. "How do you propose we enter?"

Mara peers through the lens to scan the circle of the camp. She hands it back to Nikolas. "We'll have to enter the way Spero and I did."

"What's that?" It's hard to concentrate. Nikolas asks her to marry him, and she tells him to wait for an answer?

Mara glares over her shoulder. "I said, I'll have to go in the way I did when I came here with Spero."

Nikolas knows he's not going to like it. The camp is preparing for something. But what? There's too much activity. Mara will be seen. "No. It's too dangerous."

"What do you propose then?" Nikolas doesn't know. But not that. Not this time.

Sometimes the most simple solution is the answer. "Why not walk in and request an audience?"

Mara steps down from her perch. "Do you really believe it will be granted?"

"I do. You have history with Pasha and Kyria Vasiliki."

"True. But still. I don't believe we should risk being denied."

"Come." Nikolas walks around her and heads for the gate. "Pasha will see us." He stops. "Mara?" Nikolas looks behind and sees her standing still. In the same spot. He walks back. "What is it?"

"Is this how it will be?" Mara's eyes squint below her pinched brow.

"How *what* is going to be?"

"If we're married."

"I don't understand what you mean." Mara bustles around him and forges ahead. He jogs to catch up. "Wait." He grabs her arm to slow her step. "Explain."

"I simply do not wish to be married to a man who doesn't take my views into consideration."

"Of course I take your views into consideration. Do you mean to say *no* to my proposal?"

"What do you call this?" She swings her arms out and up. "You didn't even acknowledge my way may have been the better option." Her pace quickens again.

"Mara, please. You must see how dangerous it would be if you were caught?"

"There are many things I see." *Fwap*! An arrow separates the air between them. Mara screams and jumps back. Nikolas draws his pistol to fire. *Crack!* A whip slaps it from his grasp. They're surrounded by Turbans.

MARA WRESTLES WITH the rope tied around her wrists. Their captors drag them behind like cattle on a lead. She swallows her words that are burning to come out. If Nikolas had listened to her. Who knows if they will be given an audience with the Pasha? The camp is different since the last time she was here. There are more soldiers. More tents. More tension. More men.

Nikolas breaks her thoughts. "I know what you're thinking."

" I doubt it." The swell in Mara's stomach reaches her throat. Her voice is hoarse. Visions of the last time she was bound in a Turkish camp force their way forward. The men yank the ropes, causing them both to stumble. Nikolas steps closer to her so his arm rubs against hers as they walk in unison behind the guards, his eyes fixed on her. Mara shakes her head and closes her eyes. She refuses to cry.

Their trek through the camp stops at the entrance of a large circular tent with two posts pointing skyward in the center. A guard is stationed in front. Words are exchanged before they're jerked forward and shoved to their knees. The man in front of them is not Ali Pasha. Mara raises her eyes to meet his narrow black slits. The wallop on the back of her head causes her to fall on her elbows.

"Do not touch her!" Nikolas receives a similar blow to the back of his head.

"You will show Ambassador Efendi respect." Respect? She'll give him respect. Right through his overstuffed chest.

Efendi lifts his right hand. "Raise them up so we might talk." The skin along her hairline pinches tight. The pull on her hair snaps her head back and forces her body to follow. Nikolas is shoved down at her side. "Tell me. What is your business here?" Efendi glares at Nikolas. Mara keeps her eyes to the ground.

Nikolas speaks firm and direct. "We wish to have a meeting with Ali Pasha on a matter of importance."

"And what matter is this?"

"Is Ali Pasha no longer the leader of this camp?"

The guard standing next to Nikolas thwacks the side of his face. "You will not address the Ambassador of the Sultan in this tone." Nikolas rolls his head in a circle and shrugs each shoulder.

Efendi's slithers around them when he speaks. "You will tell me and I will decide if you are to have an audience with the Pasha."

"We have information regarding the Klephts' plans to ally with Maitland against you."

Efendi clasps his hands behind his back and paces the length of the floor then stops in the middle. "Maitland? The British will not dare come against us. They have made their position known. What is this plan?"

Mara coughs. Nikolas won't look at her. He straightens and glares. "Further information will only be given to the Pasha himself." This earns another blow to the side of the head. Mara gasps. A confusion of voices are jumbled outside the door. One female is louder than the rest. Vaso.

The flap of the entrance flies wide and Kyria Vasiliki enters. "What is this? Efendi?" She turns and sees Mara and Nikolas kneeling before him. "You dare treat the daughter of Pasha's Dragoman such as this?" She points to the guard. "You!" She motions back to Mara and Nikolas. "Untie them. Now! His Excellency will learn of your actions and be displeased."

"You are mistaken." Efendi bows his head before her. "I have done nothing to warrant his displeasure. All visitors are brought to me to screen before given access to His Excellency."

"We see." Vaso motions to the guards. "Free them from those bindings and bring them." The guard does not obey her.

"Efendi? You will not unbind them?"

"Eh, no. They may walk of their own accord, but the wrist bindings will remain."

Vaso loops her arm with Mara's on one side and Nikolas walks on her other. Their wrists remain bound in front. Efendi follows behind. Vaso bends to whisper in her ear. "Things have changed since last you were here."

"What has happened?"

"The Sultan has sent his Ambassador to report on activities here. They are concerned about the uprising." Vaso peeks over her shoulder and smiles at Efendi.

Nikolas leans in front to add to the discussion. "These soldiers are not Turks."

"No. Souliotes."

Mara raises a brow to Vaso. "Albanians loyal to the Pasha."

They reach Ali Pasha's tent and the door is held open for them to enter. Ali Pasha is sitting cross-legged on a couch against the back of the tent. His white turban raises with his head when Vaso places herself by his side. "What's this?" He scans the faces in front of him. "Efendi? Why is my Dragoman's daughter and her escort bound with rope? Untie them immediately." Mara twists and rubs each wrist with her hand to calm the burning flesh. "Tell me, what brings you back?"

Nikolas steps forward to address him. "We need your help and we believe it to be in your interest to help."

"Hmm. How is it?"

"The Klephts are holding Wingrove and Lovina ransom to gain the support of Maitland and the British." Pasha remains silent. He looks at Mara. Nikolas. Efendi.

"Efendi? What do you believe? Will this ploy work for them?"

"It is my belief we must do what we can to prevent such support. The Sultan does not want Britain involved here."

"Mm. I am not sure I agree." Mara's stomach flips. He's not going to help. She pleads a look at Vaso.

Ali Pasha glares at Nikolas. His eyes contemplate. His face brittle and hard. "What possible motivation will Maitland have to get involved? What is Wingrove and his house companion to Maitland?"

Efendi clears his throat. "They are British citizens. Might that be enough?"

"No." Pasha's voice is firm. Kyria Vasiliki strokes the side of Pasha's face and whispers in his ear. He looks at Mara. "No. I do not wish to become involved in this. The Klephts are useful and help keep order. I don't wish to interfere. Nothing will come of this."

"Wait." Mara's voice is weak, everyone looks at her. She must tell them the truth. It's the only way.

"Mara, no." Nikolas begs.

Vaso shakes her head. Mara knows her meaning. She chooses not to listen. "Maitland is my father and Lovina is my mother."

Everyone is silent. Pasha motions to have the nargile brought before him. He inhales. He exhales. "This is different." Pasha's brows furrow. "Maitland will not stand by and allow his daughter and mother of his child be held captive." Another swell of his chest and release. "Efendi, you will negotiate their release."

"I?"

"Yes." He turns to Mara. "Stand up." He looks at her from head to toe. "You will stay here with me. With Vaso." Pasha then points to Nikolas. "You will take Efendi and the Souliotes to retrieve them."

"With respect, I will not leave Mara here. She must come with me."

"She will stay here or you will not receive what you request."

"Nikolas. It's alright. I will stay with Kyria Vaso." Mara nods in her direction and Vaso smiles.

"But, Mara..." Nikolas turns her to face him, holding her hands in his. He touches his forehead to hers. "...I can't leave you here."

Mara shakes her head. "No. Go. You must free them." Nikolas kisses each cheek and leaves.

CHAPTER NINTEEN

Katafigio

NIKOLAS AND THE SOULIOTES lead the horse drawn carts and the entourage carrying Efendi. Silver haze hangs over the Bay of Navarino. The closer they move, the more distinct water and land become. The Island of Sphacteria is also clearer with each step. A ship is anchored some distance from the shore. Best not to draw attention to it. Who might it belong to?

Nikolas raises his hand to stop the procession. He walks over to Efendi.

"From this point it will be only you and I."

Efendi's brows crunch together. "This is unacceptable. I must have my men."

"I don't think you understand. It's not negotiable. I will not bring you to the village and show you the way."

"So, this is a hidden village?"

"It's not hidden, but it's well protected from invasion. I'll not make it easy for anyone to destroy it."

Efendi sits atop his carriage and scowls. "No. You will listen to me. I will take ten foot soldiers and no less."

Nikolas folds his arms across his chest. "I suggest you decide now what you will tell Ali Pasha when you return."

"What I will tell Ali? I think you misunderstand the arrangement. I am here at the pleasure of the Sultan. Not Ali."

"Then I suggest you decide what you will tell the Sultan when Maitland allies himself with the rebels."

"Hmpf. We will meet again, you and I, and it will not be favorable."

"Please." Nikolas bows and extends his arm in a half-circle in front.

Efendi nods in acknowledgement.

"You will need to descend from your carriage and ride in one of the carts with me."

"What? It is outrageous. I cannot, will not, ride in *that*."

"We cannot ascend the passage via horse drawn carriage. It will need to be in the cart." Nikolas leans against the cart, crosses one leg in front of the other, and flattens one hand out to inspect the skin of his knuckles, then flips it over to check the length of his nails. He'll wait. Serves him right. A little payback for the way he treated Mara.

Efendi exits the carriage and slams the door shut. He walks over and waits to be lifted up into the cart. Once situated, Nikolas walks over to one of the Souliotes and asks for his head scarf. Nikolas hands it up to Efendi.

"What is this?"

"You must put this on to cover your eyes."

"Cover my eyes?" Nikolas is enjoying the game.

"Yes. I told you I cannot risk putting the village in danger. I'll not have you remember the journey. Put. It. On."

Efendi grabs the scarf from Nikolas' hands, wraps it around his eyes, and attempts to tie it in the back. "It doesn't fit."

Nikolas jumps up beside him. "It fits." Nikolas folds the cloth across Efendi's eyes and ties the back in a tight knot before taking a seat beside him. He calls out instructions to the Souliotes to continue to the shores of Navarino Bay and await them there.

"May I remind you the Souliotes are in my charge. Not yours."

Nikolas slaps the reins to begin the ascent to the village.

"YOU MUST NOT WORRY yourself. Come near to us and relax." Ali Pasha is almost kind. Vaso moves to make room for Mara on the couch. "No, I wish her to sit on my other side." Caution grabs hold in Mara's stomach. Ali Pasha's voice is odd, fatherly? No, not quite fatherly either. Mara sits where he directs. He wraps his arm around her shoulders and squeezes, pulling her tight against his billowy chest. His beard tickles her nose. He squeezes Vaso on his other side and they meet face to face. Vaso splays a closed lip smile and eyes her husband.

Mara blows air out her mouth to attack the beard then squats to the ground and stands up fast. It's very clear. Not fatherly. Not friendly. It's disgusting. An old man. His face is red and grunting sounds gurgle in his throat.

Vaso shoots a glare at Mara. "Do not be mad, my love. Mara is tired after being handled by Efendi. May we take leave and I will see to her comforts? We can join you again later after we are refreshed?"

Ali Pasha grunts some more before waving his hand in the air. "Leave. See to her comfort and you will return to me. I have need of your attentions."

"As you wish." Vaso stands and drags Mara by the hand, out of the tent. It's not far before they enter another. Vaso's.

It's the same as she left it last. Pillows line the edge of the tent. Mara wants to sink into them and cry. "What was he thinking? Papa would never approve of his conduct."

Vaso turns her around to face her. "Listen. I told you. Things are not as they were. A lot has changed. I don't know why he did what he did, but I will leave you here to rest while I go back and try to find out his plans."

Mara hears Vaso, but exhaustion overwhelms her. Emotional and physical. She stares at moving lips, hears a feminine voice. Vaso shakes her and she is focused on her eyes. "What?"

"I said, you must lie down and rest while I go back to attend to Ali. I will find out what I can."

Mara looks at the pillows and does exactly that.

"WILL YOU PLEASE SHUT up? I can always bind your hands the way you bound mine." The man must believe he's the Sultan himself.

"How dare you! I will not be insulted." Efendi raises his hand to remove the blindfold.

"Uh uh. No." Nikolas slaps it down. "If you want to continue on you must leave it."

"Hmpf." Efendi sits up straight. "You will be sorry for this mistreatment."

Nikolas slaps the reins. "I can always gouge out your eyes and then we will not have a problem."

"I will see your head on a stake before I am done. This, I promise."

"I'm not worried. You will have to find it first."

"I am not a man to be trifled with. I warn you."

"And, we are almost there."

The shuffle of dirt and breaking gravel begins to lull the silence. Nikolas waits for the air to clear and notices a person walking the edge of the path in front of them. He reaches to pull his pistol and lay it across his lap as he approaches. The person turns around to look at him.

"Rachel!"

"Nikolas, a fine sight you are. Heading home for a break?" She looks over at Efendi, who faces straight ahead. Nikolas stops the cart and locks the brake before jumping down to give her a hug.

"Not exactly." He walks her out of earshot before telling her what the Klephts have done. He watches Efendi lift the edges of the blindfold as he tells her his story. It doesn't matter. They're far enough into the passage and almost to the village. Efendi won't know where he is.

"What are your plans? You know your father and uncle will never allow any negotiations."

"I know, but I need to get Wingrove and Lovina out and then get back to Pasha's camp and get Mara. Was that your ship in the Bay?"

"Yes, and reinforcements are coming."

"Do you think you can free them and then make for your ship?"

"I don't know. We have orders."

"Rachel, please. I need this. I promised to get them to Kerkyra. You know this isn't the way to force a hand. Maitland will be more inclined to help if we get them to safety."

Rachel kicks the dirt with one foot and then the other. "Alright. I'll help, but you'll owe me for this."

"Anything."

"You go ahead and I'll hang back. I'll need to signal my ship. When I see you returning, I'll head in to get them out and meet you on the shores of the Bay."

"Make sure they're prepared for a fight. Souliotes are waiting for our return."

"Ugh. Nothing is easy with you."

"MARA. HURRY. WE NEED to make preparations."

Mara opens her eyes to see Vaso bustling around the tent. Mara wipes the edges of her eyes to clear her vision from sleep. If her slumber could be called sleep. "What is it?"

"We must leave. Now."

"What happened? Is he all right?"

"No." Mara's stomach tumbles upside down. She's lost him. "I mean yes. No, I mean I don't know if Nikolas is alright."

Mara stands and places her hand on Vaso's shoulder. "Please stop for a minute and explain."

"We don't have time."

"How can we not have time? It's dark out already. I need to know what happened."

Vaso takes Mara's hands in hers. "He means to make you his wife."

"I know. He has asked me, but I haven't given him my answer. How do you know of Nikolas' plans? Is he back?"

"What? No. I told you. I don't know anything about Nikolas. I mean Ali. He wants to give you this. It is my favorite of all my collections."

The Spoonmaker's Diamond. Mara wore it the night she danced for his favor. "I cannot accept such a gift. Besides it's yours. Why would he wish to give it to me?"

Vaso places her palms on each of Mara's cheeks. "He wishes to take you as wife, child. Are you not listening?"

"But you're his wife." Acid builds in Mara's stomach.

"A Pasha may have many wives in his harem. I know what he plans. We must go." Vaso continues to lay different items on top of a piece of fabric including the diamond.

"What are his plans?"

"He has sent Efendi to negotiate, but he intends to marry you, and ally himself with Maitland."

"That's absurd. How can he believe this plan will have success? My Papa will not allow it. Maitland will not either."

"He has sent Souliotes loyal to him to enforce his wishes." Vaso ties the four corners of the fabric and slings it over her shoulder. "We must leave now while it's dark. We'll rest overnight once we're some distance away. The moon is bright. We have enough light.

"*Na parei euxei!* You bring him to our village? What have you done? He will destroy us!"

"Relax, uncle."

Kolokotronis slaps Nikolas across the face with the back of his hand. "You will not tell me to relax, *nephew*."

Pain radiates through Nikolas' jaw. The reflex to fight back surges. Nikolas' nails dig into the palm of his hand. He must resist. He stands bolt upright, ready to swing back, but doesn't. He drops his eyes to the ground.

"Forgive, me. I took every precaution. I assure you."

"There are no negotiations. Once a decision is made, we do not negotiate."

"I do know this, but I thought there might be an exception."

"And how is that?" His uncle's voice barrels through his ears.

"His is directly from the Sultan. Not Ali Pasha."

Kolokotronis crosses his arms across his chest and blows a large puff of air from his cheeks. "We see. Come. Let's meet with the other Captains."

CHAPTER TWENTY

Navarino Bay

"INFIDELS. ALL OF YOU. The Sultan will not be pleased with your refusal of his wishes. I shall take pleasure in your punishment."

"Steady, now. I would be careful what you wish for." The cart rumbles across the gravel descending the passage.

"It is you who will be wishing for freedom."

Nikolas looks over to the man bobbing in all directions beside him. "Do you not see how it will be viewed?"

"How what will be viewed?"

"Your failed negotiations with the Klephts."

"My failed negotiations? Your requirements are unacceptable."

"If you believe so."

Efendi twists and wrangles with the bindings preventing any movement of his wrists while trying to scratch the edge of his eyebrow where the blindfold now covers his eyes once more. "You will regret your actions."

"I've no doubt I will." Efendi turns to reply, but doesn't.

The Bay of Navarino is becoming clear through the evening light. The lit torches of the Souliotes camped on the shore provide a homing beacon in the dusk of the evening. Nikolas' efforts to ignore Efendi's continuous commentary regarding the future of his head are met with silence and the distant whine of a lone dog calling out in the night. Efendi is still blindfolded so Nikolas takes a minute to survey the area and scan the open waters. Two ships are present now. Rachel said reinforcements were coming. Nikolas pulls out a spyglass. He recognizes Rachel's frigate anchored in the distance. He's not sure who the second one belongs to. He scans the ship's hull. It's the Agamemnon. Bouboulina is here. He presses on toward the burning fires of the shore. Darkness surrounds them now. Nikolas hopes Mara is safe. Will she eventually accept his offer? She must. As soon as they reach the Bay, he'll not wait. He'll travel all night to get back to Ali Pasha's camp.

GUNFIRE REVERBERATES in the distance. Mara's insides clench together like sea anemone protecting their prey. "That doesn't sound good."

Vaso nods in agreement. "Let's get a closer look."

They crouch behind the trees lining the shore of Navarino Bay. "Maybe it's not them."

"No, it must be. I recognize the Souliotes."

Mara prays Vaso is wrong. "They could have come across bandits, yes?"

"Maybe. But doubtful. I heard the messenger's report to Ali. He said they wait at Navarino Bay for Efendi to return from their efforts at negotiation."

"How long do you think we have before we are discovered missing?"

"We have some time, but not long. I told my hand maiden we were not to be disturbed. You needed rest and I was attending to you. She will not be put off for long."

Mara begins to head for the battle. "We need to help."

Vaso grabs hold of her arm and pulls her back. "Wait. We can't go in there."

"You may not, but I can. And will." Mara shrugs her arm free and heads for the open shore. The only light is from the moon and bonfires.

The Souliotes are fighting with swords and pistols. Where is Nikolas? Mara heads in the direction of two men fighting with swords. She passes a slain body, grabs the sword, and looks around. Two lone fire lights bob on the water. From this distance, Mara can't tell if the boats are heading out or heading in. She turns her attention back to the two men fighting. It's not two men at all, she recognizes one.

"Rachel!"

"Mara? What are you doing here?" The Souliot doesn't miss a second. He takes advantage of Rachel's distraction. Rachel doubles over grasping the side of her cheek. "*Na pate sto Diabolo!*"

Mara steps up to take Rachel's place against the Souliot. She slams her blade hard against his. He blocks her every attempt to disengage his weapon. Mara can hear the clang, clang of the blades behind her. She sees Rachel sparring with two more Souliotes, blood dripping from her face. Bodies and shadows move in the dark light of the fire on the sand. Where is Nikolas? Rachel joins her and they fight back to back every Souliot taking their turn. There are too many. One drops his sword and pulls out a pistol aiming it at Mara's face. Another one is aimed at Rachel. They have no choice but to raise their hands to surrender.

More shots are fired. The one holding a gun on Mara drops to the ground in front of her, revealing Vaso with an outstretched arm holding a smoking pistol in the backdrop. The one aiming at Rachel turns to fire at Vaso, but he falls to the ground before he can.

The yelling and shooting is overwhelming. Men run from sea to shore in intervals, fighting as they emerge. Mara covers her ears with her hands and drops to the ground. She has never been faced with a pistol point blank. One strong hand raises her to her feet.

"Mara." His voice is forceful, strong and welcome. She wraps her arms around Nikolas' neck, pulling herself tight against him. She's never going to let go. He lifts her in his arms and runs, carrying her all the way to the waiting boats. He sits her on the seat and fires back, then throws the spent gun in the boat. Vaso steps in opposite, followed by Rachel. Nikolas shoves them into the waves of the sea and jumps in next to Mara. He leans forward to grab an oar before falling face down at her feet.

"NIKOLAS!" MARA BENDS over to try and pull him upright. She can still hear the gunshots firing from the shore.

"Mara!" Rachel's voice is shrill. "Help me. We must move him so I can row." Mara can see Rachel's blood-caked cheek in the gloom of darkness. Shadowed men splash in their direction. Rachel snaps her fingers in front of Mara's eyes then pats her fingers across her face. "Look at me. We must hurry if we want to save him."

"Yes, save him." Mara helps Rachel move Nikolas to a forward seat and Mara sits next to him. Rachel takes their place so she can row the boat.

Rachel struggles to get the boat to move in the right direction. "Mara, you're going to have to help. I can't do it alone."

"I've never rowed a boat before." Mara looks down at Nikolas' limp body.

Vaso looks at one and then the other. "You cannot expect me to...to how did you call it?"

"Row." Rachel pulls the oars leaning all the way back as she does so. Her breathy voice repeats her command. "You're going to have to help or we won't make it."

Mara carefully finagles her body sideways and slowly balances her way to where Rachel sits. This time around it's pure adrenaline coaxing her every move, every thought, every action. Mara takes one oar and follows Rachel's example as they flow into a regular rhythm. The exertion is intense, speech impossible. All Mara sees in front of her eyes is Nikolas. Nikolas lying limp along the floorboards of the boat.

Rachel snaps a look behind her and continues rowing.

Mara can't even ask how much further. She doesn't want to know. Exhaustion is pressing hard on her chest; her arms are burning. Hesitation for one second may stall any effort to continue.

Push down, forward, pull back. Push down, forward, pull back. Push down, forward, pull back.

Voices echo across the water. Is she imagining it? No. It is voices calling out. Rachel stops rowing and lets go of the oar. Before Mara can react, it slides into the water. No!

"Leave it..." Rachel stands up and reaches for a rope flung from the side of a ship they banked. She quickly tethers their lifeboat. How can Rachel move so quickly? Another rope falls from the sky. This one is tethered at the other end of the lifeboat. "Mara, time to climb aboard."

"I can't. My arms won't raise above my head."

"You have to. Don't think. Just do it."

"But, Nikolas, how will we get him aboard."

"Don't worry. My men will get him aboard."

"But..."

"Don't argue. Go." Rachel shoves Mara to face the roped ladder thumping against the side.

Mara grabs on, puts one foot in the rung and hauls herself up. One foot, one arm. One foot, one arm. Each one trembles and burns. She reaches the top and two men she recognizes from her previous stay drag her over. Mara lays flat on the wet, wooden deck. Unable to move, her vision blurred. A woman kneels beside her, takes her hand and kisses her fingers. "Nana?"

CHAPTER TWENTY-ONE

Ionian Sea

FAMILIAR VOICES SURROUND her. Compression points engulf Mara's body, heavy and light, at the same time. Points on her back and shoulders and arms, even the back of her legs. Is she floating? To where? Outline images of people bustling around her blur in the shadows of darkness, front to back and side to side. She sees Nana. Doesn't she? Softness envelopes her. Nana *is* next to her, holding her hand. Whispering. "Mara?"

Mara turns to the sound of the voice. Her vision blurs into focus. Nana's dark black hair frames her face. Mara lifts her body to reach for her.

"Shh... *Nooo*, lie still. You need to rest."

Mara doesn't listen. "I'm fine, I assure you." She sits straight up and hugs her mother. Her mother. "Papa? Is he here too?"

"Yes."

"But, how?"

"Your friend, Rachel."

"Rachel?"

"She is your friend, no?"

"Yes." Mara blows out a deep breath. "She is. Where's Papa?"

"He's confirming our arrangements for Kerkyra." Mara swings her legs to the side of the bed. "What are you doing?"

"I need to find Nikolas. Where is he?"

"Mara, you need to rest." Lovina places one hand on Mara's shoulder and the other on her cheek.

"Nana. He was shot. Because of me. I must see him."

"Rachel is with him and the ship's doctor."

Mara covers Nana's hand with hers. "Please. I need to be sure he's all right."

"Fine, Maraki. Let me help you." Lovina wraps her arms under Mara's shoulders to help her from the bed, straightening her clothes in the process. "We need to get you something more suitable to wear."

"Hmpf. I don't know. I believe I like the salwar."

"Yes, well they need a proper cleaning. Your Papa will not approve."

Silence carves the open space between them. Which Papa? The one she's known all her life, is not. Mara faces Lovina and swallows. She needs Nikolas. She must give him her answer.

SOFT FINGERS MINGLE with his. Smooth skin brushes along the edge of his hand and forearm. Nikolas half opens his eyes. Locks of brown hair flow across his chest. He reaches to touch her, twist her hair around his fingers. Mara lifts her head to meet his.

"You're awake." Before Nikolas can respond, her mouth finds his. Silky lips hover above him. "How do you feel?"

He reaches to hug her close. "Much better now." The pain in his shoulder stabs him, but he doesn't want her to move.

"Good. I was afraid you wouldn't wake up."

"Not wake up? How long have I been asleep?"

"Not too long, a day maybe two? I've lost track." Mara lays her head against his chest.

Nikolas keeps her hair entwined in his fingers. "Tell me what's happened."

"What's the last thing you remember?"

"Seeing you and Rachel fighting the Souliotes. How did you get there?"

"Vaso. She learned of Pasha's plans for me, for Nana, and for Papa."

"And?"

"It seems he wanted me for his harem. He wanted to ally himself with Maitland. He thought to get Nana and Papa to his side."

"What?" The nasty blackguard. Nikolas sits up. Pain in his shoulder jabs. Pinprick lights in front of his eyes follow.

"Nikolas, you must stay relaxed."

"How can I stay relaxed? First, it's Ibrahim. Now, Ali Pasha himself? He must be 80 years old!"

Mara's eyes glisten and her nose scrunches. "Don't let Vaso hear you. She may take offense."

"I don't care what she takes. He'll not accomplish this." Nikolas tries to sit up again and this time succeeds. He wrangles his legs to the side of the bed.

"Nikolas, love. Please calm yourself. We are far out to sea, making way to Kerkyra. Nothing will come of it now. Bouboulina flanks us all the way to Kerkyra. She has arranged with Papa to see us there safely."

Nikolas snaps his head to hers. The only word he hears is *love*. Dare he hope she will give him the response he waits to hear?

"Mara..." he takes her hands in his, "...do you wish to give me your answer?"

Mara glares I-want-you straight into his eyes, leans forward, and kisses him. His stomach flails like an octopus avoiding capture, but will she capture him to her heart like he has captured hers?

"Yes."

He folds her close to his heart, raises her chin and kisses her back. "I love you."

"And I love you."

Nikolas skims the back of his fingers along the length of her cheek. She's beautiful. "I believe we will need to ask Rachel's assistance once more."

"Rachel?"

"She is the ship's Captain."

"MARA, ARE YOU SURE this is what you want?"

"Nana, I've never been more sure. I won't wait another day."

"But, your father."

"My father will have no say in the matter. I'm determined to have control of this. He has controlled my entire life, until now. It's time for me to determine my own destiny."

A tear drops down Lovina's cheek. "It was not our intention to keep you from your happiness. I only wish you might wait. What if the ceremony isn't recognized?"

Mara hugs Lovina tight. "If there's one thing I have learned from these last weeks, it's that life is short. Surely, you must understand the heart. You would not want me to be separated from my love?"

"Of course not, Mara. I only want you to be sure."

"I am sure. Very sure."

Lovina helps Mara step into her dress and laces the back. "And, if it's not recognized?"

"I'm sure the Lord High Commissioner can do something." Mara twirls a wisp of hair between her fingers. "And, if not, we will have another ceremony that *is* recognized."

Lovina steps back and dabs the corner of her eyes. "It is settled then."

Mara turns around. An ivory silk gown, gold lace trim with black and gold roses, graces her image in the frame of the mirror in front of her.

"Rachel tells me this dress belonged to the daughter of a princess, although she won't tell me who."

Lovina squeezes her daughter's shoulders from behind and stares at both of them in the mirror. "I would say it is a princess who wears it now."

A soft knock at the door breaks the spell of joy shared between them. "Nana, will you see who it is? I don't want Nikolas to see me before the ceremony."

Lovina cracks the door, then opens it wide. Wingrove enters. His arms envelope Mara in a circle of warmth and love. "My dear, I have something for you."

"What is it?"

"Here." An object folded in crimson silk is placed in her hands. "Vaso wishes you to have this."

Mara unfolds the corners one at a time. The Spoonmaker's Diamond. "Papa, I can't accept this. It is too much."

"She said you would resist taking it, and wanted me to impress upon you it is hers to give." Wingrove places the pendant around Mara's neck. "It is beautiful, my dear. You are beautiful."

EPILOGUE

Kerkyra

WAVES CRASH HARD AGAINST the rocks of the cliffs below. In this spot, Kerkyra's cliffs are not as high as Cerigo, but the sea is the sea. The salty wind, the spray, the rolling roar, and the colors of a sun dipped in blue. The climb to the top exhilarates. The difference now? Nikolas is not alone. Mara's hand is cradled in his. Their trek along the jagged edges entices. They reach the top. Nikolas steps to the edge.

"Are you sure?" Giddy ripples in Mara's voice challenge him.

"The question is, are you? A rogue eel may be hiding in the crags."

"Your attempt to scare me will not work. I've been doing this for years."

"Yes, but now I fear we may be dealing with a more formidable foe."

"More formidable?"

"Poseidon."

"You're joking?"

"No, my dear. I'm afraid not. In Cerigo, your beauty was mistaken for that of Aphrodite herself."

"Ah. I see where you are heading with this. It is said that Cerigo was the favorite of Aphrodite. You mean to imply Kerkyra belongs to Poseidon?"

"Eh, not exactly. Poseidon fell in love with the nymph Korkyra and brought her to this island. So, you see, Kerkyra belongs to her."

"I still don't know how this concerns us?"

"Why, Poseidon may mistake you for his beautiful nymph Korkyra." Nikolas runs his fingers along her cheek.

"How about this, instead." Mara closes her parasol and removes her walking boots. "You will be Poseidon and I will be Korkyra." She turns her back to him, motioning him to unfasten the back of her dress.

"You don't mean to dive as you did in Cerigo?"

"Why not?" She begins to remove the pins from her hair, allowing it to fall to her shoulders, shaking her head in the process.

"Mara, we may be seen."

"No one is around and besides, the trek down is instant." She raises her hair off her shoulders. Her playful smile entices him to follow her lead. "Come. You'll see."

Nikolas unfastens her dress and it drops to the ground. "Have you thought about the time it takes to get back up here for our clothes?"

She removes her undergarments and piles them on top of the heap beside her feet. "Hmm. No, I hadn't thought of that. I'm used to having clothes stashed in the cave."

Nikolas is frozen, his naked wife standing in front of him solidifies all rational thought. She is a Goddess. His Goddess. He pulls her close and kisses her. "If only there was a cave near here."

"There's only one way to find out." Mara pulls his white tunic over his head. "Are you going over like that or will you be bold and remove it all?"

"Mara, wait." He picks up his tunic from the ground. "Put this on, please. It will not do if we are seen."

Mara scrunches her nose but does as she's told. She pulls the tunic over her head. "If you insist." She flips her hair out of the collar. "Happy?"

"Much better." It barely covers her bottom, but it's preferable to nothing. Nikolas likes the look. He may have her wear it more often.

Mara pulls him close to the edge. He can see the excitement in her eyes glisten, full of mischief. She squeezes his hand and smiles. "Ready?"

He doesn't answer. He looks down. He's never jumped that distance in his life. It's higher than jumping off the edge of Rachel's ship. He looks at the ground he's standing on. "Wait."

"If you don't wish to, it's alright."

"No, that's not it."

"I need to remove my boots."

Mara helps him tug one, then the other. She stands them next to the heap of her clothing. He stands back up and moves to the edge again.

Mara sucks in a deep breath, closes her eyes and exhales. "Remember to push off at the same time you jump to land far enough out from the side of the bank." Mara points to an area below them. "There. That's where I want us to land. Ready?"

His blood is rushing through his veins. He can hear the pulse between his ears, feel his heart beat hard and fast. Mara holds on tight to his hand. She holds it up between them and kisses the top. "Don't let go."

"I promise. You're going to love it. Trust me." He holds her attention for a brief minute. "On three. One. Two. Three."

Free.

THE END.

If you enjoyed reading **Aphrodite Mine**, please consider giving it a review.

READ MORE BOOKS FROM **IreAnne Chambers**:
 Majestic Estates Series:
 Storm Chasers of Wentworth Hall.
 Folly at Sausmarez Manor
 Mystery at Harlaxton House
 Wolfe of Toddington Peaks
 Regency's British Empire Series:
 Aphrodite Mine
 Isle of My Man
 Aliens of Extraordinary Ability Series:
 Nightingale Song
 Bollywood Bargain
 Seasons Bliss Series:
 Countess who Kissed a Count
 One Man and a Babe

Find all books by IreAnne at:
www.IreAnneChambers.com
Join the The Cozy News for New Releases.

ABOUT THE AUTHOR

IREANNE CHAMBERS' BOOKS contain the spirit and tone of the traditional Regency with the promise of mystery, adventure, and mishap weaved in to create happy-ever-afters with plenty of fun and surprises along the way.

IreAnne looked to her Scottish and Irish heritage and discovered the name Eireann (Erin). Eire means Ireland in Gaelic and IreAnne was born.

IreAnne also enjoys writing poetry and song lyrics, but her love for the Regency romances of Jane Austen, filled with dashing heroes and feisty heroines, spurs her desire to write Fun, Cozy, Historicals, and Then Some...

As novelist and Nobel Prize winner Toni Morrison said, "If there's a book you really want to read, but it hasn't been written yet, then you must write it." IreAnne does just that.

Follow **IreAnne** here:

BookBub

Amazon

Goodreads

Instagram

Facebook

Pinterest

Twitter

Don't miss out!

Visit the website below and you can sign up to receive emails whenever IreAnne Chambers publishes a new book. There's no charge and no obligation.

https://books2read.com/r/B-A-FKKH-ZYVVD

BOOKS 2 READ

Connecting independent readers to independent writers.